Praise for *Swim Home to the Vanished*

"*Swim Home to the Vanished* is a lush and fantastic journey through strange lands and minds from an incandescent new voice full of my kind of melancholic brilliance and unromantic magic. The book devastates buoyantly, sensually, like some culinary chimera rising from heretofore unknown waters to take you under and wrap you like a song. Brendan Basham's novel is the announcement of an emerging writer fully formed."
——Tommy Orange, author of *There There*

"Basham shines in his depictions of Damien's yearning and catharsis. . . . Readers will find much to admire in the author's unique voice." ——*Publishers Weekly*

"*Swim Home to the Vanished* is a lush, soulful saga about profound loss and the mysteries of carrying on under its weight. An audacious debut novel bristling with insight, imagination, and real heart."
——Claire Vaye Watkins, author of *I Love You, but I've Chosen Darkness*

"Sumptuous, mysterious. . . . [Readers] can revel in being swept away by Basham's creation of a sensually rich world in constant and often violent change." ——*Booklist*

"In *Swim Home to the Vanished*, Brendan Basham has delivered a profoundly moving novel of originality, full of grief and hope. It is a bold and powerful new work of fiction."
——Brandon Hobson, author of *The Removed*

T0197890

"Basham's debut novel is complex and enigmatic, featuring a mythic sensibility and elements of magical realism, including the early stages of Damien's metamorphosis into a fish and other characters' taking on the physical characteristics of lizards and insects. The novel's prose is lush and evocative, and there's an almost erotic charge to Basham's writing about food, a central element in the story."   —*Kirkus Reviews*

"Basham has a particular gift for transmuting inner intangible turmoils into corporeal form; the various characters' physical transformations from human to creature are a creative epigenetic exploration of the ways in which trauma and grief shape who we are."   —*BookPage*

"An incantatory trip through place and time, fueled by grief and animated by magic. . . . Right away, we know we are to be guided by a writer (Basham is Diné) with an ear for poetry who also is attuned to the lasting scars caused by westward colonial expansion in the United States. . . . Out of this emerge scenes full of natural wonder, deeply imagined and described in bravura prose, the novelistic equivalent of a big-screen final reel."
                                    —*Minneapolis Star Tribune*

"*Swim Home to the Vanished* powerfully explores the lasting impact of grief and redemption by interweaving Diné history and traditional myths."
                    —*Electric Literature*, "16 New Books by Indigenous
                                    Authors You Should Be Reading"

SWIM HOME TO THE VANISHED

SWIM HOME TO THE VANISHED

Brendan Shay Basham

HARPER ⬤ PERENNIAL

NEW YORK • LONDON • TORONTO • SYDNEY • NEW DELHI • AUCKLAND

FOR TRISTAN

HARPER ● PERENNIAL

A hardcover edition of this book was published in 2023 by Harper, an imprint of HarperCollins Publishers.

SWIM HOME TO THE VANISHED. Copyright © 2023 by Brendan Shay Basham. All rights reserved. Printed in the United States of America. No part of this book may be used or reproduced in any manner whatsoever without written permission except in the case of brief quotations embodied in critical articles and reviews. For information, address HarperCollins Publishers, 195 Broadway, New York, NY 10007.

HarperCollins books may be purchased for educational, business, or sales promotional use. For information, please email the Special Markets Department at SPsales@harpercollins.com.

FIRST HARPER PERENNIAL EDITION PUBLISHED 2024.

Designed by Elina Cohen
Illustrations © MattGrove/Getty Images

Library of Congress
Cataloging-in-Publication Data has been applied for.

978-0-06-324109-1 (pbk.)

24 25 26 27 28 LBC 5 4 3 2 1

Contents

Part I

Fish Smoke	3
Migration Patterns of Desert Fish	12
The Goatherd	17
The Bus	25
Hwéeldi	29
The Church of Bees	32
The Funeral	36
The Village	46
Burial	54
The Archivist	62
Eddie Caro's Chinchorro	67
The River	82
Paola	85
A la Parrilla	88
The House by the Woods	99
Morning	105
Catch of the Day	112
Soufflé of Sea	128

Part II

The Lure   133

Communing with Worms   168

Jardín   177

El Dedo Perdido   191

The Blind Albino Miner   194

Cariña Marta   196

Subaqueous Foragers   201

Part III

The Storm   207

Gravedigger   216

Wasp   218

Hashtł'ish   221

What Fish Remain   225

Acknowledgments   229

Part I

BUT THE RIVER IGNORED THE FISH AND THE FISH IGNORED THE RIVER; THEY REFUSED TO EVEN DIE THERE. THEY SIMPLY VANISHED.

—James Welch, *Winter in the Blood*

Fish Smoke

Damien did not prepare a eulogy. He stood under the flickering green fluorescent lights in a room at the back of a church filled with people who probably never met his brother. If they were there to support his parents they must have forgotten his parents went missing a long time ago. He wanted to say, *My brother was a left hand, left leg, now severed above the knee.* But he choked. The only thing to come out of his mouth was a garble of words about the last movie they watched together. His throat closed. He couldn't speak. He couldn't breathe.

Damien has been working on a revision ever since.

If he could stand up there again he might say Kai wouldn't have been caught dead in this place (wrong choice of words, but doesn't make it less true), he would have hated this church service; here he is, ashes in a cedar box, grinning maniacally. He sees right through you, laughs at how ridiculous and absurd you look, mourning in an overheated church that reeks of bleach. Life is a tragicomedy, Kai would have reminded them, and it is futile to live any longer in suffering and defeat.

Sometimes he addresses the eulogy to *You* in a fruitless attempt to dissociate himself from the embarrassment at the wake; the eponymous second person feels less contrived.

Dear You is how it would begin. I don't know who the *you* is, but today it is *you*.

Dear You, there is a story I need to tell you and I don't know how.

There is a bridge with two little towers and complicated cables and pulleys that lift a road for fishing boats on their way in from the harbor to moor upriver. From Kai's trailer, you must cross that bridge to get to the only bar in town, one of the few remaining businesses struggling to survive like the rest of the county, a zone of shuttered lumber mills surrounded by swaths of forest swiped at as if by a blind man with a razor, cursed by poisoned salmon and opioids and dead Indians.

He scribbles only a line or two down before balling up the page.

Dear You. My brother is a fish. He became water, and water became him. Now when I swim, I am him, and he is me.

We are Tó Tsohnii: Big Water Clan.

We are from the high deserts of the Colorado Plateau.

We are drawn to water.

⟡

It is morning, a restaurant kitchen, that quiet moment before Damien's prep cooks arrive. He is hunching over topographic maps of the Olympic Peninsula on a prep table, follows with his fingers the snaky trails of thick brown rivers from their headwaters in the mountains to their estuaries downstream, rivers with short life spans, their names culled from extinct languages. The rains fall three hundred days a year and everything smells like rotten leaves and green needles, the sweet stink of decomposition and rebirth. He feels for elevation changes by scratching his nail along

4

alterations in the map's texture. The mountains are close, but the ocean is closer. A fish does not have to travel far to find salt water in the harbor.

After his brother died, Damien's body went too. He simply goes through the motions as he cooks. I lost a piece of myself, he says to the potatoes, to the rising bread, to anyone who will listen. He is losing pieces of his brother because his memory is fragmented, tossed into the silty river, too. He tries to speak to him, admits to his brother that it feels like dismemberment. "Dismemberment" is the perfect term, the opposite of remember. It is a complicated process, re-membering. It is impossible to tie everything back together, sewing together parts found on the roadside in Nevada, New Mexico, California, Arizona. Damien has an arm or a leg, it is all that is left. He bathed the limb in the Colorado River, the Hoquiam River, scrubbed it in Grays Harbor. If you were a limb to me before and your death was the severing, why do I carry this one with me now? It stinks of rot. It grows barnacles that slurp for air when the tide is out. Damien sprinkles the limb with corn pollen. Pours whiskey on it any chance he gets.

Some days (most) he feels like he has run out of words. Not enough poets can summon his brother, the vocabulary of loss. Grief has claimed his capacity for language.

After boning the rainbow trout, Damien rinses and pats dry their slime-shod bodies before sprinkling on a cure, a blend of salt and nitrites, brown sugar, juniper berries. Normally he feels nothing around these fish. They are more corpse than food, farmed for their tasteless meat in an overstocked pond somewhere far away from here, their eyes coated in a white film. They arrived in plastic packaging, pre-gutted to save time, but Damien does not worry about time in the kitchen anymore.

Swim Home to the Vanished

The trout still smell like lake water. It makes his mouth tingle. He tastes the leaves rotten at the bottom, hears a stream trickling into it. He sticks a gloved finger into a trout's mouth and feels all its prickly little teeth, when suddenly his back seizes at a sharp pain at the tail of his spine. A shock runs down Damien's sciatic, his right hip into his femur. A new kind of pain, a longing, which makes Damien nostalgic for a drive, the kind he and his parents and brother went on every few months when he was a kid, a several-hour hot car ride to their grandmother's crumbling government home or Auntie's double-wide in Diné Bikeyah.

From the backseat window, Damien's and Kai's heads bobbed as they watched power lines bend to the tops of poles, then dip below the horizon. They watched birds line up on wires like music notes on a staff and wondered why they didn't get fried. They laughed when tumbleweeds stuck themselves to fence lines, mocked perplexed cows grazing empty lands while their mother raced mile-long trains along I-40, a race she always won because she did not have to drag railcars full of oil or coal or cars or logs, while Neil Young, Robbie Robertson, and Linda Ronstadt guided them around dust devils and vermilion cliffs and smelly Mack trucks.

Kai told stories featuring his invisible friends: Garlic Balls, Uncle Zippy, a third one Damien can't recall. They joined Kai on his adventures and their parents laughed along, but Damien understood the apparitions, he knew that they were conjured from real weirdos in town—a dirty cowboy who smokes too close to the railroad tracks; that one Indian guy who loiters for popcorn by the corner newsstand.

The boys waved hello to the sad single yucca in their grandmother's dirty front yard as soon as they arrived, a plant that lived for decades, until the family used its roots to wash their hair after their grandmother died. Then they tried to coax mangy dogs subdued by heat and hunger out of the shade for a head scratch. Their grandmother, a beautiful woman born for land where red dust coats plateaus and sagebrush blooms like winter horse breath, spoke to the boys excitedly in Diné Bizaad, a language Damien could not yet shape with an untrained embouchure. But they understood more than they admitted. They felt like time travelers. They were young, and they were old. More than anywhere else, Damien and Kai felt both at home and lost at once.

Damien has cleaned hundreds of fish and mammals, yet he feels different about these rainbow trout now. He considers their consciousness, how even these stupid rainbows must have had a spark in their tiny brains, a cold thought squeezed through their two-chambered heart. For a moment he feels close to the fish, especially as they lie wide open and boneless.

He and Kai had always liked dead things, but his brother was braver than Damien. Squeezed the grasshoppers, fed them to ants. Captured spiders and made them fight to the death. Powdered his cheeks with the sparkle of moth wings.

During summer rainstorms, the brothers played in ditches lined with volcanic stones, used G.I. Joes to build dams with mud and pine needles, and when the dams broke waved at Snake Eyes as he went scrambling down the spillway into the street.

"Goodbye," Damien said.

"Goodbye," said Kai.

⸺

Damien slides hotel pans filled with salted ice into the bottom of the oven and then seals the vents. He splays the seasoned trout onto wire racks to place in the oven above the ice.

He feels a gurgle in his chest, finds it difficult to breathe, as if he were a fish who has been out of water too long. He doesn't belong here anymore, but he doesn't know where else he is supposed to be. Maybe that is how steelhead feel before they head out to sea. When anadromous fish return upriver to spawn, how do they know where to go?

In an iron skillet, Damien heats wood chips until they combust into flame, then smothers the fire and tosses the smoking pan into the oven. He wonders whether he is preserving life or death, if the smoke is to purify or embalm. He realizes this preparation is a kind of ceremony, like many of the repetitive tasks he chooses to take on rather than assign to his cooks—roasting veal bones until the fat and marrow spit, simmering them with mirepoix and wine and spices for fourteen hours; straining, degreasing, simmering another half day until the stock has the viscosity of blood. Some rituals are monotonous. Others are an observance, a sacrifice.

Damien blames himself for his brother's death. Reason fails to convince him otherwise. Those first days Kai went missing, Damien figured he'd finally run away. How could anyone know that he might harm himself? Kai had carried an intensity that agitated and occasionally terrified Damien, but he always felt his little brother was more likely to hurt somebody else before himself, somebody who might well deserve it. Maybe Kai's death would be less difficult to comprehend if he'd ended up being some kind of martyr.

When Damien thinks of his brother as a toddler, he is: bumps on a big head, red-faced and bawling. Sharpening a butter knife. Eating cold soup from a can with the sharp lid still attached. Damien once caught Kai sitting on top of the kitchen table playing with a Tabasco bottle, specks of red on his arms and chunky knees, about to bawl when it got in his eyes. He thinks of that show they put on for their parents, the clown trick where they impersonated a tiny man—Kai's hands were legs and Damien was the arms and when he pushed a penny whistle too far into Kai's mouth Kai gagged and tried to beat Damien up. Or how in kindergarten Kai didn't take off his pirate costume for two months after

Halloween. His class holiday photo captured him poised with his back to the camera in puffy pants and ruffled half-sleeve shirt, a red sash around his waist, plastic sword probably confiscated.

Kai was a good artist, but Damien felt like the world tried to punish him for it. One year, a teacher recommended counseling after Kai drew a realistic portrait of a Rambo rhinoceros, ammo strapped across his muscled chest, a hunter's bow slung over his thick shoulder, and a bandanna cocked sideways on his head the way the medicine men wear it; but the teacher's main point of contention was the rhinoceros's cigar dangling from his enormous lips, not the rhinoceros's potential for gun violence.

Kai is a piece of graphite in Damien's arm, the left one, from 1989 when Kai stabbed him with a Ticonderoga #2. Damien does not remember blood, only a red spot, a speck surrounded by a purple patch of swollen arm meat, though an eight-year-old does not have much arm meat. They were jumping on the bed, arguing. They might have been playing some version of school, and Kai, in his insolence, attacked Damien, the teacher, maybe because Damien pretended to reprimand his brother for refusing to do his homework, or for refusing to play school in the first place because what child in his right mind wanted more class time after he had already spent the day in school? A child with few friends, perhaps, or one whose only friend was his little brother who was still in first grade; a child who did not yet know how to placate his hyperactive imagination if there were no woods to play in and there was no mischief to be had, especially if Dad was around, because even when he seemed to have his back turned he never took shit from these wild animals, these not-yet-savage beasts.

Are these memories all that he has left of his brother? As if twice isn't enough, Damien thinks he is losing his brother again. First was when they grew up and moved out of their house sometime after their parents left them there. The second loss was in death. Now this, his memory, fading. Damien can remember only a few of his smells today. The sweet alcohol of fluorescent-green ninety-nine-cent hair gel. Old books swiped from a used bookstore. Cloves from the kitchen cabinet. Lasagna in his pits. Damien sees him reading on the couch in the morning sun, cat behind him lapping at the back of his head (she liked the taste of his hair gel). Dust motes and cat hair float around his still body. Smells like pine, the night's fire gone down to embers, coffee burning because the machine's been on since five in the morning. Damien feels there is more of his brother out there. He needs to find out. He needs to know.

"It's time for me to go," Damien says to the trout as he removes them from the sweet smoke. "You guys are gonna have to find a new caretaker."

The pink meat shines and the fat drips white from the skin, still too cool to have fully deliquesced.

"I am you, and you are me. Let us take a trip together."

⋙

When you lose someone close, you travel to a place of the dead. You enter the river, you swim in it, it takes you out to sea. The fish seem to know. It is sad there, lonely but necessary for closure, if closure is what you want. You might grow, you might return to where you came from up those dirty sloughs to small mountain streams. Then when you return to spending time with the living again, you feel guilty for knowing. They cannot feel where you have been, yet. You believe the living world does not understand what it means to be in between like that. You don't belong anywhere anymore, more than you ever felt before.

To be haunted by a memory and to be haunted by the feeling that you have lost all memory are nearly the same thing; it is all loss. You are never getting the real thing back. You lose something while you simultaneously gain something else. A dirty limb becomes a clean limb hanging around your neck. But the smell is not his. It is a clean rot. The stench of life cycling and decomposing into life again.

Damien must find all the limbs. To reassemble, to re-member.

～

What he believed would be his last day as a chef is a mellow one, and after dinner service Damien says his good nights like he does every night, returns home to stare at a bowl of ramen because he forgot to eat at work again. The scrape of his fork against the bottom of the bowl echoes in his empty apartment, shudders his blood. He thinks of his brother. He thinks of the fish, his cooks. He thinks he hears someone in the bedroom. He goes in to check, flicks the light switch on and off, smells the sheets even though he's washed them several times since Kai last stayed here. Damien crawls around on his hands and knees, searches the corners and under the bed for more hints of his brother, but there are only spiders and lint down there. All trace of Kai is gone.

He was last seen in the bar on the other side of a swollen river.

Damien's chest hurts again. Something feels different this time. He starts to cry; at first it's only a couple of squeaks, but soon he is on his knees again, heaving, like an ache in him wants to escape but is trapped somewhere inside his body.

The following morning, Damien is about to shave when he feels the slits behind his ears for the first time. He thinks he has developed some kind of infection caused by stress, or a bad portobello. Grief is real and sudden but quickly fades, only to grow into something different over time: an abscess, cancer, a rash.

They are hardly noticeable at first. A few days pass as they lengthen and change. They begin to look a little like thin-lipped mouths. Soon, Damien is able to lift the flaps to reveal tiny filaments, like whiskers almost, just beneath the surface, and he finds himself longing for water, for home, a journey to sea.

Swim Home to the Vanished

Migration Patterns of Desert Fish

Six months after Kai's death, Damien quit his job. If he'd had to explain it, he would have said he was fed up with the long hours of restaurant life and had endured enough pain in his calves and hips and back. The repetitive tasks of a cook's Sisyphean life exhausted his mind as well as his body. But the real reason was that he felt as if the contours separating the present and the past were out of focus. Kai's migration has pushed him farther underwater.

A ringing grew louder, not in his ear this time but from his belly, so he packed his pickup and drove south until its motor seized, then he wet his handkerchief and wrapped his gills and stuck a fin in the air for the next tidal breeze (still a hand, really, but why not call it what it wants to be?), the air moist enough to lend some flavor to sea.

Damien thought he might find a new family following the path of bleeding rivers and winding sloughs from cold streams where families are born, down the cold estuary where they feed, and off to bigger water, where they grow fat and bored before attempting the long trek home however many years or lifetimes later.

Damien hitchhiked until he found a rail yard, where he put his ear to the ringing steel and listened for the wheel discs a thousand miles away, hot and close to molten somewhere in Iowa, Illinois, one of those I's, a place that smells like dusty mice and slaughterhouse. He feels the friction of a continent wiggle atop beams of tarred pine, the pain and yearning and endless chase for land and gold and blood over a wounded country.

Each night he half sleeps in dust; in the mornings he pulls his boots over crusty socks and ties his sack of sandwiches to his walking stick and continues south, drawn by the scent of salt. His boots are calloused above his toes and the soles have worn to a thin sheet of gum. To pass the time, he attempts to change the shapes of clouds with a flick of his wrist, or flings stones deep into the ravine and listens for the shatter. Sometimes Damien pretends his shadow is Kai. As the sun goes down, he is thankful to have someone join him, a friend to speak to, someone to overcome if challenged to a race.

He is not suited for desert life anymore, though his sense of smell is especially acute in this dry air. He senses water but the ocean is far away. When the sun gets too harsh, he searches for a tree or bush to lie under and swallows lunch in three bites; or, if there is no bush or tree, he removes his bandanna and uses his walking stick to forge a small enough tent to shade his blistered face. Each night before dark he sets up camp, removes his boots, and sets his socks out to dry beside the fire, where he tries to sleep without thinking.

One day the tracks lead him to a sweet-smelling tunnel in a mountain. He can feel the moss breathing from a hundred yards out. Damien screams into the darkness. His voice echoes back. He throws a stone and it sparks against the tunnel wall, clinks a rail where the light chokes off. For a moment he thinks he should find another way around, a path where he can count lizards and kick dandelions, but maybe it would be nice to walk through a mountain. He has never done that before.

As the light behind him begins to dim, Damien tries to think of things to distract himself from the darkness. A river winding across the backs of dead things, its black soil beneath; its tributaries and how they are fed by springs flowing from the depths of dormant volcanoes where whispering trout gossip in caves. He wonders how the river tastes upstream before it gets tainted by shitty cow fields in sad towns, meets the drainpipes of manufacturers spewing heavy metals and aborted slush.

He panics at the sound of gravel crunching beneath his feet, remembers that he has been in a dark tunnel for some time and realizes that a train could chug along at any moment from either direction without warning. He removes his shoes and balances himself on a rail to feel for the vibration on his bare feet. Maybe if he pressed himself against the wall when the train swooshed by he would be okay. In his blindness, Damien feels the movement of the earth's bowels, its billion-year evacuation. He leans against the walls, touches them. They are damp and soft, covered in moss but along with what feels like human hair. Damien is not scared in the dark, nor does he feel lost. He finds comfort knowing that nobody would find his body or miss him if he somehow got smashed and sliced by a mile of train cars full of consumer goods or tanks or lumber cut from the remains of old forests.

A spear of light finally pierces through the other end of the tunnel. Damien runs toward it, trips over ties until the damp stink evaporates. He looks around, gulps the dry air. To the south, the steep cliff descends into canyon, and beyond the canyon is a desert lying hopeless—a hundred miles dotted by spouts of dust devils pushing against the zagging blue shadow of a mountain range. On his right is more cliffside and mountain. A goat trail winds its way to the crest. He already misses the tunnel, the coolness of the burrow, because he is unsure again which way to go.

He turns around.

"Thank you," he says, but he is too far for an echo.

Damien struggles to get his boots on because they are too

ragged, the worn soles and holes threatening to rip at the seams, the laces shredded. He ties what is left of them together and throws them over the cliff and they chop through the air until they are swallowed by the shadow of the canyon. He then follows the trail to the top of the ridge, the burnt tree line, a boneyard of pines missing their skins and needles. The farther he walks the bloodier his feet become. Why did he throw away his boots so soon when they might have lasted to the summit? He rips his handkerchief in half to wrap his smelly arches. His skin still reeks of dirty bleach water, burnt fats, garlic.

He doesn't miss the kitchen yet, but he'd love to cook something—anything—right now.

The mountainside is silent except for the ruffle of his pant leg, a nosy wind in his ear. Damien feels closer to the sun the higher he climbs; he can almost touch it. The breeze at the top of the ridge is cool and dry. Flies hum above the crackle of cicadas, the wind-jostled aspens. Damien thinks he might be able to find evidence of life from up here, a bit of smoke from a village, the clap of a hunter's rifle, but there is nothing. Only canyon, desert, a distant range on the horizon. The only sound is the scurry of lizards running late.

He senses that his father had been here once, maybe when he worked for the lumber company, but that was a long time ago.

Damien stops to bury his face in ponderosa bark, inhales its butterscotch. He counts the tall mounds of needles piled like funeral pyres before the trail sinks into a meadow where blond grasses soothe his burning feet.

From the meadow, the path winds into spruce and ferns. The weather changes with the elevation, and the light grows softer, the air like cooled glass. He ran out of food the day before, and his clothes drape like sacks over his body. Hunger weakens muscle, but he continues up the peak anyway. Clouds pucker at the summit and the mountain vanishes. He is the only person up here, the last one in the world, and it makes him want to shed his skin for scales.

Damien removes his clothes, feels compelled to. He rolls them into a pillow and rests against a boulder, wishing the clouds away. He wants to feel the world on his skin. He wants to feel something other than what he is feeling, but even that has started to fade. Maybe I should die, he thinks. If I close my eyes they might freeze shut, let my skin turn pink; my joints already creak louder than my chattering teeth.

He rips up clumps of short mossy-looking grass, chews it for water, its green flavor resembling some sort of nourishment. He reaches into the cold soil, rubs a handful of dirt around his neck and chest to slow his heart. He thinks somehow this will get him closer to Kai. Perhaps his own death is necessary to be with his brother again. Damien's hesitance says enough. He is thirsty and alone, but he remains as curious about life as he is about death.

Damien gets dressed, teeth poised to shatter. He descends the peak as quick as he can, sliding over loose gravel and hopping boulders down to the tree line. He wanders through the forest for some time before he finds a small meadow surrounded by aspen, a decent spot to set up camp. There is a stream, a small lake some-where; he can smell it. Damien nearly collapses in the tall grasses and meadow flowers, but he is distracted by the cluck of a tongue.

The Goatherd

Across the meadow, under a crop of aspen, an old man rests against a dilapidated wagon. He sits up, squints at Damien, and clicks his tongue again. There is an old mule lying beside him who looks like she has collapsed under the weight of her own skin. The wagon's canvas cover is tattered; the wheels are detached. Notches in the wooden carriage bleed ochre where a metal frame had once been. Hooved goat legs dangle like prizes or talismans from the side of the carriage.

The old man waves Damien over. Damien dawdles, peeks into the cart first. Dozens of small jars filled with leaves, grains, spices, spiders, liquids of varying color and viscosity all sit neatly in little cubbies along the cart's frame next to small moldering oranges and branches of plantains bundled with twine. Among the fruit are muslin-wrapped jars filled with bees.

The old man wheezes, spits, swats at the flies. His crusty linen and burlap clothes cling desperately to his emaciated frame. His wrinkled grin is off-putting yet sincere, a smile neutralized by dark, sorrowful eyes. His glacial joints pop and crack as he tries to rise, but after he swallows a handful of dried sliced mango and a shot of liquor, his eyes brighten. The mule's tail flaps, suddenly alive.

"Hungry?" he asks.

Damien is tempted to refuse out of pity for this skinny man and the saddest quadruped he has ever seen.

"I could eat," says Damien.

"Help me up."

Damien lifts the old man off the ground like a half-empty sack of potatoes.

"You look like you're headed somewhere," the man says. He shakes a stale pant leg free of pine needles and dirt and leaves. "It'll take a few days, but if you keep heading that way, you'll reach the sea." He points south to where the mountain path descends, the way Damien has been heading all along.

Damien pokes around the cart. He raises one of the jars of bees; their crooked hairy legs reach for the sky.

"Take those," the man says.

"They're dead," says Damien.

"Just resting. I am resting, too. Waiting with Ishka." He slaps the mule's ass, then pours a cup of smelly tea from a kettle beside the fire and offers it to Damien. "You look terrible," he says. "Drink. You must be tired. You look tired. I know I am. Let's rest a day or two, then we'll point you in the right direction."

The spoon clinks the tin cup as Damien tries to shake the honey off. After a few stirs, two bees float to the surface. His fingers tingle. He sips the tea and nearly spits it out for its bitterness. The taste is familiar, and before he can shake her away, he thinks of his mother, who, near the time of her disappearance, began to steep teas from bitter plants and found objects when she ran out of tin cans of imported loose leaf. Sometimes she would sip hot tap water thick with slate, stare into the garden, and whisper secrets in French or Diné Bizaad. Said "Déjà vu" like a curse when she saw the robins pecking for worms in the garden beds because she swore she saw the same bird every morning, but she could not remember from when or how long ago. The robins scavenged daily, though she would act surprised each time. It occurs to Damien now that her mind might have been stuck in a loop. He understands, or thinks he does, or so desperately wants to that he can only pretend to understand what his mother went through.

Near his toes, the tops of his black and sooty feet, Damien feels the warmth of his blood pulse. His nerves twitch, as if searching for a pocket of memory.

"Do you have a name?" Damien asks.

"Not one you'll remember. People just call me the Goatherd," says the old man. "I can get people things."

Damien scratches at his ankles. "I need shoes," he says.

"Huaraches, sí," says the old man.

Damien closes his eyes, picks at a sticky patch of cold sap on his arm. He nods off but does not realize it until he opens his eyes and sees the old man kneeling before him unwrapping the dirty rags from Damien's feet. The Goatherd then begins to scrub Damien's feet with soap and a river stone. He takes a pull of pitorro and spits into his hands to rub between Damien's blistered toes.

"Fuck!" Damien screams.

"I used to have many goats," says the Goatherd. "I use their skin on my feet."

The Goatherd tries to smush on a pair of goatskin huaraches but they are too small.

"I can fix this," he says. "Go rinse your feet while I trim this out."

Damien hobbles to the nearby lake. He feels like he is losing control of his muscle and bone, as if they disagree on what his brain is telling them to do. He dips his feet. The water is warm. The pine trees hiss. He wants to close his eyes and lie on the soft moss again at the summit of the mountain. He is a long way from the desert, but he likes it here, the coolness of this elevation. The mountains and forest feel familiar.

Swim Home to the Vanished

He cups a handful of lake water and sips at it, slightly sulfuric on the tongue. He pulls his ears forward and there they are: his gills, moist and glistening. He splashes them in the lake. By the time Damien returns to the camp, his legs are less wobbly but his vision is blurred, his stomach prepared for ejection.

"Don't worry," says the old man. "Put yourself down—you've traveled a long way. We'll be down the valley in no time. Or you will. I have to stay here. I grew up here. Hope to die here, too. Soon, por qué no? It is where my memory belongs. Stay resting; we're not in too much of a hurry. We've waited this long anyway, what's another little bit?"

The Goatherd hums and chuckles as he cooks a trout in an iron skillet over the fire. He fries eggs in the leftover grease, pulls a charred potato from the embers, and pours two cups of thick, grainy coffee. Damien licks his lips. It will be the most he has eaten in days.

The Goatherd coughs and picks at his teeth with a branch he sharpened. He looks, in this light, to be shrinking.

"There is a village," says the Goatherd, "a land for the grieving. Is that who you are? Maybe the people you are looking for, the people you have lost, maybe they are there."

The old man coughs and food flies out and catches in his beard. He takes a handful and wrings it out.

"The village is a place where memory goes when you think it is lost. A place where mothers are born, then leave and wish to return to but don't know how."

Damien nods, and though this cryptic place doesn't sound like a place he would normally want to go, he is intrigued. He scratches at his ears and lies next to Ishka, whose warmth is inseparable from her stink.

"I imagine I will have to retire one day," the old man says, "if I don't die up here in the mountains. If I do, tell them to bury me with all my little bells and whistles—I want to be buried with sound. Throw Ishka in there too. I only hope she doesn't fart when she's dead like she does when she sleeps."

The old man coughs and laughs and spits again. Damien smiles politely; he doesn't want to be rude, he just wants to rest a while longer. There is something about this air he loves, a crispness. He could watch his breath float around all evening. He sees his mother doing the same thing. She was on her way to another world before her sons got to truly know her. Maybe that was for the best. Damien can't seem to remember anything before he had a brother. Kai has always been there. All Damien's life, a limb, now missing. But it is still there, the ghost of a limb. It is there all the fucking time and it stings like a grease burn on your chest that melts through to your lungs and heart.

The old man throws a log on. The fire snaps.

"Since you are still young," he says, "maybe you haven't lost yours yet—but our memory fades. We long for nostalgia, crave its pain, for in that remembrance is a kind of cure, a beautiful handful of a gift, like a handful of dirt, joy running through our fingertips, and what better gift than a handful of dirt?"

The Goatherd's cackle spooks Ishka, and she hops up with a snort. He leans against a pine tree and shaves bark off another branch with his hunting knife.

"I used to grieve," the old man mumbles. "If love is grieving, that was me. Down there in the village, I don't think they know the difference. Time shifts for the grieving. Our bodies change; things don't quite appear the same anymore. We grow numb. It's almost like fate to have found a place you think you belong which is nowhere—*but it is everywhere!*—this place for the grieving."

The Goatherd spreads his arms and looks up at the canopy and sky and nearly tips over.

"I thought I understood the world once or twice in my life," he continues. "I thought I knew what faith was, and love, and carnal and venial sin. Here, eat this bread, it's my body! What kind of hilarious culty priest would tell his flock to drink watered-down wine and call it blood! But to each our own. If only you seen what I seen. Body and blood ain't the half of it. They see the world differently down there, you'll see. Conquistadors, famine, drought. Possessed by ghosts, human lust after excess. It's in their blood, passed down generations. Might fit right in if you're not careful."

The sun drops, and soon the mountain's shadow envelops the camp. It is a cold night, but Damien does not miss the desert. The last light fades, and a waxing moon peeks out and ignites all the fluttering leaves and needles in the forest. He watches the forest inhale wisps of warmer air catching in their nets of moss and branch. The pines are slow breathers. An inhale might take months, but the exhale is quick.

"The smell of trees makes my mouth water," Damien finally says. He is surprised to hear the timbre of his voice restored. It had gone raspy and nearly vanished altogether.

"Sí, this is a timeless place," says the old man. "Let's live here a moment."

The Goatherd puts down his whittling, pulls his straw hat over his eyes, and before Damien has a chance to thank him, the meadow is filled with his snores.

Damien clears a spot under a sap-gorged spruce and sleeps restlessly. He dreams of opening one of the jars: hundreds of bees drift out and fly into Ishka the mule. She inflates into an exaggerated form of her younger self, ribs neatly hidden under a supple, glowing coat. Her hooves twitch with excitement. The bees carry her up a trail and they float over boulders and weave through the trees to a small syrupy lake. She drinks from it. Instead of dragonflies, the lake feeds hummingbirds gathered at the corners where the lake is sweetest. After Ishka drinks her share, the bees pour from her body and swarm playfully above the water. She is a young mule again, prancing along the sticky shore, chasing the kingfishers, nudging black rocks with her muzzle.

<hr />

Damien wakes to cooing, doves in mourning, wood popping under a pot of green banana bobbing in boiling water. His skin is steamy from the fire. As he stretches, he hears the hum of his nerves stretching, as if a song boils in him, like the roiling of bees in Ishka from his dream last night. Damien is warm, full; there is a buzz in his marrow, and it is all that matters to him now. He tries to draw in a deep breath, but he coughs violently on the harsh vinegar fumes of boiled green banana.

The old man laughs. "That's the secret," he says. "Vinegar is said to soften their bite, make them more palatable. You know where these things come from? Can't believe they're still green—should've ripened a long time ago. Here, add some heat."

He hands Damien a plate and a jar of tiny peppers soaking in more vinegar with garlic.

"In one of those buckets I had some coffee fruit to grind for coffee, but I can't find them. Sometimes I eat the cherries and save the seeds in a spit jar, but Ishka must've found them. She may be old, but she still looks younger than me! Must be those coffee beans."

Ishka flaps her mangy tail.

The old man takes a tally of goods in his cart, then he sits with Ishka, who has happily fallen to her side in the sun on a bed of old leaves. The Goatherd runs his shaky hands along her bones. He whispers into her ear; her tail plays in the ferns.

Damien takes a couple bites of green banana. He feels it in his fingers first, then wrists and shoulders: small shocks of light passing through arteriole into capillary, a sizzle in his muscle, clouds of static.

Swim Home to the Vanished

Before he can cry out, Damien's eyes roll back and there he is on a boat listing in a storm. A wave tumbles and tosses him into an amniotic sea. He is a child, weightless, reaching out, but his arms and legs are roots that stretch wildly into dark water. He can breathe underwater, though. It seems so natural. As the storm retreats, the ocean drains and gravity returns. The earth pushes up all the other fish so that they gasp around him too, each with another fish in its mouth. Damien's body sinks, and now he is a big fish gasping on the desert floor. The desert and the fish and the broken wormy boats are all that remain once the ocean recedes.

The Bus

The Goatherd's face, inches above Damien's, smells like mildew.

"It's time for us to go," he says. "No more time for wallowing. Didn't I tell you the consequences of remembering? The pain of it is lodged in you and remembering won't clean you out. You said you're looking for something but didn't know what. And then I said you were more likely running and didn't know what from. We were probably both right!"

Damien does not remember saying or hearing any of those things.

The Goatherd lifts himself from the earth with grunts and bone cracks. He hands Damien a chunk of salmon jerky and the bottle of pitorro, but something is lodged in Damien's throat. It hurts to swallow. It hurts to breathe. He takes a bite of the stinky fish anyway and forces it down with a swig of liquor.

The old man packs Damien a small satchel with food and water, plus a jar of bees to deliver to his friend Wilmarí, who grows corn in a wash near the village. He draws a map in the dirt and tells Damien to descend the mountain to a bus stop—a boulder painted orange with white stripes. He is to wait there as long as it takes. The buses are erratic because there are no villages up here.

"All you need to do is follow that trail," the Goatherd says, pointing between two paths. He hands Damien another cup of tea with two dead bees floating on the surface. "Drink up—you'll be there in no time."

Damien is relieved that the wait is short at the big orange boulder, where a screeching bus slides up cloaked in dust. He climbs aboard the rattling shuttle with "La Playa Oeste" scribbled on a small square of cardboard at the driver's window, and the first thing Damien notices is how the heat has raised all the devilish stinks from each passenger. Damien gags on the smell, purges a few drops of bile into his handkerchief. The chickens look restless stretching out their wings the way they are, but at least they do not complain, unlike an old muttering woman who clips her nails shorter by the mile, first her fingers then her toes, back again to her fingers, which have started to bleed at the cuticle; nor do the chickens express a single cluck over the decaying fish in a bucket sliding between the legs of a bobbleheaded sleeper in the back row. This journey might have been that sleeper's last if his studious daughter (who must have been lucky enough to have been born without a sense of smell) was not protecting him from angry passengers prepared to eject him and his stink out the emergency exit.

Next to Damien is a chicken sitting on the lap of her owner, a short balding man whose legs flop like a marionette's with each jolt of the gravel road. The bird on his lap is struggling to breathe; her mouth gapes stupidly, her zombie eye pierces Damien's with something primordial. As the bus descends the steep ridge, he watches the vines and jungle go dry, trees lose limbs and leaves until they become grassland, then the grass turns to dust and sparkly stone; and if death has a smell beyond the putrid and rotten, Damien thinks, it is this land of chalky bones, this bus barreling through the center of it.

They are far from the mountains now. The vents blow hot air, and the open windows only let in more hot air.

"How much longer?" Damien asks the little chicken man. The little man stares out the window, violently petting his mouth-breathing chicken.

"No sé, un día?" he squeaks.

The land through the tiny window is unrecognizable, but the window, like the landscape, is concealed by a thick layer of dust. Damien is relieved to see he is not going the way he came. They are traveling more south than west, though the driver, who has a helmet of brown hay for hair, seems to be aiming directly for the sun.

"No hay peces en el mar," the chicken man says to his reflection in the window.

"Is that right?" Damien says.

"Sí, no peces. Dicen que los peces nadaron por la carretera submarina."

The man speaks much too quickly for Damien to understand. Damien gets up to stretch his legs but catches a whiff from where the air is hottest, and nearly retches. The bus hits a hole, and a dozen heads bounce in sync with the clang of the undercarriage. He flings up his hands to steady himself but the aluminum roof is oven-hot, so he grabs the luggage rack but it has nearly ripped from its rusty sockets. Damien feels the eyes of other passengers on him, feels tall and imposing and out of place, but when he looks around no one is paying attention to him except for the rotting-fish guy's guardian daughter. She smiles as if she knows Damien is lost. How considerate of her, Damien thinks, but his smile quickly flickers away, because who can trust any salty passenger in this sardine can?

The girl noses her book. Damien returns to his seat. He is hungry despite his upset stomach, thinking now about canned sardines, oysters, razor clams. There are a few treats left in the Goatherd's satchel, including fried crickets that he claimed were a delicacy, a canteen of water, and dried fruits. Damien goes for the breadfruit chips, careful not to wake the neighboring bird from her seizure, and washes them down with the last of the tepid water from his thermos.

Damien lifts the jar of bees to the light. They still look dead to him. The chicken next to him opens an eye. Damien turns to hide the jar, but the chicken is only half-interested and returns to her dreams of corn kernels and mealworms and seed.

By the time the bus reaches its final stop, Damien's ears have popped for the millionth time. He is the last one to exit. He thanks the driver, who is much younger than Damien had guessed from staring at the back of his head, and steps out into the sun. He stares at the bus schedule. His Spanish comprehension has not improved beyond the blasphemous tongues of his kitchen staff, though Damien can interpret enough of the sign to figure out that there is only one bus a month and that one must call a number in advance, but the number has been scratched out in a dramatic frenzy.

The heat unsteadies Damien. He wants to scream. Beat the phone booth to smithereens. Blood pushes veins to surface, the pulse in his temples causes him to smack himself in the forehead and cheeks and hit the side of his head and temples, as if that might bring the pressure down to a simmer.

It seems as if Damien's aches arrive in swells, cresting when the weight of his bones and brain becomes unbearable. He finds it difficult to see hope between sets. This had been happening long before Kai's disappearance.

When Damien's urge to fuck something up subsides, he leans back on the concrete bus stop bench under shade of a willow tree. He closes his eyes with his shirt over his face, if only for a moment, to gather his wits.

Hwéeldi

Damien has that feeling again, a moment of recognition: he has been here before though knows it is not possible. This heat. His body misplaced, misshaped. This is not the same land as his, but he senses the history of blood and resentment and loneliness. The landscape reminds him of his mother, of a story she told Damien and Kai when their father was away.

A long time ago, she said, our people were forced to leave our lands because a man shot a horse. Before they took our sheep, they took our homes. To make their home, they needed sheep. They did not need us. They did not want us. They sent us to a glittering world but not the one we know. Dragged by the hair, pulled by our skin. Beat forward under a sun that never blinked. A vulture and her husband followed the line, waited for us to fall face-first. The soldiers who pushed us sat on sweaty-backed horses, smell of rot baked into their hide.

When we saw a river, it meant we were half-dead. If death is home, then we were halfway there. Women raped. Men shot. Everyone starved. Some women ran with their children to hide in the cliffs, sometimes a forest. Mostly sand. Sand. Sun. Blood curdled into it. We walked until soulless but somehow became heavier.

Carried the weight of our despair. The women who escaped smothered babies quiet. How many hundreds we were. Thousands. Hunted, captured, homes burned. Beat and beheaded. Get up, said the stick. March on, said the gun. Die if you want, you're dead already. Carrion crows shaded the weak.

One man hid corn mush in his scalp. When government soldiers walked the lines with buckets of water, he used his share to rinse his hair and fed us with the drippings. He died of thirst for us. Another man chewed tumbleweed, wiped the paste on children to trap in what life they had left. Soldiers left pregnant women behind, too slow for the starving. Damien's grandfather was inside one of them, forced born by the desert. They named him Yazhí. His people buried his umbilical far away from any home he would ever know. But his mother was to suffer, wrapped in a shawl and shoved behind. Told him not to cry or he would be tossed for beaks to peck. Maybe his mother survived, but he was passed among the still-living. They hid him from the sun. From soldiers on skinny horses. From the scorpions, from the snakes.

Three hundred miles felt like three hundred years. By the time they found the river land, Diné Yazhí had hair. Winter froze mornings, afternoons burned, stars on the darkest nights howled hollow. A camp of thieves broken by the army's scorched-earth policies. They were called thieves when all they stole was another day to live. They were called a successful failure. They were told to farm the desert for the army. But the land was sand and they were not farmers.

Language is resistance but we could not speak, Damien's mother said, or our mouths would be stuffed with chunks of lye soap. We concealed defiance in our mouths. Lulled tongues to sleep until our return. But after four years, the soldiers were shipped east, and we were sent home. A war had broken out between bilagáana. By the time we returned, Diné Yazhí could speak the language the government tried to wash out of him. His mother's language, the sounds she hid in his throat.

Out of ten thousand, one in four of us did not make it back.

But it did not end there. Years later, our people were shipped to other camps, where nuns cut our hair and bashed our knuckles. Sent us commodity goods: old fruit in sugared water, yellow cheese that tasted green, vats of lard, wormy bags of flour. They shipped in rosaries from the east and pushed people to their knees to pray to crosses also shipped in from god knows where. Our people had never seen a ship but learned that whatever came from one made us sick.

To survive, Diné Yazhí had to become one of the invaders. He read their holy book to make them believe that he believed so hard until he really did start believing. It offered him a story to flush nightmares of his violent birth. He began to read other things to escape, too, and soon he learned that their world was not as big as ours, nor were there as many of them.

Our people did not bury your grandfather's umbilical in a place called home, Damien's mother said, so now home can be anywhere we want it to be.

The Church of Bees

The sun is heavy. Damien's throat burns; he has no spit left to swallow. It is hard to breathe with his gills all dried up like this. He rises from the bus stop bench, scrapes vomit off his huaraches with a branch of rabbitbrush. He doesn't remember throwing up. Where's his bag? His last handful of chapulines was in there.

He does not know how many days or miles have passed since he left home. His rags cling desperately to what little of him remains. The stank of the stranger's satchel and goatskin feet has grown on him. Feels like only yesterday he was cooking brunch for a bunch of thankless idiots. Despite everything, Damien feels lighter now, detached. He tastes salt, finally. The ocean. Hears gulls screech. And singing, somewhere, like a million bees rehearsing their hymns.

Up and down the coast the view is obscured by cliffs and rocky outcroppings, but in between the wilderness there is a small harbor and jetty nestled in a bay. A short walk down a rutted dirt road, Damien is blinded by the sun's reflection off the bay's glassy surface. Two docks jut out like rabbit teeth. Wooden fishing boats blanketed under sheets of yellowed canvas huddle close, tied together with tattered rope. A cone of gulls, drawn by the stench of fish guts and blood in the water, swirls and squawks above the hooded men below. Near the boat ramp, shirtless men in rubber fishing pants try to stay balanced as they unload a haul of dorado, but each time the captain revs his motor to keep from getting pulled out with the tide, the fishermen topple over their asses into bloody bilgewater.

The sun is oppressive. Damien wants to swim, but he is beckoned by the singing. He goes down the cobbled street that hums the loudest. The streets are bare except for a few people desperate for relief from the heat this time of day. A small man with splotchy skin furls himself into a square of shadow, cowers at the sun's touch. A woman blistered from radiation shades her eyes and waves Damien away with a caw. He picks up his stride, thinking maybe he should heed her warning, but his body is ravished. He needs a cool place to rest or hide and eat.

Down the street, a lopsided sign pieced together with scraps of driftwood reads NUESTRA SEÑORA DE GUADALUPE in front of a sun-bleached church. A broken wire fence wrestles with the cauldron of flailing cactus arms. Damien attempts to kick the gate open without getting poked. Up the steps, he cracks open the big wooden doors and slides into the buzzing church.

The adobe structure is dark and cool. His eyes adjust slowly, painfully, to the darkness. The first things to come into focus are the beams of knotted pine crisscrossed above the nave, sanded baby-smooth and polished a dark varnish. The benches, too, are shiny enough to be frog-less ponds absorbing the warmth of the reds and yellows and blues from the Guadalupes and saints of the stained-glass windows looking down upon the parishioners as if to sentence them. Incense burns Damien's nostrils, but he thinks it is sort of pleasant, like a dying fire.

A few people turn to him, then spin back around just as quickly. The priest is speaking.

"Dios te salve, María, llena eres de gracia: el Señor es contigo;

bendita tú eres entre todas las mujeres, y bendito es el fruto de tu vientre, Jesús." The priest wears an eyepatch and slouches like a cane. He has the husk of a voice that can carry only in a church like this. "Santa María," he continues, "Madre de Dios, ruega por nosotros pescadores y pecadores, ahora y en la hora de nuestra muerte."

The parishioners hold their rosaries with whited fists to their mumbling lips, an eye to some god or another. Damien dips his chalky fingers into the cold holy water and runs them through his hair, dabs his lips and gills. He stands at a back pew. The hum is soothing. He smells the stink of sweat on him like piss.

He leans into the aisle for a closer look. A casket lies open at the altar. The woman inside holds a crucifix to her chest, a bundle of driftwood tied together with fishing line and kelp. Bees swarm above her. Her lips are curled like a smushed slice of bread, as if she is having a pleasant dream, but her hands have been messily folded, perhaps to hide from the mourners the stump where her pinkie used to be.

Damien slides into an empty pew and unfolds the hassock and kneels. The dead body makes him think of all the bodies he has seen, dead, or close to it. The first was when he was six, a sheep dangling upside down from a juniper tree in the desert, three men standing around with thumbs in their belt loops. They drained the blood, then sliced the belly open, let the purple guts spill into a bucket. He saw a man's body at a cadaver lab splayed on a stainless-steel table with a sheet pulled halfway up to hide the sutures, whose tattoos stretched from life had shriveled in death. The third was his grandmother in a hospital bed, life forced upon her by beeping machines and a superstitious family. Damien held her hand. It was cold and plasticky, as if molded from a sheet of dried glue.

He did not see Kai's body, but he feels the weight of it every day. Damien squeezes his eyes shut and listens for the buzzing of the bees, the murmurs of prayer. He lost the meaning of prayer years ago, never understood its usefulness. All these people mumbling devotions is collective madness. Love for all but none the one, "Ahora y en la hora de nuestra muerte." But he should try to pray, he thinks, might make his mother proud, wherever she is.

The Funeral

Marta smells the congregation's fear rise above the censer smoke. She wants to spit on all of them. All of them.

"This is a house of God," they say, those wives of drunks, lazy congregants.

"A tragedy," they say. "At least Carla's in a better place. What happened to her—and your poor mother, just terrible! How could she ever get through this?"

"The power of the Lord, no doubt," says the priest. "Only He knows, can offer benediction."

None of them knew Carla, Marta thinks, let alone Him.

Marta sits next to Paola in the third row, both sisters itching to get out of there, when a man opens the church doors, letting the cool stale air rush out of the building. He enters with his arms clutched around his rib cage and beltline as if his insides are about to spill out. He dips his fingers in holy water and dabs behind his ear like it's perfume, then takes a seat in one of the back rows behind the handful of mourners, most of whom are old women swaddled in their blackest blacks and veils.

There is a short pause; heads swivel around. The man in back bows his head, lets it sway like a broken pendulum, seeking or sleepy, red-faced but not drunk, not yet: a hungry fish who surfaced too quickly, eyes bulging under burnt lids.

The priest continues: "Santa María, Madre de Dios, ruega por nosotros pescadores y pecadores, ahora y en la hora de nuestra muerte."

A woman behind the sisters pokes Marta's back with a bony finger. "Do you know him?"

Marta leans over, brushing the woman's big ugly hat aside to see the man who wears his skin like a sheet in need of an iron.

"The hour of your death, here to deliver your soul," says Marta.

The woman in the hat sucks her breath and crosses herself.

Marta scans the room for her mother. Her eyes land on Tito, Carla's husband, squirming in a back row in the shadows. She waves but Tito does not see her, or pretends not to.

"Mamá isn't here," Marta whispers.

"Are you surprised?" says Paola, her sister, straining to hear the priest's remarks.

The woman behind them nudges Marta again with a Bible. "Not a terrible thing," she says, "that your mother not show up."

Paola shushes the nosy woman. "Don't you touch her," she says.

But the woman in the hat goes on: "It's not so unbelievable, but her own daughter, nonetheless!"

Paola nearly jumps over the bench to crush the lady. "Who are you? Get the fuck out of here, friends and family only."

"Puta. Your hat is stupid," says Marta.

"Everything okay?" croaks the elderly priest.

Marta signals for him to continue, winking for good measure.

"You almost took her out," whispers Marta.

"Who are these people?" Paola says. She sits back and slides her strong fingers between Marta's, clenches them until both their hands turn red and purple and white, flashing like a deep-sea creature.

Swim Home to the Vanished

"Mamá must have hired them," says Marta. She winces.

Paola shakes her head, and doesn't stop, it just keeps rolling side to side, nearly tumbles away. Her body shudders as if she is holding in a cry or a sneeze, saving it for later to let it all out at once when nobody is around to witness the mess.

Marta wants to tremble with her, to show her sister how much she cares, but she thinks Paola will shrug her off; Marta's performance of grief might be unconvincing. She wants to be a good sister. Paola is now Marta's only sister awake on the surface, soon Marta's only sister aboveground, soon her only *only*. Marta does not know how to be a good sister because her sisters were not good sisters to her. Paola and Carla treated Marta like an indentured servant, that's what it felt like, ganged up on her not only because it was convenient but because they enjoyed humiliating her in intricate, premeditated ways.

One time late at night they convinced Marta to sneak into the church and pound on the organ keys, then Carla and Paola locked her in from outside. Marta was furious, tossed the organ bench off the balcony because the organ itself wouldn't budge (she had to try). She attempted to break a window by tossing Bibles at them, but the books fluttered and collapsed like frightened flightless birds; she drew flames and wasps fighting fanged hairy beasts between their chapters and verse instead. Marta eventually discovered a room behind the altar where the priest stored his wine and crackers. She got drunk for the first time under the pervy eyes of those decaying idols.

The priest struggles for words again, estúpido, old fucking man. No one in this town knows nothing except for the dead, Marta thinks. It is so sweet that the dead cannot speak, yet the living can still point fingers.

Marta turns around; her eyes briefly meet the stranger's. His are so twitchy. He mumbles to himself. His chest heaves like a trapped sparrow.

"You think Mamá is cooking?" Marta whispers. "She must be feeling guilty."

"Or maybe sad and sick to her stomach?" says Paola. "Stop obsessing."

Marta can't stop. She won't. It's been ten years since their father's funeral. This service feels familiar to that one: a story cut short, Ana María's a no-show, everyone acting suspiciously. Thoughts of her father catch Marta off guard, and her eyes twitch back up to the ceiling, she tries to hold back the tears by staring at the old beams up there, pine from a lifetime ago, and the glass-work so colorful spraying across the pews, the reflection of saints in the tears of villagers who never met her sister. Never met her for *her*. They did not know Carla's strength, how elegant her hands were with wood and stone and yarn. They did not know how much time she spent in the wilderness; they should have interred her in the clouds of a mountain canopy. Who convinced Paola to purchase a casket? Carla was claustrophobic.

She was also a sleepwalker. Marta saw her one morning before sunrise slow-dancing on the beach. She looked peaceful, lit by dawn, gown waving sweetly in the breeze. Marta felt threatened by that image of Carla, as if Carla alone had the ability to escape their tyrant mother. Even in a narcotic state, like now, in the casket, Carla looks so peaceful and dreamy.

Paola clamps onto Marta's hand as if it is Marta who needs consoling. Marta wishes she could comfort Paola, too, but she doesn't know how. That was Carla's job; she was a natural care-taker. But did Marta's sisters forget how distraught she had been when Papá died? Where was Paola's comforting hand then? Forget Carla—she acted as if their father's death was a godsend.

Last big hurricane, when Marta was ten years old, Flaco didn't return home from sea. Some nights Flaco returned hot and stinking of liquor, but at least he came home. The night he did not was the first time Marta had these flashes, whatever they are. Not visions or spells, though; she hated when her sisters called them that. She saw her father standing barefoot in her room, salt water dripping from the bloody fishing pants he never changed, fishing coat unbuttoned, too large for his skinny frame. Bulbous scratches scarred his rib cage and sun-splotched chest, wounds that seemed to breathe on their own.

"Papá, ¿qué pasó?" Marta had cried.

Flaco had tried to speak, but only water spilled out. She walked toward him; he stepped back. The room stunk like burnt seaweed. She knew the smell from when she built bonfires on the beach with her sisters and they used to throw whatever they could find into the flames. Seashells and starfish, kelp stipes, driftwood and old rope nets. The bodies of crabs hollowed out by the purple-mouthed eels.

She took another step forward, but her father raised his hands. When he tried again to speak, he collapsed into a puddle and slipped through the cracked tiles. Her room felt like it was about to fold in on itself.

"Papá!" Marta screamed. She ran outside, down the street to the square. The statue in the plaza snickered in the dark. She peeked in store windows, checked the bar, then the docks. If her father was not at the chinchorro singing, then maybe he did finally sink to the bottom of the ocean.

The rain couldn't decide on which direction it should fall. A surge heaved itself into the harbor. Boats squeaked anxiously. The ding of ropes against their masts said a storm was coming, was already here.

Then Marta heard claws on wood—that is what it sounded like, she swears. She climbed into a yola and hid under the canvas. Through an eyelet she could see two silhouettes talking; on the dock was a third. The taller shadow picked the third body off the ground, folded it in half, and stuffed it into a barrel. The other shadow raised a lantern. It lit her face orange. It was Mamá, Ana María, hijáeputa.

She set the lid, and the tall shadow sealed it with a wooden mallet.

"Row out with him," she said to the shadow. "Light him up."

Marta thought her father tried to warn her, but it was too late. Papá was in the barrel, flammable from all that mescal Mamá had poured into him.

"Ship him into the storm," Ana María said. "Watch him burn."

The tall shadow rolled the barrel down the planks to the boat, then raised the sails and pushed out of the marina. The lantern light dwindled into the dark, flashing as the ocean swelled.

Flaco's flammable body lit the boat up in a brilliant light. By that time, Ana María had slipped into the water and wagged herself away. Caimanes hunt only at night. Marta did not tell her sisters. They would not have believed her anyway. They would have said she had fish in her throat, said she was the pelican who couldn't keep it down.

If Carla and Paola were Ana María's favorites, Marta was Flaco's. But Ana María buried him at sea, alight from within, without allowing his daughters to say goodbye.

❦

Marta raises her hands, entangled in Paola's, and presses the bundle to her mouth. She starts to shake. Not for Carla, but at the thought of her mother's betrayal. The anger toward her mother has been so relentless that sometimes she thinks she can't feel anything else, convinced nothing will her make her feel anything anymore.

"She should have made an appearance," Marta says. "Mamá should be here right now. She made this happen. Bruja bitch."

"It's okay," Paola says, gently, but she squeezes Marta's hands tighter, afraid her last sister will flee, disappear. "It does not matter where Mamá is."

Marta tries to release herself from Paola's grip, but Paola's hands are too strong.

"I've been trying to tell you," Marta says. "Blame must be cast, guilt assigned. Do you think she knows how to relinquish her power? We have to be prepared to—"

"To do what? What do you think Carla would have wanted us to do?"

"She would want us find out why this happened, find out who did this, and take care of it," Marta says, unsure if she herself is convinced. If they were born in another world, another time, products of different sets of egg layers and seed donors, would Marta and her sisters have a less reptilian way of looking at the world? Instead, maybe they were dancers, wrestlers, bakers, gardeners harvesting corn pollen, corn, sweet silk in their skirts. They may have even been the kind of sister-cooks who honed each other's knives.

"Let us pray!" says the priest.

"Sí," Paola says; "No," says Marta; "Pobrecita," they cry (for the wrong mother); and the strange man cries for himself.

Paola kneels. Marta follows. The wood, the backs of benches, so salty and saccharine. Nose into hands into wood, faintly like tobacco. Only thing Marta likes about this place. She finally peeks over the pew at the casket. Carla was not one for painting her face, though here she sleeps, pale but rouged, lips stained from crushed raspberries. What wounds under awful clothes. Old-fashioned, bib-like, nearly pink, an injury unto themselves.

"Whoever dressed her like a doll might be next in the casket," Marta says.

She is sure it was the priest. Makes her face burn red. Maybe Ana María told the priest to dress Carla up like this, makeup and all. Carla wanted to be nothing like Ana María. Carla was no bully. She made plans with Tito to crawl out of this desert one way or another before it turned her into something she didn't want to be.

The praying hat behind them whispers, "She looks at peace, wouldn't you say?" It nods toward Carla's body.

"We don't think so," says Marta. "You're next, by the way."

"If it be my time," says the lady, tugging at the mushroom on her head, "I pray for Him to take my hand."

"Take your hat, more like it," Marta says.

"Both you, shut it," Paola whispers.

"Let me hurt her, please?"

"We can't protect the village if you kill everyone," says Paola.

"What do you mean by that?" Marta hesitates. "Not everyone. Just this woman, asphyxiated by her own church crown."

"Fine, I'll help you with that, then no more. Now be quiet."

Paola's glare, those powerful eyes which can crawl into a heart with sweetness only to stab it to death, shoos the hat away.

The priest looks up and clears his throat. The sisters (and the hat) bow their heads in silence. The man in the back hiccups.

If Mamá was out of the picture, Marta would realign the village priorities; she has been honing her platform for years. Tell the people to prepare for desertification. Prepare to find new crops to grow, drought-resistant grain and rice, drought-resistant animals, drought-resistant minds. White coral means get used to no more fish in the water, could be any day now the last of them decide to go. All of it enraged Marta. That, and that her town had adopted customs, costumes, from a culture force-fed to them, sweetened and chased with a bit of monotheism. Oh, there will be changes, thinks Marta, once it is her turn to be on top. It must be Carla's death giving her this confidence, to lead, to step up, to fill the vacuum of loss.

The parishioners stand, straighten their backs. As Paola rises, she tries to hold her hands steady, but her hands will not comply.

"The woman in the hat is just like everyone else in this place," says Marta. "They'll say and do anything to stay on our family's good side."

"Are you still thinking about her?"

"We have to stick together," says Marta, "no matter what happens."

Paola wishes she could agree, wishes she could believe that Marta is capable of sisterhood.

The priest clears his throat again, louder this time. "Would anyone like to add anything before we line up and say our private words to Carla?" he asks. He leans toward the bickering sisters.

Marta nearly takes the bait, wants to tell the parishioners: I do not fear death, nor should you; we should not worry so much where the dead go when they die, and though it is a safe bet we are swarmed with spirits, your blind trust in religion is bothersome, faith as a blanket to hide beneath for when the *real* storms come won't keep you dry.

The sisters wait for the line to shorten before joining. Marta can't keep her eyes off the casket.

Paola reaches for Marta's hand and grips it tight, tighter, like a big sister should, until her nails dig into her sister's flesh.

Marta pinches the back of Paola's arm to ease up.

"Sorry," Paola whispers. She doesn't know what to do with her hands. She tries rubbing them on her thighs, tucking them into her armpits, but they still won't stop wiggling around like flounder.

Marta rubs the back of her wrist. "Now I'm bleeding," she says.

"Liar, that's not even where I pinched you."

"You broke through my skin."

Marta's face changes into something more pitiable. She'll remind the priest, remind the whole goddamn village: after we pay our respects to the oldest daughter of Ana María, they will agree that Carla's death was their mother's doing.

Paola turns away, faces the casket. When it's their turn, they step up and peer down at their sister's dolled-up body, her sleeping face. Marta, fuming, remains an arm's length away. Paola wonders if Carla would have seen past Marta's performances. Sympathy for the dead seems easy enough; empathy for the living is another thing entirely.

Paola pulls Marta closer but Marta resists. She defeats the urge to yell, scream, cry.

"I'm sorry" is a sound Marta breathes; it is so faint as to be nearly meaningless, but it tamps down enough of Marta's sorrow into her burning thorax, for now.

Paola reaches out to touch Carla's cold hand, but Marta flicks Paola's hand away and slams the casket shut.

The Village

Damien looks up from his prayer-turned-slumber in the back row. Nearly everyone has left the building. The hum and buzz that filled the church earlier has been replaced by crackling candles spitting wax. His stomach groans, his face is peeling; maybe that is why the woman in the enormous hat several rows away scowls at him. He has not been warmly received here so far.

"Cuidado con la familia de las brujas," she groans. "Esas mujeres tienen poderes."

Damien does not remember how to properly conjugate verbs; in his kitchen, none of his cooks had the patience to teach him, or he had lost the patience to learn. He understood enough of what the woman said to know it was a warning, but what's a family of brujas even look like? Damien nods at the woman as she exits, her hat nearly swallowing her whole. He wonders if she speaks to all the filthy transients, if her judgment of character is as wretched as her taste in fashion.

Damien splashes his neck and gills with cold holy water once more and steps out into the dry heat. The procession has already started. Speakers stacked on a little red pickup blast mariachi horns behind a parasol-spinning crowd. They look like black ants marching to a picnic. The air is filled with fish smoke. Palm fronds flap wildly in the wind. He watches the procession climb the hill to the cemetery, but he turns toward the village plaza.

At the center of the square is a fountain filled with corroded pesos and stained tile and a statue of a woman in robes fighting off some serpentlike creature with an invisible weapon. She is pockmarked, weathered to a calcified base, limbs and phalanges eroded by her combat with time. Cacti sit around her scattered haphazardly in large clay pots, and a giant cottonwood rises from broken brick, walling off half the square.

Damien climbs into the fountain and finds a spigot. It hisses at him when he gives it a turn. He smacks his splitting lips. He crosses the street to a pay phone, but he doesn't have any coins. There is no dial tone. Who would he call, anyway? His cooks? What brief hope he has evaporates. He cannot think of a single person to call. He has no more ties to that past life.

Damien finds himself back at the dock. Half the boats must be out fishing or don't exist at all, while the rest look ready to sink. The pylons have a mossy shine beneath their suit of barnacles. Tiny mussels gasp for the tide to return. Some of the pylons are rotted, others have sunk so far into shoal that the boardwalk has rippled into helices.

Damien sticks his nose in the air and follows a plume of smoke. He runs his dry tongue over his cracked lips, stinging them. On a pier, beside two leaky coolers overflowing with ice and fish, is a woman with overbaked skin, fat but sprightly, who flips meat on a grate that looks like a xylophone resting on a small charcoal fire. She mumbles something to herself while holding a glass of liquor in one hand and a pair of tongs in the other, with which she occasionally fans the smoking grill. Whole snappers and little pulpo spit into sizzling coals. She wears a sarong, bright yellow with blue flowers, her hair tied in a tall bun and wrapped in yellow ribbon. All sorts of vianda and fish rolled in banana leaves sit on a side table ready to fire. Pots bubble over in the corners. Everything has an oily green sheen, some sauce she bastes with.

"Señor?" she says. She puts down her glass and waves Damien over. "You look hungry."

He stumbles closer. She pours him a glass of liquor from an unlabeled bottle. He takes a whiff. A peppery burn runs from his top lip into his nostrils and up between his eyes.

"Gracias," he says, retreating like a stray. He raises his glass, swallows it in one gulp. The bones in his hands relax. He hears the buzzing again. He cranes his neck, expects to see a swarm of bees from the church. He is not fond of bees. Prefers them over flies, though; a sting is nothing, but when flies land on him he feels like he is rotting.

She pours another. A smile crawls up her fat cheeks. Damien sips at it this time while the smoke of the first one burns his esophagus.

"This is a new batch," she says. "Aged well, just opened."

"It's delicious," he says, "but I don't have any money."

"Don't worry. You look to be misplaced." The woman gazes at him with something like pity, but he cannot hold her stare. He still doesn't know what he looks like; he could even have a dorsal by now.

"Let's get you a plate." She serves up sausage and rice with peppers, whole grilled sardines, blackened lemon, and boiled cassava. The woman's food is vinegary and garlicky and sweet, swimming in oil. It reminds Damien of something, but the drink and exhaustion have fogged him up.

"Thank you," he says. He spoons a heap of yellow rice into his mouth.

"You're welcome," says the woman.

He sips another bit of liquor.

"My name is Ana María." She reaches out to shake with a big greasy hand.

"Damien." He raises his fork.

"Where you from?"

He doesn't really know anymore. Did it matter? "I should lie down. I feel light-headed."

He sits at one of the tables with umbrellas, and after he takes a few deep breaths Damien shovels in a mouthful of the woman's food. He senses it will stop her from eyeballing him. He chews slowly, tries to imagine where each ingredient comes from, breaks it down to the numbers—how much each ingredient might cost, the color of soil where the vianda grew, the tall plantains, their protectorate of bees. He feels them swarm above him. One curious bee separates and swoops down. Damien's initial reaction is to run or shoo it away. But instead of attacking, the bee shrinks its flight path around Damien, as if for further inspection.

Ana María pours another drink. Sweat drips from her temples. Her eyes narrow.

"Your scars," she says, examining the lines on Damien's forearms.

"Looks clumsy," says Damien.

"Sí, pero I have them too," she says.

She pretends to roll up her nonexistent sleeves. She has large hands, but still they don't reach around the excess flesh of her wrist. He recognizes the pale splotchy scars splattered across her wrists and forearms from hot grease. And the backs of her dark arms have pale lines cut into them, like notches on a baseball bat. Knife slips, maybe, though some look like claw marks. A cat would be too small. A rooster, perhaps.

"I'm looking for a cook," she says. "You look like you might know how to grill a fish."

How dumb of him to think he could ever run away from a life in the kitchen.

"Fácil." Ana María points out the fish fillets cut into perfect portions, the sauces, the pots of simmering roots. "You clean, scale,

grill. Only a couple rushes a day; we stop serving at sundown."
The job supports her family, cooking for the fishermen and villagers, serving them beer and flavored water. Her daughter Paola does most of the prep in the mornings at home; her other daughter, Marta, runs the hot side. But if anyone wants the mescal, they must come to Ana María. They might say they don't want it, but they do, they just wait until sundown so their wives won't see.

Ana María snorts and grins wildly. Her teeth look like they've recently been sharpened.

Damien nearly tumbles from his chair, but Ana María catches his arm and whips him around like a dorado.

"Careful there," she says.

"I'm okay, it's okay, you can let me go." Damien shrinks from her grip. He can't believe he feels this drunk already.

"If you need to rest, I know a place," Ana María says.

"Just need to walk it off."

"I have a room."

"Like I said, I'm fine."

"I'm about to close up." Ana María clasps her heavy hands. "I can take you around, show you the village."

"Thought you closed at sundown?"

"I close whenever I like. And you can sleep later. Vamos." Ana María reaches for him again.

"No." He steps away. "Don't." He feels the burn again in his throat. Something deep below searching for a way out.

"I insist," she says. "First we clean you up, then——"

"No, let me go." His eyes are watering. He can't keep it down. He runs to spew off the side of the dock but misses. Little bits of orange meat and rice invite a flock of eager gulls.

Ana María fills a pitcher from a cooler of melted ice and dumps it over his head.

"Fuck!" Damien screams.

"Better?"

It is.

He looks up. She smiles, her gaze distant. He recognizes that faraway look. It runs in his family. The eye moves blindly across a field of pastels. The preoccupied smile fades and folds itself in half. His parents' gaze, their struggle, which Damien and Kai didn't notice until it was too late. Instead, the brothers built forts in the forest to hide in when their parents argued, returned when they were hungry, or after enough time had passed for their parents' tempers to cool. They had been so preoccupied with their own loneliness that they didn't recognize it yet in their own sons.

Now that the acidic bits have left his body, Damien feels less lethargic. He rinses his mouth with a wash of beer.

"My daughter is being buried today," says Ana María. She wipes her sweaty brow and looks out at the water. "I couldn't bring myself to go," she continues, "because my family, we're leaders in this community. At least I am. I must remain open and available; the people must be fed. We must be careful not to show weakness." Her voice is quick and agitated, like that ache in that muscle in your neck when you push down a sickness or a cry until it rises into your glands under your jawbone, and forces you to talk like she is talking now, choked and trembling and hot.

Damien nearly spits his drink. "Sorry to hear that," he says. Be polite, he thinks, refusing to acknowledge he was at the funeral.

Damien watches Ana María wipe down surfaces, hum and click her tongue. He sees the brightness beneath her lazy walk, as if the lower half of her strained for light from beneath her shadow.

He considers Ana María's offer. He could take the job until he figures things out. An easy job with room and meals. Isn't so bad being this close to water. Could swim every day if he wanted to, isn't that why he was drawn here? But scarier than someone with power, he thinks, is someone who believes they have some when they don't. He never liked working for anyone else in the kitchen.

Dizzy, Damien collapses under the shade of the umbrella and

picks the salty pieces of regurgitated fish from the back of his teeth with a skewer. A splinter pierces the inside of his cheek.

One of Ana María's crusty eyes tears up. She wipes her long face with a meaty thumb.

"Carla was a good cook. Hard as you try, you won't replace her."

"I have no interest in staying long, anyway." Damien stops himself from asking what happened to her daughter. Perhaps the less he knows the better off he'll be.

"Who knows, maybe you'll like it," Ana María says.

She clinks open a bottle and drinks almost all of it in one go. Damien watches the muscles in Ana María's cheek contract, her teeth clench, unclench. He thinks, How terrible a feeling it must be to lose a child, to have to fill a daughter's shifts with a random worker when the daughter's body isn't even cold yet.

"Okay," he says, "I'll do it." It is unlike Damien to be so trusting. But he has nothing else on him, no place to sleep, money, food.

"Bueno, that should settle it then," she says, and pours them each another drink. "Salud."

They raise their glasses. They drink, and the liquor lights Damien's heart, warms it up. He coughs a little but holds it down this time.

"I'm not crying because of this," Ana María says. She flips the shot glass. "This I can handle." She pours two more.

"No, no," Damien says, "no more for me."

"This one's not for you," she says. "It is for the ones we have loved and lost or left behind." She blows her nose into the crook of her elbow, leaving a slug trail.

The alcohol hits him hard, but he is grateful for the numbness. It makes him want to keep going. He forgets his pain, all of it. Legs and back, neck and shoulders. Hollows him on the inside too.

Ana María finds a clean dish towel and soaks it in ice water, then she carefully unfolds it and wipes down her face. When she reappears, she is glistening and revived somewhat, though now with a predatory eye, as if she has emerged from a dark river.

"After this, I will show you where Eddie Caro's bar is," she says.

Damien raises his glass to make an offering. Ana María raises her shot, too. He knows an offering doesn't really mean anything, but he looks up at the sky anyway, contemplates why or for whom he is raising his glass so high (for the dead; he hasn't forgotten completely), and suddenly he feels self-conscious in this pathetic stance toasting to the unknown, and the ensuing awkward silence paralyzes him. He blinks and doesn't know what to say as Ana María gulps loudly, and he nearly mutters an "amen" just to break the silence, but he snaps out of it and slurps down the burning liquid, and the fire crawls into his chest and coils deep into his belly like a sleepy fox. He cannot help but think they are drinking together for the same person, or maybe it is for the same loss, or maybe it is guilt, but for whatever reason, for this brief moment, he feels seen for the first time in a long time.

Burial

The pallbearers close the casket and carry the body outside into the heat and load Carla onto the mule-drawn hearse. Tito, some elderly seat-fillers, and several bees follow. Marta and Paola exit the church last, heads bowed, fists clenched. They are greeted by a small crowd grinning too eagerly. Marta sees their show of teeth not as respect but as a sign of cowardice, submission to her mother, who isn't even here. Or is it us they are frightened of? she wonders. The daughters of Ana María will take their mother's place after this breach. Their mother, Ana María, once a savior, now a black cloud weighing on the shoulders of a weakened village. Someone must set them free. Marta will be her people's emancipator.

As the procession marches up the hill to the cemetery, Marta watches her circus-mirror reflection in the fenders of the shiny hearse. It makes her look funny-shaped and bulbous, pinned together in black segments, like a carpenter ant or a wasp (had she any wings). Paola is sniffling under the shade of her sombrillo. She had insisted that the caravan have a band because Carla would have loved this as a celebration, a lovely stroll up the hill, but Marta had wanted the procession to be only her and her sisters.

Instead of musicians, large speakers on a tiny truck blast Carla's favorite chinchorro songs.

Paola stops halfway up to let people pass so she can speak to Marta alone.

The bees, sensing the parishioners' fear, lead the way forward.

"What if I could have saved her?" Paola sniffs. "Every piece."

"Don't say that," says Marta. She feels phony saying it. A pat on the head in lieu of a Band-Aid. "What do you mean 'every piece'?"

Paola pinches Marta, leaves nail moons in her skin.

"Will you stop, please?" Marta tries to pull her arm from the nook of Paola's armpit.

"The scene is repeating in my head. I can't turn it off," says Paola.

"We don't know everything yet. Your imagination is filling in the blanks. Imagination is your enemy." Marta kicks a dandelion head.

"Please, Marta, I'm not picking a fight."

"Your tone says something else."

"What do you expect? How fucking polite to do you need me to be, today of all days?"

"Why are you yelling at me?" Marta reddens. Her remaining sister is turning on her; she should have known this was coming. Marta will be left alone, as expected.

The procession is nearly to the cemetery's entrance, but at the steepest part of the road, the mules grow stubborn. Marta tucks her hands into the pockets of her bulbous robes, where she rolls beads of dried mud with her fingers.

"Paola, I'm sorry," she whispers, "but you don't need to worry about me. I don't expect you to."

"Anymore?" Paola says. Dubious of Marta and her games of charm, Paola does not fall easily for these apologies.

"No, you're right," says Marta.

Swim Home to the Vanished

"If Mamá asks you to do something, tell me. For now, we have to play it cool with her."

"Why?" Marta snaps. "Why would she ask me something and not you? Do you think I would help Mamá? I'm nothing like her. I want nothing to do with her. If only Mamá knew how talented I was—"

"Jesus." Paola drops her sombrillo down, just enough sun to blind Marta. Paola looks deep into her eyes. "Don't get upset about it, Marta. I didn't say you're like her."

"I can take care of myself," Marta says.

"I only want us to be careful." Paola raises the shade back up. "Don't do anything stupid," she says.

"Like what?"

"Like that time after Flaco died," Paola says. She remembers Marta was so upset, she ran around during a big storm, lucky she didn't get hit by a falling tree. Instead she got so sick she was bedridden and delusional for days.

"That's a different story," says Marta.

The mules finally get off their knees (after a bit of sweet talk by the Pallbearer) and they lead the small crowd into the cemetery grounds to Carla's plot. The hole in the ground is damp and sparkling. The Pallbearer, the black cowboy (he came from a place that does not know fish), the toothless one who can't drink without a straw, puts the bodies away. He has kind, fidgety eyes. His face looks sculpted from stone, and they hear he chiseled out his teeth.

Pallbearer stands tall, waits for the hearse to straighten out. There are two helpers to keep balance, but he is the muscle. They remove the casket from the hearse, place it on the ground next to the hole. He leads the straps through the handles of the box with his huge hands, then lowers the casket, one handful at a time, each release an eight-inch fall. He does not smile unless rum-drunk, nor does he bring flowers. But he is a sweet man. He wears those hands only for these occasions, to aid in the descent, to drop bodies into holes, then he'll pocket them and waddle back to the chinchorro to suck beer from a straw and dart his curious eyes among the living.

"Marta," says Paola, "the bees."

They trickle in at first, then start to build themselves over the casket. Some try to sneak into the cracks of the lid.

"They mourn with us," Marta says.

"Or they warn us," says Paola. We drop our sister into the earth when she dies, but to bees, birth and death are reversed, Paola thinks. Bees drop eggs that turn wormy in golden-walled cells where they're fed pollen vomit. They feed on the nurse bees' custom liqueur until they grow wings and mandibles and chew their way out.

Marta shoos some of the bees off the casket with a flick of her hand. The swarm weaves fearlessly through the remaining quivery parishioners, then buzzes far away, enough to no longer be a nuisance but close enough to keep an eye on Carla.

Ana María had lectured her daughters countless times about the Church of Bees. Nature shares a grief, she said. To some people, the bees act as a guide, to others a gauge. Bees hold their setae to the ground and report on the emotional state of the land. We are supposed to pay attention to them. This land, this earth, has endured enough turmoil at the hands of the blind and will one day rise up in vengeance. Their family's role, the village assumed, was found in their ability to understand or communicate with the bees, thus keeping a pulse on when the earth decides to revolt.

Paola and Marta stand over Carla's sparkly grave. Paola takes Marta's hand, quickly this time, before she can slide away. Despite Paola's anger and resentment, she will protect Marta, even from herself. Paola holds Marta's hand tight, tighter, like she thinks a big sister should.

"Stop hurting me," Marta hisses. She attempts to peel her

sister's fingers back, but Paola's hands are still too strong and sweaty. She panics. "Let me go."

"You can tell me anything," says Paola, "you know that, right? Let me help. You only need to ask." Paola twists Marta's arm like it's a wet rag.

"You keep saying that. It sounds like you're fishing for a confession." Marta cries. Paola doesn't understand; her sisters never have.

Paola loosens her grip.

"It's only me and you now," she says.

Marta nods.

"If you think Mamá can't be allowed to take everyone down who looks at her funny, neither can you."

Marta laughs. "We have to do something about Mamá, though, right?" she says.

"Not yet," says Paola.

The priest says some words. So-called friends of Mamá say some words. Carla must be getting squirmy, Marta thinks.

Paola looks around at the dwindling mourners, too distant to listen in on their conversation. None of them will look at her or her sister anyway, except for that weird man at the church.

"Where do you think that guy went?" she says.

"Still praying when we left." Marta shrugs. "Are you going to the wake at Eddie's?"

"No, I shouldn't," says Paola. "Come home. Come back with me."

"I can't risk seeing Mamá. If she's there I don't know what I'll do." In Marta's imagined scenarios, none ends without bloodshed.

"Por favor, Marta, don't stay there all night."

"Why, you think something like this will happen to me next?" Marta looks down into the glistening grave. "Unlike Carla, I can defend myself."

"Don't be like that. You knew she could fight," says Paola. "It's strange, right? Carla should have an attacker's meat under her nails. She was stronger than both of us."

Marta flicks away a bee that is more agitated than the others.

"Or, the attacker didn't pose any threat," she says, "at least initially. Could have been somebody she knew."

"Carla knew everyone," Marta says. "She trusted everyone, everyone trusted her, the only person in our family worth trusting."

"Exactly."

"What do you mean, 'exactly'? We've narrowed it down to everyone in the village and the valley, probably mountains, too."

"Not *that* many people liked her."

The onlookers have started to meander to other gravesites, searching for shade under tall coconut palms as the day heats up. Many trees remain stumps left over from the big storm that snapped them in half years ago. Nobody bothered to replant them because when the coconut fruit dropped, their thump on the ground sounded as if the dead were trying to knock their way out to quench their thirst or else finish some unfinished business, so the villagers left the graveyard as it was.

Paola cups a handful of soil from the pile beside Carla's grave. Marta follows, finds a spot in Carla's hole where something seems to be wriggling, and tosses the soil at it.

Some bees scatter, but most stay, as handfuls of dirt knock on Carla's new roof. Then shovels sound like ocean: scoop, toss, thump, crash, over and over like they are rowing into the earth. The sun will soon bake Carla's grave into a tasteless cake.

On her way home, Paola turns down a different path, the long way.

"Marta," she says, "don't drink too much."

Swim Home to the Vanished

"Sí, Sister," Marta says. "Te amo, tú lo sabes."

Paola continues down the old road in silence. Marta is tempted to cry out to her, tell her she misses her. How could she miss her? She sees Paola all the time, every day, too much. Maybe she misses the old Paola, the Paola before their father's death.

"I miss you," she says under her breath, but Marta is alone again. "Go on, then, go home. I'll be at Eddie's because over there, they know me. They understand."

Marta used to think she was close to Paola, though never as close as Paola was with Carla. Growing up, Marta became the victim of their alliance. Sisters grow apart; perhaps they could come together again. But her sisters did not understand how everything changed for Marta the night Flaco died. Flaco's death gave Marta's life new meaning. It revealed to her the weaknesses of her enemies. She discovered a modicum of self-worth. She would no longer be a child after witnessing such events. She kept it a secret, and learned from her mother's strengths, for soon Ana María would be nothing but teeth and scales flushed out with the tide.

<hr />

The remaining mourners had maintained a wide berth around Marta and Paola when they walked down the hill from the cemetery. They shuffled along behind them, whispered their gossip, though neither sister seemed to notice or care.

"One of them found Carla's body," they said, mother's minions, scapegoats and real goats and phonies.

"Not only beat up but stabbed, too, a hole the size of a fisherman's blade."

"Tito would never do such a thing," they said, those wives of fish slayers.

"Never, but what of love?"

"This was obviously Ana María."

"She made a lot of enemies over the years."

"Including her own daughters."

"Each of them has a bit of Ana María in her, too."

"Who else could have done it than one of the three?"

"Or worse, who else might be next?"

The Archivist

Paola gets home from the funeral, runs upstairs, slams her bedroom door shut, and locks it. She does not want to be interrupted. She expects the others to seek refuge here after the wake at Eddie's, so she might have a couple of hours to find comfort alone among her curiosities. She flutters her nails along glass jars, tapping a xylophonic song. She removes an eight-ounce container of dried black beans from a shelf in her closet, and with one hand on the lid and another on the bottom shakes it like a cocktail. She loves the sound. A shuffling like footwork from an old dance. These are not beans for cooking, these she collected from a field on Marta's second birthday. Paola snipped and dried the tender bean pods herself when she was seven years old, and when the husks were shriveled, she carefully pinched the beans from their cadaver bags like they were black rubies.

Paola has a bitter relationship with time. She collects pieces of it—memories, dismembered moments—as if to hold on to whatever remains of her family. Her collection started when Marta was born. Paola wanted to drop her newborn sister into a container and save her in that state forever, tiny and shriveled and unaware of the violent place she'd been born into. Marta was born thin and light, with a full head of black hair. Paola clipped a little bit off her fontanelle and stored it in an envelope. On it she wrote the date and time, then hid the envelope in her bottom dresser drawer.

As Paola grew older, she did this with rice grasses, buckwheat, hopniss, using whatever containers she could find: tiny paper bags, empty glass bottles from alleyways, plastic jugs or buoys washed ashore after a storm. She constructed boxes by gluing together twigs, and she wove baskets with palm fronds or seagrass. She stumbled easily into kitchen work before she could reach the kitchen counters, though her mother would have insisted she learn to cook at that age anyway. In Paola's quest for what would become her family's compendium, she discovered pickling, canning, preserving, fell in love with the sweet pain of boiling vinegar, the burn of it in her nostrils and esophagus, saliva on her lips.

Ana María reminded her daughters daily what they were born to do. This was their land to protect; that meant maintaining the land, which meant asserting power, which ultimately led to cooking by way of corruption. Paola believed that because Ana María and Flaco were terrible cooks, they required their children to learn how to feed and clean up after themselves. Ana María and Flaco would disappear after a meal, presumably to go hunting or fishing, yet never seemed to return with much.

But Paola did not mind her tasks. Rather than play outside, Paola preferred to rearrange the herbs and spices according to phylum and kingdom, though much of her parents' stash had been reduced to bundles of sticks, weeds, and seeds rolled in brown paper bags, tossed into a stinky drawer. She created what would become the household spice cabinet in the downstairs kitchen, where each item was meticulously labeled with time, place, and weather on the day it was harvested. Bright powders glow now in clear containers on open shelving, a canvas of spice organized by hue. To Paola, colors are their flavor: the yellow of a wasp, the orange of a monarch, red from a velvet ant.

Paola reaches for a jar of stringy pods (*Elettaria cardamomum*), opens the lid, and inhales deeply. She thinks about why she collects anything at all. It began as a way to preserve the time of Marta's arrival, who, though she was no surprise, was no planned child, either. In Paola's five-year-old mind her sister slid out wet-eyed and hissing, like how the lizards hatch in the reeds by the river. Paola had to safeguard the world as she knew it. She began to save everything in little jars because Marta's birth changed Paola's future, and it was essential to her that the past remain the same.

Paola never shared her collection with anybody, not even her sisters.

She opens another jar. She sucks out air infused with a seed-pod from a rare orchid. Tears come to her eyes. Her mouth waters, smiles.

Of course, some things did not change after Marta's arrival: the bruises on their mother's thick skin, the bite marks on Flaco's arms and crooked fingers. Marta was too young to have known the severity of their fights back then. She did not know the kind of man Flaco could be, the man Paola knew. For this, Paola collected for her sister sludge from the Red Clay River and cactus spines and fishing hooks found snagged on Flaco's pant legs.

Paola was fifteen when Flaco went missing. It was not rare in a community of fish people to lose their loved ones at sea. Flaco, the village's best pescador, required the most destructive storm anybody had ever seen to wash him away. It troubled Paola, but she was not as devastated as her little sister. Marta was still young enough to revere their father, still thinks of Flaco as a masterful pescador and a village hero; it's no wonder she was drawn to stories about nihilistic fishermen fending off toothy creatures in billowing seas, the mythical heroics of wife-beating drunks.

Sure, Paola and Carla were afflicted, but Marta had suffered something more severe. She has always acted as if her sisters did not understand or care about her. Could it be only because they did not love Flaco like she does?

To ease the suffering caused by her parents' negligence, Paola began experimenting with insect preservation (one process: hang them to dry on thin threads of fishing line found in Flaco's tackle box). Parasitic Hymenoptera were best kept in 90 percent ethyl alcohol, but adult bees were not allowed to swim in alcohol because it matted their hair. Adult moths, butterflies, anything with scales and long fine hairs were worthless in the liquid, too.

But the soft-bodied, and poisonous, wasps kept well, especially if the alcohol remained chilled. She gathered washed-ashore cephalopods to store in a homemade ethyl alcohol gelée. An individual fish could be harvested into a dozen jars alone (see items #35–47: scales, swim bladder, eyes, gills, bones from head, bones from tail, ingested items found in stomach, etc.). Some creatures were dried and pinned to whiteboard displays under thin glass, others pickled in chemical sludge. What was once coping became compulsion.

It was not long before Paola ran out of drawer space, so she converted her closet into a museum of dead things as a way of preserving life. There are days where Paola feels like she keeps time as a pet. History is alive. Why not ensnare it, claim it as your own? Next generations learn only if we survive this one.

Paola cut sections from her closet walls with rusty scaling knives to make room for shelving. It took years, because she worked secretly, quietly, with tiny saws, afraid of what her mother might do to her if she discovered her obsessions. Neither Ana María nor Flaco had shown much interest in their middle child, too preoccupied by Carla's fierce independence and Marta's colicky years, which were quickly followed by years of Marta's unabated complaining.

Paola's human samples began with snips of Marta's newborn hair, and over time she curated her entire family. Paola did not plan on losing them. She did not expect this tragedy; that is not what fuels her interest in preserving their memory. Her father did not leave much behind except some old clothes and fishing gear, fish scales grown thick around the ankles and wrists. Fortuitous, though, that Paola had harvested from Carla a vial of drool during her afternoon nap a month ago, and that she had filled a wooden ring box with shavings of her calluses. Paola extracted Carla's hair from the drains, dried it into spirals of black pasta. In a tiny salt-shaker, she had her yellowed toenails chattering with a box of vials of other people's nails, each meticulously labeled with a description of the person from whom the keratin had been harvested, sub-organized by digit, in Paola's minuscule script.

Some jars in her exhibition contained intact fingers. Toes, too. Paola starts to cry. This is all she has left of Carla. Paola's life's work and nobody knows a thing. To a novice, it is hard to distinguish pig hooves paddling in brine from, say, a school of ears floating in formaldehyde. Or to tell the difference between the shed skin of an iguana and the shriveled remains of an arachnid's carapace. To discern classifications of mammal skin after its hair has been shaved, degreased, salt-cured.

Paola is not hoarding trophies, soused souvenirs. She captured the life of one sister's intrusion, and preserved the death of another. To Paola, the jars contain ingredients of truth; memory often fragments the present tense into fiction. Someone must record this life before it is gone; how else will they remember Carla, or any of their dead?

Eddie Caro's Chinchorro

All the regulars are there. Retired fishermen, men without dreams, no longer dreamers, no longer pescadores, happy in this shithole swelling up their livers to purge a memory. Most of these borrachos have been there all day and will be until sunrise. The Pallbearer, El Mariachi, Benny, Fredo the Gimp, the Hunchback and his wife Lorena. El Mariachi is propped against the jukebox singing at the top of his lungs for half the village to hear. When the mourners enter, the patrons turn to acknowledge them; even the Hunchback offers something of a nod. But when Marta follows, they all swivel back. She wishes she could hate them, but they are all tíos to her, mad uncles who once respected her mother as a leader in their village. Now Ana María rules by fear. That is how Marta wants them to see her, as if she is next in line.

For now, though, she will lurk at a table in the back of the chinchorro with a bottle of mead Eddie orders special just for her, and she'll keep an eye on all the swimmers trapped in the whirling room throughout the evening. A few customers paddle by to offer their verbal and facial condolences. Marta raises a glass to the Pallbearer in his spot at the end of the bar, sucking at his straw. When it gurgles, Eddie, who rarely removes himself from his office chair, not unless you're a loyal customer, gets up with a painful grunt to slide a beer down the counter, flaunting his catfish smile. He has made the throw thousands of times, but still he leans back and strokes at his whiskers with pride, perhaps wondering why his customers do not cheer for him more often.

It is then that the man from the funeral flops into the bar. He looks around idiotically, like he's never seen a watering hole before. A smile crinkles up his burnt face. He looks drunk already, like a fish in search of water who just got spat on, enough to breathe through the night. Schools of borrachos swim around the stranger, but they do not make eye contact. He finds an open stool and orders a beer and leans into Lorena as if he wants to tell her a story but forgot what language his tongue makes. Lorena turns away from him, throws her heavy arms around her husband, and nuzzles his hump.

Marta is embarrassed by the old couple; she feels herself go hot and turns away, maybe because it reminds her of Carla and Tito when they made out at the bar. It was the sound of their smacking and the places they let each other's hands touch and fumble over, all happening right in front of Marta and these drunks, Carla not even afraid that Ana María might walk in. Seeing her sister with anybody grossed Marta out, but for some reason she hated that Carla had picked Tito of all the men here. Carla seemed to put on these shows just to tease Marta, make her mad and blush, and it did, she made Marta livid, both her sisters did, and then they let Marta stew in her own insecurities and hateful juices for long after.

Marta and Carla did not get along, and it was more than their age difference. What pissed Marta off about Carla was that she did not earn the villagers' confidence, as if she were bequeathed good faith simply by being Ana María's firstborn. If Paola is the shy and quiet sister, Carla was the one who got away with anything, in addition to being considered the beauty in the family (if one could call it that; she had a little bit of a tail, but that didn't seem to bother

Tito). Who cares about the symmetry of a face when Carla could rouse a crowd like her mother. Both her sisters and her mother can get along with anybody, or at least fake it well enough. Not that Marta wants to have that skill, she thinks she's doing fine, she would make friends if she wanted them thank you very much. But while Ana María collects allies and creates hostilities and bargains for her ear, Carla was selfless, never demanded anything in return for her friendship and kindness. Carla was respected because she was genuinely curious. She helped customers feel welcome, listened to their stories and complaints about the village and Ana María's bullying. But Marta saw through all that, thought her sister was still a charlatan. Still, she wishes Carla were here in the bar now. A room came to life when she showed up.

The drooped heads of mourners come alive, and the regulars start to get a little rowdy. Marta wants to mourn Carla, she really does, and that day will come, she knows it will, but she cannot purge the memory of her father, Flaco. What happened to him has long twisted her view of the world. She locked him deep in her thorax so as not to warp or distort his pristine image. The attempted murder and erasure of her father only made his presence permanent in her body.

If Marta heard unflattering stories about Flaco, her love was not swayed. If it were not for what Marta witnessed on the dock ten years ago, she would be forced to agree with her sisters that their father was a lazy drunk and would rather fuck a ray than his wife. Sure, Flaco will forever be remembered as a great pescador. But if Flaco didn't die, Carla would still be here. None of this had to happen.

Had he survived, would Marta have accumulated bruises of her own? Perhaps she would finally feel like she had something in common with her sisters and mother.

Marta scans the room. In brittle daylight, the customers are cadavers sipping away their last years, but as evening cools, Marta sees the drunks for who they really are. Eddie is truly catfish. Pall-bearer some bigmouthed, no-toothed bottom-feeder. Benny like a seahorse who recently discovered legs. Lorena and her crusty, discolored husband, barnacled like whales to the bar. Even El Mariachi's baritone resonates like a deep-sea song. In a corner, Tito and his crew circle like hammerheads, who knows over what, maybe his dead wife, but coded in fish talk. Then Eddie swims by with a paper plate full of toothpicks baited with cubes of ham and cheese. The new guy grabs several toothpicks and stuffs his mouth, then he starts getting chatty with a sea cucumber. The cucumber makes it known that she cannot hear him. The juke is too loud, plus all the voices ricochet off the high ceilings. He leans in closer to speak. He smells the sea cucumber's neck by accident. He looks surprised, probably because she does not smell like a fish. Someone should warn him they can be toxic.

Still in the back of the bar, empty bottles clanking, the room spinning around Marta, the wobbly table not helping. She keeps an eye on the stranger. She is determined to meet him; it is rare to have visitors. And because she wants him before her mother can get to him; Ana María has probably set her squinty eyes on him already. Not that she wants to be her mother. Marta hates her mother. Her mother makes her nauseous. Does that mean Marta hates herself? Marta is her mother through blood and sheer need, direction. Without an enemy, what is her purpose, or her mother's?

Damien looks up from the cucumber and orders from Eddie, so uncanny a catfish that Damien can't avert his stare. The thin comb-over, beady eyes, slick whiskers poking out the sides of his mouth. Eddie's hands are only hands, but what type of fins for feet might be hiding in his mud boots? Across the bar, Tito points to Damien with his lips, whispers something to the Pallbearer. The Pallbearer then sits next to Damien. Even mounted on his barstool the Pallbearer looks taller than everyone else in the room.

"Hey, you fish too?" the Pallbearer asks. He smells like old fryer grease and mouth rot.

Damien shakes his head. "I don't think so. What are you supposed to be?"

"Hey," Benny yells from the other end of the bar, "he don't speak, you know."

"Sí, Benny," Tito yells from a game in the corner, "maybe not to you. Mind your business."

"What, you wanna do this now?" Benny makes every effort to climb down his stool, but his tiny legs, shaped like parentheses, tucked into knee-high rubber boots, are weighed down with globs of dried cement. Tito acts ready to box, and everyone laughs at this seahorse dance routine they put on.

The Pallbearer taps Damien's shoulder, towers over him like a long-necked goose. Damien reluctantly turns away from the boxing match.

"If I average one burial a week," the Pallbearer says, "for twenty-five years, that would be thirteen hundred cadavers I've buried: twenty-six hundred eyes, times ten for fingers, times twenty with toes, give or a take a few dismemberments (part of the trade of pescadores), it adds up to the population of the living."

The smell of the Pallbearer's toothless mouth nearly pushes Damien off his stool. He checks the math on his fingers.

"For every body I bury, there are innumerable Criers. Miracle the graveyard isn't underwater already." The Pallbearer pulls beer into his straw, then tilts his head back and lets it roll down his throat.

"Is there something I can help you with?" Damien asks.

"We don't know you."

Damien eyes the room, sees them see him. That woman Ana María led him here. He had not considered he might not be welcome.

"Some people," the Pallbearer continues, "when they grieve,

Swim Home to the Vanished

they don't have a choice about how. Some are violent grievers, some get drunk and vow silence, others convert to the religious. Blame the dark, blame a god, deny it ever happened. I seen some Criers turned on by tragedy and they grieve through sex or love or some version of one or the other. It happens to a lot of us. Know what else?"

As Damien shakes his head, the Pallbearer reaches out with his long arm and brushes Damien's sebaceous hair behind his ears.

"What the fuck?" Damien slaps the Pallbearer's hand away, his enormous cracked fingers.

"Ah, sí!" The Pallbearer starts to laugh, but it looks like he is choking on a chicken bone.

"¡Mira!" yells Eddie. "Look what the guppy did. Made the monster spew beer out his nose!"

The crowd, inciting the ill-matched shark fight between Tito and Benny, turns and points at the Pallbearer, who covers his gummy grin. He chokes on his laugh; it's like a donkey's bray.

Damien violently smooths down his hair, seals it with grease from behind his ears.

"No, no, ¡diles que paren!" Pallbearer shoos the crowd with his free hand.

Damien cups his ears and gills. He darts his eyes around in fear and agony, not knowing why they would laugh, not knowing if it is him they are laughing at. Of course, they are not laughing at him, it was that big dirty man with a donkey in his throat who puts people in the ground for a living. Why would they laugh at Damien? He has no bray left in him.

The Pallbearer finally catches his breath. His pungent words emerge braised low and slow. "I wasn't laughing at you, entiendes?"

Damien nods. "Why would I think you were laughing at me?" He squirms, motions to Eddie for a drink. The crowd resumes their chanting behind him. One woman, who was grimacing at Damien earlier, now smiles at him with yellow teeth.

The Pallbearer waves the nosy ones away. "If we are suspicious of you, apologies. You understand."

Damien removes his hands from his head. He unwraps the damp bar napkin from around his beer can and uses it to moisten his throat and jaw and gills.

⚬

It is the middle of the night, and the music and laughter pouring from Eddie's is still at its peak. Scratchy horns blare from the juke's old 45s, bass thunderous, trebly guitars a touch too deafening. Voices sing along with their own ricocheting echoes in the cavernous bar, full tonight with the addition of the vespertine critters who bloom brightest in the evening.

Marta roams the room with wobbly grace, and while the crowd opens for her, they do not make eye contact. Most of their red eyes twitch restlessly in their sockets in search of moisture in this dry place. Bees bump around the ceiling to the cadence of a slow song now playing on the jukebox. The Hunchback is bent over his straw. Tito is in the back playing dominoes. The Pallbearer has stepped out for a piss. Everyone seems happy, oblivious.

Marta signals to Eddie. He rolls toward her in his office chair but kicks too hard and rams into the liquor rail.

"He might be able to help us," says Marta, pointing her thumb at Damien, who is sitting a couple stools down sipping his beer like it's whiskey.

"Not us, you!" Eddie grunts, clicks his tongue, wags his finger.

"You haven't even heard what I've got to say!" Marta says.

Eddie hands her a can wrapped in a cocktail napkin to soak up the condensation, and he rolls away.

Marta visits Lorena next. "You know what Mamá is up to," she says.

"Sí, pero no, Marta," Lorena sings, "let Ana María be who she is and no one else will get hurt."

Eddie wobbles out of his chair, a ratty old thing with orange sponge leaking out of its sides. He lifts his head as if he can smell something a long distance away. He tilts his head back farther. His thick whiskers quiver above all those chins where his gills are most likely hiding.

"A storm's coming," Eddie declares.

"What, you predict the weather now?" jokes Lorena.

The entire room bubbles up with laughter, except Mariachi, who is still singing a sad one with a six-tooth smile.

"You don't smell that?" Eddie smiles. He rolls over to the liquor shelves and grabs a bottle of rum and pours everyone warm shots into tiny plastic cups.

"That's you, Eddie," Marta says, "you're full of shit."

"The nose knows. Sixth sense. Feel it in the bones. Remember that last one? I felt its pain months before it hit." Eddie crosses himself with the rum bottle. "Let us stay dry, huracán," he says.

Benny comes up to Marta, says he saw her asking questions, scheming. "You need help? I'm your man," he says.

"Not yours," Marta says. "Leave us alone, Benny. We didn't ask for anyone's advice."

Benny pokes Damien's arm with two of his tiny fingers so that it feels like one regular-sized finger. "You've got to keep those gills wet," he says, "jump in water with eyes open!"

"Salt stings eyes," says Lorena.

"Close them, then!" Tito yells from behind.

"I said never mind," Marta says.

"No, please go on." Damien motions for the crowd to continue their banter. The rousing circles. The hunchback and porpoise, a catfish in brine. Damien feels like bait.

"How do we see underwater if we keep our eyes closed?!" Benny yells.

"It is all darkness under there," says Lorena. "Darkness and algae. Darkness and big-eyed fishes and weightless words and sharp teeth."

"You want advice?" the Hunchback croaks. "If you never leave this place you get rum gum. It's when your teeth get numb and loose. It's like they get cold. Like they want to vacate your mouth, pack their plaque bags and storm out the place, leaving sockets in the dustup, sore sockets to soak up the crumbs of Eddie's stale bread."

The room fills with more laughter.

"Hide the leftover ham in there!" cries the Hunchback. "Hide your half-chewed yellow cheese and let it dissolve overnight, a drip in your throat, a midnight treat!"

"Don't trust *his* teeth," says Lorena. "Don't trust any teeth. Don't have them when we're born, don't have them when we die, maybe weren't meant to have them at all!"

Lorena hocks a loud loogie and spits for punctuation, but she misses the door and her phlegm drips down the frame like a jellyfish.

"Don't stay here," says Benny. "Don't stay in this dry place with us, the toothless and sun-hardened. Don't believe this is where teeth go to die."

"To be stuck among lizards, huddled by tuna and coils of rope with blood on your hands," says another old fisherman, "don't believe you got no choice in the matter."

"Don't listen to them," says Marta. She pulls Damien aside. She recognizes that he has no more faith in the benevolence of drunks than she does. "They've never asked what *I've* had to say. I've known them my entire life. What they're saying is you need protection."

"From what?" Damien says.

"From the sea cucumber over there, and from Mamá and the rising waters, from the colorful snakes in the reeds." A man will do anything for a bit of direction and safety, Marta thinks, especially if stranded out at sea. She could use this man to help her depose Ana María of her lizard crown, and if that be his purpose, he may be collateral damage, sacrificial. She knows exploiting a stranger sounds like something her mother would do. Marta would not be surprised to discover that her mother sent Damien here already drunk and stupid and hooked on her mescal.

"Have another shot," says Marta. "Eddie, three more, por favor!"

Eddie lines them up and fills them to overflowing. Damien, distracted, lets his eyes meander from Marta to the ceiling to his drink, his torso and shoulders swerving half a beat out of time with the cantina song. He nearly slips off his stool when he hears the uproar in the back where Tito and his friends are slamming their last tiles down on the rickety card table. One man stands and laughs before he slinks over and sinks his head between his knees in defeat.

Damien feels the room get watery. Benny slaps him on the back.

"Look at this poor bastard! He's no longer here," Benny says.

Damien doesn't know why he is crying. He dabs at his tears discreetly with a cocktail napkin. Marta punches his arm.

"Something wrong with you?" she says.

"You made our new friend cry already, Marta?" Benny asks.

"I didn't mean to, he's an open wound."

"What'd you say to him?" Tito joins in from his win.

"Nada, no sé," says Marta.

"I'm sl-fine," Damien slurs.

"He is stranded in some dusty memory between the living and the dead," says the Pallbearer. "His pain brought him here."

"What are you going to do with him?" asks Eddie.

"Don't know yet," Marta says, scratching her chin.

Tito grabs Damien's arm and hoists him upright.

"Hey," Tito says, "do you know where you were going before you got here?"

Damien shrugs and burps up something salty.

"You can't just leave him like this," says Eddie. "Safest to let your mother take him, at least for now." He raises his wiry eyebrows and his reading glasses slide off his nose. His thick whiskers protrude from his jowly face—a warning sign, a show of aggression. He wipes his small nose with the back of his hand and slides them fresh beers.

"I didn't know where I was going," Damien finally says. "To die, maybe?"

"Funny guy," says Lorena.

"You're stuck here for now," Marta says, petting Damien back down to his stool. "We'll keep you company while you figure it out."

"Just let me work," Damien slurs. "As long as I can work I can ignore them." He sits, calmer now. He burps something foamy, this time into his fist.

"Ignore who?" asks Eddie.

Damien tells the bartender an inebriated story about how he gets itchy under the skin no matter where he is, that something is crawling around under there, that he scratches at it mindlessly, sometimes with a sharp point, a blade or stick or pencil. His story is misinterpreted by the pescadores as something far more severe. No, no! He wants to peel all his skin back! he explains, lie down and fillet himself blade parallel to table, peel off the layers one by one starting with epidermis, dermis, hypodermis, the false borders between us and the universe, thin margins of error. Seals water in, keeps water out. Keeps bugs out and some bones in. Despite this thin skin, these weak margins, he wants to believe they are all one big amalgamated bloom, the stuff of stars fluttering in the ether—

The bar laughs.

"Hippie," someone says.

Swim Home to the Vanished

"I think it's the dead," says Damien, "ghosts or something, I don't know. Why do you keep looking at me like that? Like I'm nuts. I'm not nuts." He gulps his beer.

Marta smiles a polite, menacing smile, as if her teeth refused to do as she asked.

"You're right, the dead are not gone," she says. Her tongue feels heavy in her mouth. "Ignore them all you want, we still live among them. All the time. The dead, the spirit of the dead, ghosts, whatever the fuck you wanna call them, they're here all the time, and there's no running from them. Happens all the time, right, Tito?"

Tito is not listening. He is thinking about Carla, Carla, his corazón. He takes a shot of rum (he asks for it chilled this time) and stares at patterns in the countertop, mapping out Carla's freckles and moles in the laminate.

Marta has nearly forgotten she's supposed to be mourning. She hopes Tito hasn't noticed. She drapes her arm over his shoulders. She bows her head. Tito bends his, too, and whimpers something Marta can't make out. She attempts to pray but she doesn't remember how, though as a child she had found praying so easy. Perhaps she was able to feel more, back then. Was she capable of showing love? Receiving it? She knows there was fear, she was able to express that much. Marta no longer wishes to acknowledge her fear, thinking that will make her bolder, brave.

Tito comes up for air. "It's like the fish," he says, looking to Damien. "I know, I say it a lot, but it always comes back to the boat, the net, the hook, the gaff. Blood in the hull, bellies ripped open, air bladders plucked and left in the current for the bigger critters. The men on the water, in calm seas or vicious, with a caneca as their crown, king only of what they've known all their lives because you can't be king of something you know nothing about."

"What are you talking about?" Damien sways on his stool.

Marta realizes she was wrong about the bar. Idiots. Nobody will help her conjure a plan. They're too drunk to agree on what number of beers they're on, or what song to play next. These fish are drunk and riled enough to be convinced of anything, only to forget moments later. Besides, there is no way they'll agree to take action against their enormous matriarch. They find comfort in this obliteration. They will not risk the one life they think they have left to live, but the hypocrites act as if they do not know what lives among them. If these borrachos die, they're not going anywhere, just like those before.

"I guess I'm saying that in order to appreciate the good, a lot of people have to die," says Tito. "Animals, too."

"Storm is coming," Eddie states again. Nobody bites. "Will be here soon enough. The last one had her chance, and the next one won't make the same mistakes."

"Here, we continually relive our pain," says Tito. "Brujas did this to us."

"Isn't that just part of life?" says the Hunchback.

"So is dying!" someone else adds.

Marta thinks her mother does not care for these expendables, prefers them simmering in their stupor. They may know this already. It may be why they spend all their time at the chinchorro in the first place.

Damien goes to piss in the alley (less foul than Eddie's bathroom), wonders who the culprits are as he steps around the piles of shattered glass canecas. Everyone in the bar seems capable of drinking this much shitty rum. How many times had he done it himself? Pound a bottle of liquor in an alley to thin the blood, hide in shame for sneaking a drink.

Damien returns to his seat, orders another beer, and half listens to Benny argue the benefits of copper over brass fixtures. Mosquitoes attack Damien's ankles—only his. The villagers must have an immunity. He decides to leave the chinchorro without further harm or humiliation, and stumbles through the mob.

Marta is set on following him. Sneaks out the back door after realizing just how drunk she is, hoping not to puke. Damien is gone by the time she loops around. She goes home and sits in the middle of the street to listen to the night creatures and watch the pinholes in the sky spin and spin. She does not want to go inside, does not want to be reminded that her sister is dead, or that her mother is a cabrona, or that she forgot to do something Paola asked her to do days ago. She goes up the stoop, drapes her body along the steps. Legs curled in, head tucked into her arms, a moment she wishes her father were still alive (never mind that he'd be at the chinchorro all night). Before Marta is able to cry for him (or Carla), she hears someone walking near.

A hand shakes her lightly. Marta's body freezes. She is in no position to move, no position at all, a pile of thumbs. Some sickly rooster crows in the distance.

"You okay?" the voice croaks.

Marta expects some borracho, and recognizes Damien's voice.

"You need water?" he asks again, kindly.

Get the fuck away! is what she wants to say. She turns to squint and spit at his shapeless silhouette, but he is already tripping through the front door of her home.

Still in her black dress, eyeliner smeared, she smells oil burning from a lantern. Hears the waves strike shore. Crickets chirp as if it is their final song, like they are all being crushed at once. The star will be up soon, Marta's sun. It is now that dark part of morning when the sea conceals everything in a coat of salt. What does he want from me? Did he follow me here?

Damien returns with a mason jar of water. He trips again, spilling some on himself.

"Drink this," he slurs.

Sometimes, when Marta closes her eyes, she sees things clearer. Like now, she imagines this man going for a swim in the bay and it does not take long for him to get pulled under. A caimán (Mamá!) rises to the surface. She takes an arm and leg and spins her tail into the black water. The village knows that the big fish swallow the little fish and she swallows the sea.

"Do you need help?" He steps closer. "I have a key . . . I live here now, the lady said . . . I can leave the door unlocked, in case you—"

Marta wants to scream *Fucker don't touch me I live here!* but she is too drunk to speak.

Damien leans over, offers his hand.

How the fuck did he get a key? Marta flips him off, cradling the water in her free arm. Damien relishes his wobbly retreat inside. What does he mean he lives here? Has Mamá dug her greedy claws into him already?

Marta drinks his water. The sky turns black to blue, and there is one little cirrus in the sky like a stroke of horsehair. Marta forces herself up the banister. The world is still whirly, so she curls back up on the top step and falls asleep, and in her dream she loses her nose and lips. She runs around holding her hand over her mouth, but the parts keep falling off. She tries superglue, bubble gum, duct tape; still the parts won't stay put. Then Paola comes in and piles Marta's body parts into some arbitrary system, then Carla shows up and attempts to put Marta's face back together, but her pieces no longer fit right. There is a mouth where an eye used to be, and an ear for a mouth, a nose for an ear, and when Marta tries to scream at her sisters to put her back together they only laugh and act as if they did nothing wrong.

The alley smells familiar. Pez viejo, la panadería. Marta opens her eyes. She tries hard to focus, make the doubles become one. She gets up and puts her ear to the front door and listens. She doesn't want to risk running into that man or her mother or her sister, so Marta climbs the fire escape and crawls through her bathroom window. She draws a bath and slips in and watches her skin wrinkle and slowly hang loose from her bones.

The River

Kai was missing for thirty days before a squall washed his body ashore.

For thirty days, Damien lost his sense of taste. Every phone conversation with the detective made his stomach feel like it was bleeding. He hoped his brother would return from an expedition in the woods, a search for their mother and father, both of whom Kai believed could be photosynthesizing among the weeds.

For thirty days, Damien imagined hundreds of ways to die before he considered the possibility that Kai might still be alive. For thirty days, Damien's calls were not returned. If Kai had run away he would have packed first, but his room was clean, his trailer spotless.

The day he disappeared, it was raining. On the high Pacific coast in winter, the rains feel frozen even though they hardly ever are. Damien imagined his brother on the bridge where a hand gripping the metal beam had to be stronger than a storm, had to crack through the rust for a grip, had to be dry to not slip, had to be warm enough so the cold wind wouldn't numb his long fingers, which had plucked rusty guitar strings or flipped through the browned pages of a used Russian novel earlier that day.

Damien was not there, he was a hundred miles away hunched over a line of tickets, screaming at his cooks and servers with sweat in his eyes. He was not there, but he could feel his brother, could touch his arm and chest. Damien tried to whisper into his dark eyes: you are welcome to stay with me, it is safer to be in the fog with someone you know.

Sometimes Damien imagines Kai pissing off the quay after leaving the bar on the other side of the swollen river, slipping in because the rain was heavy, the concrete slick. He sees Kai's black hair bobbing in the fast water. Damien knows what lies at the bottom of that river, seen it when the tide goes. Reshaped bicycle bones trapped in oily mud next to car tires and an orange-seated Big Wheel, fishing waders, tangled running shoes.

Maybe the wind whipped around as he leaned into it, changed direction, and nudged Kai just so. The boats moored in the estuary looked constructed of brittle wood, held together by a thin coat of marine paint, like everything else in town. If Kai grabbed ahold, the boats might have disintegrated.

Was he feeling so confident on booze that he wanted to take a dip? Forty days of rain and a high tide peeling out from the muddy banks—no way he'd be that dumb or drunk. But the bridge nearby made for a good vaulting point. Damien could see Kai up there on the truss squinting and grinning, balancing above the current.

"Twelve fifteen may have been the time," the detective said, "the last time another human saw him, in the bar on the other side of the swollen river."

Damien wondered which fish saw him last as he floated into the bay.

Perhaps the bar where he was last seen was playing the Dick Clark rerun of the East Coast countdown. Maybe Kai was staring out the window rubbing his sweaty palms on his khakis, bouncing his legs. Maybe a man in the back who had been drinking since

Christmas Eve was eyeballing him, a man waiting for the right moment to act out an evil he'd been nursing his whole life.

But the detective said no sign of struggle. A trace of drugs in his stomach; Damien doesn't remember which ones he said. He wondered, though, did he take enough of something to sleep through the hardest part of drowning, the part where the lungs fill up with water and the body convulses to expel it? Were his eyes closed?

Perhaps his final words were his mother's: "Do shí tá hó t'sii da." Meaning, in Diné Bizaad: *I am without balance.*

"Whether we'll ever be able to determine what happened, we don't know," the detective said. The detective's face looked bloated the first time Damien met him. Not like a body trapped under some logs, not like he'd been sleeping underwater for a month. Too much sodium, probably, or those heavy beers on the weekends.

Damien drove home from the coroner thinking about a pact he made with Kai after their parents had left them, made permanent by a fight with kids on neighboring properties. The contract they had always known, yet that remained unspoken: one of them had to persevere if the other was gone.

Damien learned from the coroner that bodies in water at an advanced stage of decay are called "floaters"—decomposition begins at the moment of death, and the gases released during putrefaction are appropriately named: cadaverine, putrescine. A coroner can pinpoint the date of departure by when a body rises.

He also learned that only 10 percent of drowning victims die from asphyxiation. When people drown in fresh water it is from swallowing the water, which dilutes the blood. The lungs scream for oxygen, the heart pumps harder—in three to five minutes, the heart gives out. In salt water, the water absorbed draws blood into the lungs, and the heart goes into tachycardia since there is nothing left to pump.

Paola

It is late when Paola goes to bed, and nobody has returned yet from the wake at Eddie's. Marta is probably still there; who knows if Ana María even showed. Paola falls asleep counting sweet potatoes. Someone crashes through the door downstairs, shocking her awake. She listens as they feel around the room, bumping into things like they're drunk or have never been here before. Perhaps both.

Paola crawls out of bed and peers over the half wall to spy on the intruder. He fills a mason jar full of water. When he turns from the sink, Paola recognizes him from the funeral. Who invited him here? Mamá, of course, she must have rented out Carla's room already to a man no one knows without even consulting her daughters.

He leaves and is gone only a minute before he staggers back in. Paola is relieved to see he does not look capable of doing any harm, seems almost cheery in that drunk way, the way Flaco used to come home. He certainly looks more alive than he did in the church earlier today, though now he struggles to climb the stairs, holds on to the banister with his life. Before the man reaches the second flight of stairs, Paola retreats into her room and locks the door. The doorknob rattles. He moves to the next room. That door opens. He enters Carla's room. It sounds as if his clothes shed themselves from his body and fall to the floor with a loud thump.

Paola listens for the squeak of Carla's hammock, waits long enough to ensure the man has rocked himself to sleep. She goes in. The man has already got himself tangled cicada-like in the hammock's web. His arms and legs are twisted around each other, twitching in surrender. Paola kicks deeper into his room the pile of clothes he left behind. A satchel remains in the hallway. She opens it, finds mostly crumbs and cricket legs and an empty thermos, but in an outer pocket she discovers a jar of bees. She hangs Damien's bag on the doorknob, keeps his door cracked open, and sneaks away downstairs to check if anything is missing or broken. She pokes her head outside. She finds Marta passed out on the steps, curled into a little comma.

"Marta?" Paola runs to her sister, imagining in a flash all the violent possibilities, terrified her instincts were wrong, that this creep was now upstairs in Carla's room. Paola clenches her jaw. She will tear apart the streets, burn the village to the ground, and destroy whoever left her sister like this!

But then Paola notices the mason jar. She relaxes her burning cheek muscles and releases her whited fists. Paola is surprised at herself, how ready to defend and fight for her incapacitated, ungrateful little sister. Marta's bouts of down days may have become more common, but she is normalizing this behavior, nursing its bloom. Paola cannot help but defend Marta, though. She loves her family too much to let it be destroyed by a few bad decisions. Tonight, as an act of defiance, or to teach Marta a lesson, Paola does not carry her sister to bed. Instead, she kneels next to her sister, touches the crown of her head. Marta does not move.

The night before last, Paola was crouched at the river's edge, a muddy place, dangerous because the river is known to snag the unsuspecting, but Paola has been collecting cattails and sweet-grasses and red clay there for years. The other night she heard something and hid, careful not to rattle the reeds more than the wind.

Paola found Carla there lying in the mud, motionless.

She panicked. She had to capture the moment. She felt compelled to embalm the present tense. She contemplated what to do next.

She removed Carla's shoes and socks and tossed them into the river. She pulled out her pruning shears (the same ones she used to collect the thick-stalked cattails, same ones that scissored Marta's infant hair) and with a snip took Carla's left little toe. Blood trickled out. Nowhere near rigor mortis. Paola felt no remorse, only shame, for what she did.

But her pickling recipes made everything taste like the past, so for posterity she took a finger too, protected now in brine.

Swish pinkie, circle flower, swim toe.

⌘

Paola pulls Marta's hair back, at first with care, followed by a couple violent tugs.

"Maybe you can hear me," says Paola, "maybe not."

She removes from her back pocket a pair of small shears, the ones she carries with her everywhere. She wraps several threads of Marta's thick black hair around her fingers.

"I love you, but you frighten me," she says.

Paola clips Marta's hair an inch away from Marta's scalp. Marta doesn't wake or flinch. Drool trickles from the side of her mouth.

"I won't let anything like what happened to her happen to you," says Paola. "See you tomorrow, sweet baby sister."

A la Parrilla

The next morning, Marta finds Damien tangled in her dead sister's room. Marta used to wake Carla in the same ratty hammock he sleeps in now. Carla slept there whenever her husband stayed out late with his fishing buddies, which was quite often (she never could keep up with their drinking). Tito had lived with them part-time, when he wasn't at his uncle's place. If Tito didn't stay the night, or went out fishing that morning, Marta would come in to run her hands through Carla's hair, and Carla would roll slowly and sigh and smile when Marta whispered, "Time to get up, lazybones," before Paola banged through the house hustling them all out the door for work.

Marta stands above Damien this time, and though she is not worried about him, she feels an urge to run her fingers through his greasy hair. She assumes her mother poured him enough to sedate a horse in order to convince him to clean fish and run the grill for Carla's key. She could tell he was under her mother's spell already, compelled to help a hand that serves him delicacies of the ocean, drink the brew she says is digestif.

No toques a mis hijas, pendejo, Ana María probably said.

Está bien, said he, maybe. *No tengo hogar, muchas gracias, mi amor.*

She runs her fingers through Damien's hair. She rubs his scalp forward and back, rests her hand on the back of his head until he sighs a sigh that could be his last, a surrender to some affliction he brought about himself. But she knows he is not dead, because she can feel a burning rise from his body. He is in a fever. Some people lose hearts or flee from them outright. At least his is still beating in his chest.

His face turns to her, but it is still unconscious. Marta lets his cheek rest on her hand. She lifts his earlobe to inspect the gills.

Damien's eyes open furtively, as if seduced, before he realizes what is happening. He jerks, tries to smack her hand away but is still ensnared in the hammock. He squirms to unravel himself but falls face-first to the floor. His back and butt and thighs have diamonds burned into them from the braided rope. Marta thinks they look like scales.

"Water," he says. His voice is smoky from drinking too close to the fire pit. "Agua."

"You need more than water," says Marta. "Those look dried up."

Damien covers his ears, hoping to hide his gills.

"Last night," he says, "the Pallbearer grazed them with his burial hands. Do they look infected?"

"No, no," Marta reassures him. "The Pallbearer's reaction was not one of surprise, but recognition. *Ah, sí* is all he said, as in: *Yes, of course; I see you.*"

Damien stands, tries to steady himself on a lamp, but it's forged from hollowed-out cactus arms. Marta brings him water and a willow branch for him to chew on, the best cure for a hangover. She gives him one of Papá's old sweat-stained guayaberas she keeps hidden in her closet. As he slides his reddened arms into its sleeves, Marta's sense is that Damien's body was once fuller than it currently is, that this will not be the last time he will stumble in and forget what happened the night before. He will wake her scrambling drunk through the back door. He will scream or cry or break something, but it won't bother her. Marta can sleep through hurricanes, just like her mother.

And what will the village think?

He's a godless man, they'll say, those wives of drunks, hypocrite congregants.

A tragedy, they'll say, *he belongs in the mountains*.

Power of a bruja, no doubt, only she can offer benediction.

Marta will check on him, make him chew more willow branch to make the pain go away. He does not yet know he needs protection from Ana María and everyone else in this place, because whenever they see a stranger, they want to take them for themselves. But Marta will take him first. He will do quite nicely.

Marta takes Damien's limp arm and leads him out of the dark bedroom. Damien pinches his eyes shut and palms his temples, feels for the drum of blood, the pulse of flight or forget. His knees nearly buckle going down the staircase, but he holds tight to the handrail, with Marta on his other arm. Downstairs, Paola is charring garlic and toasting spices. She pulls a steel pot dangling from a hook above her, spins it around, and sets it on an open flame with water and ground coffee. She smiles when she sees Damien.

"Buenos días," Paola says. Damien has no pants on.

"Good morning," Damien replies. He does not remember if he met her last night. "Buenos días." His accent is terrible.

"Did you make breakfast?" asks Marta. Her dark eyes are crusty and swollen and her black hair shines with grease.

"You look like shit," Paola says to Marta.

Marta takes a bow. Her rat's nest remains undisturbed by gravity. Paola has nearly forgotten about the specimen she snipped last night. She snickers at the flicker of scalp at the crown of Marta's head.

Paola pours the boiled coffee grounds through a sock filter into three clay mugs, then peels an orange and arranges its sections on a saucer. Marta adds tequila and cinnamon. Damien joins them at the table and by instinct bows his head and mumbles his "gracias gracias," then Paola warms tortillas in lard and plops yellow rice onto his plate, tops it with grilled mero, roasted peppers, and maize. Marta pounds the charred ajo, chiles, limón, with cilantrillo in the mortar. She spoons the salsa onto Damien's plate. He tilts his head back, inhales all the sweetness and green notes. His eyes water.

Marta pokes the new guy with her fork. "My guess is," she says, "Mamá hired this guy soon as our sister died."

When Marta pulls back her hair she smears a spicy green stripe across her face. She waits for Damien to notice, but she is sure he sees only stars, her mother's poison. Is it jealousy she feels? Hatred clouds everything around her.

Damien shakes his head and grunts. Rice spills out of his mouth. He does not seem to remember last night. Does not seem to remember anything at all.

"Oh, is that who you are," says Paola, "hired help? I thought this might be Mamá's new toy." Paola hops to sit on the counter, and she picks deliberately at her plate, admires the care she put into her dish.

"You catch on quick," Marta says, shoveling a tortilla into her mouth.

Paola knows better than to get pulled into her sister's reactive moods. She refuses to antagonize her little sister today; it isn't fun without Carla here to laugh with anyway.

"You can start in the kitchen with me," Paola says. "See if it's a good fit."

They must be Ana María's daughters, Damien thinks. He introduces himself.

"I didn't realize I'd have to start so soon," he says, licking his fingers. "Not today, right?"

"With a bit of food and water, you'll resemble something human again," says Marta.

"Don't listen to her," says Paola. "You don't have to do anything, just watch. This is the first we're hearing of Mamá's idea."

"As if we have a choice," Marta mumbles.

"Stop." Paola elbows her.

"Right, okay," says Marta. "Paola, you get him started with prep. I'll go set up the grill." Marta drops her plate in the dish pit. She wonders if her sister has noticed how responsible she has become.

Paola looks at Marta but says to Damien, "Carla would have been set up by now and cooking for pescadores."

"Yeah, I got your point." Marta's hope for recognition dies. If she wanted to take Carla's role, Marta would need to get up earlier, pretend to enjoy the job, fulfill the daily mission, be someone she is not.

"See you later, I hope?" Marta reaches out to Damien, but he dodges her touch.

"Yes, sure," he says mid-flinch.

She looks at him with questioning eyes. Red veins shock her sclera like cracked eggshell.

"I forgot my kit," she says. She runs upstairs.

Damien and Paola scarf down their breakfasts (he has thirds) and rinse their plates. Marta stomps back downstairs with a knife roll slung over her shoulder and slams the door on her way out.

"She's been forgetful lately," Paola sighs. "Go wash up, then we'll start with the stock." She hands Damien a stiff washcloth and points him to a closet-sized shower in the back.

Damien watches brown water wash off his body and get pulled into the drain. Beneath the dirt, he is still brown, but with a reflective coating, almost. He studies himself in the mirror as he towels off. Checks the inside of his mouth because it felt scratchy in there back by his glands. He flips his ears forward. The gills have evolved into more than a blemish on his neck. Perhaps they will be useful to him, soon. He has not yet gone for that promised swim, after all these miles in this sun and heat. How did he get so easily distracted?

Damien sits with Paola at a prep table where she has set up two high stools. He swings his legs, crossing them, and hunches over Paola as she quietly separates the pebbles from the pintos. She slides the good beans to a good pile, ugly ones and stones to another, until the big sack is empty. Her hands move quickly, but she is unhurried. She sweeps the clean pile into a large stockpot filled with water, submerges her hand and agitates the beans, then drains and repeats the process until the water runs clear.

Paola is happy to have a quiet house, and Damien is calmed by her movements. The sound of the shuffling beans hypnotizes him. He sees flashes of last night: stray dogs fighting over a dead rat in a dark street; a one-legged drunk pissing in the doorway of a shoe store, howling at the sky. He saw his parents, too, on opposite sides of the street, pointing at each other, crying one minute, laughing the next. They didn't make a sound, didn't seem to even notice their son. Where'd you go? he cried out. They turned to him. His father's skin shined, his silver hair slicked back and tied into a tsiiyeeł, matching his suit in color and flair. Damien had never seen his father in a suit or a tsiiyeeł before, but he recognized the work boots, laces loose, pant legs tucked under dusty tongues. His dark mother wore chains around her neck, the ones she made by braiding wires and interlocking copper hoops. Not heavy enough to weigh her down but enough metal that she shined in the moonlight. She looked at Damien's father, who stood dumbly with his mouth open, and she shook her head, pointing at him, mocking him.

Even on this side of death they felt threatened, like they

wanted to prove to each other that they still existed despite the other. Maybe they weren't real, but he wanted them to be. He felt like he had so much to tell them if they would listen.

Damien wonders if the villagers are aware their streets are filled with the dead.

Beans washed and soaked, tomatoes diced or smoking, potatoes peeled, the ice is scooped for the coolers of portioned cuts of meat and fish. Paola also shows Damien how to toast spices *her way,* thinness of the plátanos *just so,* telling him to always use a timer since he obviously has no sense of time.

Damien admires Paola's confidence in the kitchen. Each vegetable she handles, any organism canned or dry, live or dead or somewhere in between, Paola admires it as if to ask for absolution. Do all the families eat so well? Damien wonders. Does the village know the difference between this and the other? He tasted love in the plate Ana María served him yesterday, care for the ingredients and their stories: how a yuca came from earth to leaf to root to an inevitable violent death in a pot of boiling oil topped with the charred remains of sweet onion and pepper. He felt it from the mescal. Paola makes Damien taste everything as they prep sauces and marinades, the soups and stock. He tastes something he cannot quite put his tongue on, perhaps an ingredient Paola uses in excess. But it occurs to Damien that this flavor might be found only in these bodies of water, bodies of tuna, nourished by the sea, a sea who expects to be nourished in turn.

"What else do you have left to do?" Damien asks.

"Not much," says Paola, sticking a label on a container. "You don't have to work the grill with Marta today if you don't want to. But once Tito comes in, she could use help with the fish."

Damien shrugs, shucks more corn, peels more onions. He doesn't want to leave Paola, this house. A heavy fear weighs him down, he is not sure why. He's afraid of what is out there. He has felt this way before—chest pains, hurting heart. He struggles to breathe, pictures his lung bags collapsing to expel the dust.

When Damien finally feels brave enough to step outside, the heat grabs him by the ears and shakes Marta and Paola's wonderful tortillas and grouper right out of him. He vomits in the gutter and cowers back inside.

"It's hot out there," he says, wiping his mouth.

"You're hungover," says Paola. She scoots her chair back, digs around the kitchen cabinets, pulls out a small tin. She opens it and takes a pinch of tobacco and rips a page out of a tiny Bible and rolls a spliff with skunky shake. She tongues the Scripture, seals the creases tight, lights it up. After a puff, she beats her chest, says, "You should be careful around her," with smoke still clutched in her lungs. Paola exhales and clears her throat loudly, but she does not cough. Instead, she takes another hit and blows the cloud into Damien's face, then hands him the rest.

"Careful around who?" he says. "The hangover is my own failing." Sure, Ana María had gotten Damien drunk, but he didn't feel like she was being nefarious. He takes a hit. It tastes like a freshly mowed lawn, bacon and eggs, black peppercorn.

"My mother, yes, she is dangerous. But Marta, too, may see an opportunity in you."

"You're scaring me," Damien says. He's already confused and lost. Now she's making him paranoid.

"It's not my intention. Simply a gesture of caution for our new guest. I doubt anything I say can make you feel at home. Sorry."

"I'll feel better after a swim." Damien takes another hit. He raises the spliff. "This helps, too."

"You might not be in the best state for a swim," Paola warns. "But if you must, the best place is beyond the docks, around the jetty, but only until afternoon, then it gets real choppy."

"And your sister?"

Swim Home to the Vanished

"She will steal you away from yourself."

"What's that supposed to mean?"

"Don't get caught in the undertow," says Paola. "I don't want to say I told you so." Paola pinches the roach and sucks the whole thing down, smoke and ash and crutch and all.

～

Almendro trees line the beach next to tall palms teeming with green cocos. At least a half dozen kids—eight or ten or twelve years old—laugh and splash like piranhas in the green water. Some catch small waves on their bellies and tumble onto shore, others wrestle and force each other underwater. From a distance their skin looks mottled, like tiny hammer strikes on copper skin. The children move in and out of the water with ravenous energy, a frenzy that keeps Damien at a distance.

Gulls glide by with treats in their mouths. A pelican loops around and dive-bombs a sardine. Damien removes his shirt and buries his toes in the sand and lets his skin crisp up before he wades into the salt water. He drops his arms and slumps his neck, lets it wrap him like a new skin. He dunks his head. His gills sizzle like the top of a match.

For a moment, while underwater, Damien can breathe again, as if he has been suffocating all this time, gasping for air in the mountains where the air was thin, or in the desert where it was thick and dusty and dry. Even in the kitchen he'd suffered the kind of heat where the air and food was never salty enough and a noxious foot on his chest kept him from catching his breath. The kitchen sticks to you, and no matter what you do you can't wash the soot and grease and onion out of your flesh. It crawls into your lungs and makes you heavy, toughens you, makes you mean and numb and dumb.

Something touches his leg; Damien panics. Probably just some kelp wrapped around his ankle. But he kicks, and the grip clenches; the harder he kicks, the tighter it gets. He scrambles for air, but it seems to pull him deeper. Beneath the rush of bubbles on his eardrum, Damien can still hear children on the beach, their muffled laughter.

Damien opens his eyes in the opaque water, gritty and green, and he sees a boy under the water's surface, with him, watching him. His face is swollen, but Damien recognizes it. The shape of his eyes, the shell of black hair and widow's peak . . . are Kai's. The boy reaches out with a wrinkled hand.

Damien flails. Kicks coral and stone and water until he's crawling on all fours in the shallows, coughing up the sea.

"¡Pendejo!" the scaly kids yell from the beach. None of them are in the water. "¡Cabrón!"

They laugh and roll and roll in the sun.

Damien spins and dunks back under, but his brother is gone. A warm current has washed away the cold.

A swim was supposed to make Damien feel better, but now, with the waves up like Paola said they would be, there is just too much shit floating around, and the rocks and coral are too sharp (his toe is bleeding) and those children won't shut up, so he crawls up the beach and curls in the shade of an almendro tree. His hands dig mindlessly in the sand. His hands do not feel like they are his anymore.

A pack of dogs roams past. One of them rolls on a crab carcass; bits of shell collect in her fur. The kids throw rocks, but she struts off only when she feels like it, tail high, to catch up with the rest of the pack.

Damien shields his eyes as he looks across the water and imagines swimming as far as he can go, swimming until his arms detach and fins grow out. Maybe there is a family out there for him, since he no longer has one here. Maybe he will swim and keep swimming around the planet and end up right back on this beach. Kai might not really be out there. Maybe something *of* him is in the water? Like he is a part of it. All water is connected somehow. It is infinite and it is limited.

The face couldn't have been his brother—he can't be in the water. His body washed ashore; they burned it and buried the ash. Doesn't explain seeing his parents last night, though; they must have been conjured by the booze.

Still, he must swim! Until the burn in his shoulders resembles the burn of blue flames, until he stinks of singed hair and smoking fat, until he is fish like his brother.

Hungover and stoned, Damien falls asleep in the sand, but not before he feels the bees return, perhaps sensing his weariness. He dreams they land on him and chew him apart piece by piece, turning him into a funny kind of honey.

The House by the Woods

Damien's father thought their house would hold but the chemistry was broken, the wrong ratio of silica to lime. The adhesives dissolved first, cracks in the veneer letting the weather in. He slathered grout into the seeping fractures but his compound was too thin, the mortar joints too wide. Loose sand rinsed away and the corners chipped in the spitting wind. Thinset mortar, iron truss, corner braces, concrete—still the walls began to crumble.

Damien's father was a mason who built their house himself brick by brick with red powdery hands numb to cold and immune to chemical. When he returned from work he left his muddy boots at the door, slung his sweat- and bloodstained socks over the porch banister. Mortar dried under his too-short nails, caulked his thick calluses. His eyes were rubbed red from heavy palms and calcified dust. Slaked lime cooled his gypsum cheeks. After a shower, rivers of dust clogged the drain, a smell like hot stones hosed down with milk and ash.

Their mother wasn't a good cook, but their father liked a boiled potato as long as there was salt and butter—the sand and water of a mason's appetite. She was Diné, a metalworker and jeweler who never wore or sold her work. Her workbench was hidden in a closet in the spare room. The room had an odd hum and smelled like wet cardboard under the smoke of brazed metal and hot wax. She filled it with her finds from the world: faded sepia photos, rugs and typewriters, a milking stool, instruments nobody knew how to play, boxes of Christmas ornaments and too-small clothes. The boys weren't allowed in, nor was their father.

She molded silver onto decayed corners of the house. Heat strengthened metal but made mud brittle.

"That'll never work," their father said.

They ate with plastic forks because she melted down all the silverware.

Their father was neither mean nor a drunk, and their mother lost her mind but never her tongue. They spent weekends and evenings in orbit of one another, feeding off each other's gravity. But the satellite sons changed their parents' trajectories, pushed them out of rotation.

"Do shí tá hó t'sii da," their mom said.

"English, please," said Kai.

She paused and looked out the window above the kitchen sink.

"It doesn't work like that," she said.

"Try us," said Damien.

Damien and Kai would watch her stare out the window for hours with an ear rested on her shoulder. Her gray eyes tuned her beautiful face into the frequency of a question, and her hollowed cheeks reddened with the slightest bit of attention. Her sons may have been the only ones to offer it, the only witnesses to her glow.

She taught Damien how not to make a pie. He stood on the step stool in the kitchen and peered over the countertop, watched her massage the butter and flour until the dough became resentful. Cherries bubbled over on the stove as the crust par-baked in the oven, but the house already smelled of defeat. The sugar burned black and the cherries were wasted. The overworked crust retreated from the edges of the pie pan.

"I can't believe you made me do this," she said. "This is your fault."

Their father was happiest outdoors. He took his sons to the forest, where he revealed roly-polies, worms, centipedes, and millipedes underneath boulders with grunts of excitement. As hawks rose on thermals, he pointed out the curvature of their wings, the angle of their tail feathers. He had a similar stance as their mother, the slight tilt of the head as he shaded his eyes from the sun, an itinerant hand rubbing the small of his back.

"Don't forget," he said, "we're part of nature, not its kings or possessors."

He pinched leaves off a laurel tree and rubbed them between his palms, then cupped his hands over Damien's and Kai's faces and told them to breathe deep. Their eyes rolled back, and they drooled a little. They inhaled again, huffed until light-headed. It was a kind of magic, a potion that seeped in and burned their lungs—or froze them, they were not sure which—and their father unlocked something in them that recognized the scent, as if the memory had already existed.

"What is it?" Kai asked.

"Laurel leaf," their father said.

"Makes me want spaghetti."

The brothers inherited their father's love of insects, their mother's creativity, and both parents' anxieties about the world's many oblivions. Their parents did not speak of death, which made their boys extra curious. They felt a need to destroy things. They began with red ant hills, opened their home with the scoop of a spade, watched them gather their eggs and grubs in their mandibles before retreating deeper into the earth. They flicked black stink bugs with twigs, and their leather butts shot into the air as the ants took them down one leg at a time. Then they dropped horny toads on the pile, but they were not interested in the ants at all.

Swim Home to the Vanished

A bitter powder rubbed off on their hands as they collected moths at the porch light in the evenings, ruining their wings and chances of escape. They gathered spiders, black widows and tarantulas, in an old shoebox and forced them to fight to the death. Used grasshopper spit, as thick and acidic as tobacco juice, to burn through caterpillar skin. Cut out butterfly proboscises, stole full saddlebags from drunken bumblebees hovering above the lilacs.

Their mother didn't know about her boys' inflictions upon the world, she only saw the dirt in their nails, their scratched knees and muddied faces. They played their part in nature as their father had directed.

"Equal to insects," he'd said, "only stronger and more intelligent."

After their bath, their mother set out bowls of fruit and boiled oats for dinner. She enjoyed having her sons in the house when their father was away. She sang songs in French as she paced or cleaned, cooked and smoked. The only time she seemed at peace, though, was when she parked herself at her studio desk, where wire clippings lay like dried-up maggots, tying and twisting knots from endless spools of wire until her hands were cramped or bleeding. She stared through a large magnifying glass attached to a mechanical arm that distorted her face into someone her kids would never meet nor ever could. When the red of hot rings hissed in a pool of mercurial water, when she forged steel, as she played with all her shiny toys like a raccoon rinsing shells in the bay, it must have reminded her of all the things she couldn't do if they weren't made of alloy.

One night, dinner wasn't on the table. The steam of overcooked broccoli haunted the house. Damien and his brother and father watched each other, waiting to see who would break first. Their father knocked on her door, checked the backyard, called the neighbors. Damien followed the fence line, and then he pushed Kai onto the roof, but Kai said he saw only red-tailed hawks hunting for rabbits and a couple of mourning doves.

"Maybe she forgot something at the store," their father said. "She's always forgetting something at the store."

The glue of sand and blood that kept their house intact was too soluble, and the walls finally crumbled. A builder might blame the chemistry before himself, but their father's uncertainty eventually turned to guilt, as if he realized that everything he had ever known was false.

He sat in a wooden chair in the backyard and massaged his arm under a tree full of hissing cicadas, blindly fingered the veins in the backs of his hands until the leaves turned yellow and twirled down on him. The willows and cottonwood threatened to choke him, but the brothers snipped the branches with round-tipped scissors and raked up the leaves. They peeled the slugs from his pant legs, brought him blankets in the evening. Their father's silence was a form of communication before, but now he was an empty shell where a snail used to be.

So Kai and Damien worked with the hawks at catching meals. Raptors dropped rabbits and gophers and birds at their doorstep. They learned to clean them, blanch the pigeons to rip the feathers out, skin the mangy rodents and marinate the meat. What the toads didn't eat the boys slurped up. They used crickets to bait the lizards, netted crawdads and minnows from a spring box in the woods. They collected water from the gutters to quench the corn and carrots in the garden, ripped handfuls of dirty lettuce, burnt garlic in the fire pit, boiled bay leaves with potatoes, and smashed squash with cinnamon and salt.

They trimmed their father's nails but not his beard, and checked the house again for clues—their parents' room, Mother's secret studio. She didn't even take her tools with her. When the

boys went for walks they yelled down alleys, peeked into laun-
derettes, hardware and grocery stores. On their way home they
picked rosemary sprigs, dandelion leaves, figs.

Soon all that brick-and-mortar mush Mother fed Father dete-
riorated, too, and he withered to a pile of ash, but not before the
ivy took him. When spring arrived, the brothers rubbed him with
their own salve of mud and dung to keep the itching and swelling down. Tendrils of wisteria took a leg, morning glory twined
its way up his arms and neck. Scandent beans bound him to his
chair. The boys fought them back, but for every snip two more
bines sprouted, and overnight their strength nearly doubled before they flowered. Their father was a feast of purple and green.
When he was ready, he asked the vines for abscission, and finally,
in one last magnanimous bloom, he was released, and the colony
collapsed with him.

Morning

There are no sisters, no mamá, nor fishermen to interrupt Marta as she sets up the line at the beginning of her shift. This is Marta's first opening since Carla died. It was Carla's favorite shift. The sun is low, and the cool air fills with the songs of extroverted birds. Fishing nets fly over the mellow bay and red-eyed pescadores pull them in with sinewy arms. The pescadores start early with pints of rum to fight the morning chill, then they gather sardines and baitfish for the big runs in the afternoon after the thunderstorms.

Carla used to tell Marta that the village requires that small delight, the predictability—the inevitability—of a storm. The village relies on routine for its survival. Nature can be brutal, or she can be protector. Brujas are easily upset, unpredictable. To ensure their mother's quiet delight, Carla's, Paola's, and Marta's territories require balance; balance necessitates routine and efficiency, despite how much a bruja is irritated by the customs of the fish peddler's life.

The village has suffered in the past, Carla warned her, but at least they have not known hunger, not since they married off their greatest pescador, Flaco, to Ana María, the caimán queen. On Ana María's wedding day, the women of the village fed the bride fish head stew, then washed her in a tin basin and dried her with crumpled newspaper. The bride's skin was dry and thick like pine bark. They smashed annatto seeds in a mortar with goat's milk to smear along her sutures and crooked face. After wrapping her in linens and pinning a veil to her skull, the old pescadores hoisted her above their heads and carried her through the village.

The men wore white guayaberas and white cotton pants tied with red rope at the waist, red kerchiefs at the neck, straw hats for when the sun was at its peak, and they wore their nicest huaraches, sandpapered and spit-polished. The women wore their whitest whites as well, short-sleeved dresses with poofy shoulders and woven belts braided with red, green, and turquoise string. Little girls tied their hair up in buns with red yarn while the boys brandished fresh bowl cuts. Flaco wore his synthetic purple suit it took months to raise the money for, shipped in from someplace east.

As the men marched with the bride on their backs, her mouth hung slack-jawed in a perplexed, hypnotic smile, and women and children waved palm fronds along the street. They sang and cried and prayed. At the church doors, acolytes draped hibiscus garlands on the children, and once everyone was seated, the acolytes lit the candles with wicks burning at the ends of long poles. The room filled with excited murmurs and smoke from the greasy censer.

Prayers were followed by splashes of holy water to moisten the bride's drying eyes. Father Gáagi, bless his heart, slapped her snout before she could bite Flaco, then she side-stared him with her toothy smile cracked open. Once she hissed, the priest announced them man and wife, but when the groom went in for a kiss, she snapped again. Flaco grabbed her snout and kissed her between the eyes, and gently caressed her ventral scutes, then the church filled with cheers and whistles.

The ceremony started before the sun came up and ended when

it dropped into the sea. The village dressed in their best huddled around a beast in a gown and a pescador who wore their expectations like a crown.

⚓

Marta unfolds the main grill from the larger vessel containing a trough for hot coals, a rotisserie, storage drawers and cabinets, little serving stations that flip open at the ends. Iron chains and pulleys move fish-sized baskets vertically over the coals, heat precisely controlled with the turn of a crank. She lights the fire; the coals must glow red before the first customers arrive. She warms the griddle, sets pots to simmer, assembles her line. Two prep tables with large cutting boards act as the butcher station. A waist-high table beside her sheaths wooden spoons and tongs and freshly filled oils, sauces, lemon slices and garlic and salts and peppers in homemade clay pitchers and bowls, placed neatly next to clean towels folded into tight rectangles to lift scalding handles and wipe surfaces free of blood and residue, the grease of the sea.

Marta scheduled herself to take Carla's opening shifts since Paola does most of the prep alone at home and they no longer can rely on Ana María. Their mother is unpredictable, shows up occasionally with supplies they do not need, ingredients they have enough of, and she is lethargic and sloppy on the line even when business is slow. Marta occasionally worked the line during the lunch rush, showed up early to try to impress Carla, prove to her big sister that she cared about the family business, when in reality all three sisters saw themselves as Ana María's pet projects, her acolytes gone awry. They took pride in their work, but their work did not define them.

Marta misses working with Carla. They had a balanced system. Marta's violent and brutal ways of putting together orders were softened by Carla; she had a curious way with customers. Carla treated people with respect, as if she liked them. She asked questions, simple ones: How are you doing? Are you and your family getting enough food? Have you spoken with your ancestors lately?

Marta, on the other hand, moved like a blind mad percussionist during a rush, hurling insults under her breath like a demon, but her tickets never backed up. If Ana María had witnessed Carla handing out extra portions or botched orders instead of reusing the leftovers for empanadas or weird specials, she would have slapped a welt into Carla's face, rendering her sightless for a week. But Carla was unperturbed by the threat of their overpowering mother. She was different somehow, in that she could easily subdue Ana María with flattery or quiet compliance, never outright disobedience like Marta was prone to.

Against her mother's wishes, Carla started the food line for the pescadores. Every morning, Carla began her shift by feeding Tito before he launched his boat. Black beans stewed with pork scraps bubbled on the back burner all night, or rice fried with chorizo, pulpo, and sweet plantain. Soon she was providing all the pescadores with meals nourishing enough to keep them out longer before they returned shit-faced and empty-handed in the afternoon. Carla initially fed them for free, out of her own pocket, a generosity which further set off her mother. It's rude, uncouth, that a chef feed only a few when she possesses an abundance, thought Carla, and soon Carla's popularity grew, along with a jealous rift between her and Ana María.

This struggle for power bothered Marta to no end, because it showed that they still looked at her as a young and naïve little girl. She tried to impress them, and in return they made her feel like she didn't exist.

The customers do not understand much about what goes on behind the counter. Even though it's an outdoor kitchen and café, secrets and mystique remain veiled by smoke and cantankerous cooks. Customers admire from afar the beauty of what Ana María has created over the years; her food would always be trusted even if her customers could never trust Ana María, who, despite living here all her life, is considered an outsider. The customers also have their preference as to who cooks at any given time. If you're in a hurry, Marta's food won't look as good, but it'll taste exactly like Carla's cooking; Carla was slow, but treated every plate like a sculpture.

After Marta handles the morning push, Paola arrives at her usual time with a delivery of backups and sides: beans and rice, viandas en escabeche, cucumber salad, shredded green papaya, all of it meticulously portioned, labeled, stacked on a cart Paola designed herself. She calls it her guagua. In her free hand she carries a basket piled high with fresh tortillas, wrapped in fat-stained newspaper and tied with butcher's twine.

"I can't believe she made us stay open today," Paola says, handing the tortillas to Marta.

Marta scrapes the grill with a wire brush, a little too aggressively. Bits of ash catch in her eyelashes. She was really enjoying the morning alone. She'll claim the stress of cooking breakfast solo got her worked up, not yesterday's funeral, and definitely not this hangover.

"Sorry I'm late," Paola says. She's anticipated Marta's mood. It's like Marta changes into a different person as soon as one of her sisters shows up. "It's been a difficult morning."

"I have it covered," Marta snaps. She sharpens her fillet knife the way her father taught her.

Paola unloads and counts the number of orders of pulpo and fish available and writes the number down. She wipes her runny nose with her sharp thumb.

Swim Home to the Vanished

"Where is the new guy?" asks Marta. "Aren't I supposed to train him?"

"He should be here by the time Tito motors in," says Paola. "Didn't you just say you have this covered?"

"What do you think of this—Mamá's—arrangement?" Marta asks. "Does he seem suspicious to you?"

"I saw you this morning, holding his hand down the stairs, spoon-feeding him—you don't seem that concerned," says Paola.

"Is there a problem?" Marta puts the fillet knife away and reaches for a larger one.

"I don't have a problem except we haven't decided what to do about Carla." Paola steps on a pump and water rushes into a tiny sink, where she rinses her hands.

"What about her?" says Marta.

"You don't think someone needs to be fed to the tiburóns for this?"

"It was Mamá's fault," Marta says. "Everyone knows it."

Paola bites her lip and stares down Marta.

"We should bind her little legs and arms and roast her over a spit," Marta says. "Keelhaul her."

"On a yola?"

"Tie a shark to her waist and throw her in the Red Clay River."

"You remind me of Mamá more and more," says Paola. For a second she wants to play this game with her sister, imagining all the fun ways to annihilate their mother. Paola tries to smile to disarm the insult, but she can't smile today. It is too late anyway, the fuse lit.

"Puta bitch," spits Marta, "leave me alone."

"Gladly. Where is Mamá, anyway?"

Marta shrugs. "Does it matter? She'll show up with new scratches and act like everything's just fine." Marta brings the blade to her eye, tests its sharpness with her talon.

A few new customers place orders. Marta puts away the sharpening stone, checks the rotisserie, stirs the vianda. Paola steps back to watch her sister cook. Marta may have learned from Carla, but her skills on the hot side have surpassed them all. Her sisters can't move in the kitchen like she does, like a musician or a dancer or both. Paola wants to attribute Marta's agility to her weird body shape, but Marta's secret is that she ignores her fear. You can't be scared of burns or mistakes, slipping on a mat and twisting your hip. Can't allow your muscle groups to dictate where you go or how you move just because you anticipate a fall. You don't have time to wallow in delusions, wrath, or unhappiness when your body is in a zone floating flying dancing in the kitchen, a song of its own creation taking place. Food writes itself. When Marta cooks, she has several more appendages and extra eyes dialed in on the grill and fryer and sauté and oven, and the smoker, too, if Paola is not hovering over its embers.

Catch of the Day

The shade has moved, and the sun now has Damien pinned to the beach. He peels himself up. His skin is burnt, his gills itch, and he is caked with sand. His chest and belly are mottled and pale in contrast to his darker limbs, like some kind of lake trout. But he shakes off the sand, along with the image of his brother, and returns to the docks. There is a blur of heat glowing from the grill, where Marta basks in its haze and smoke. She fans herself with a paper plate, pokes at the grill with her tongs, while a few customers await their lunch.

"You're late," she says. Every time she moves or rotates something, a flame roars with a hiss and black soot floats away like a cloud of angry gnats. She swats at them like she swats at the bigger flies. For every slap, four more land on her arms and ears and skewered fish.

"I didn't think I'd be thrown into the mines so soon," Damien says. He watches flies spit up the bile to digest the meat on the butcher table. He hears their slurping, their incessant preening. He doesn't know if he will be able to tolerate the flies like Marta does.

"Of course, you don't have to if you don't want to. ¿Quieres un trago?" Marta snaps a bottle cap off before Damien has a chance to refuse.

"No, gracias," he says.

"*Grrr*," she corrects him, rolling her tongue, then she opens her mouth wide and slaps her chin with the back of her hand. "*Ahhh cias*.

"Drink that, you'll feel better," Marta insists.

The first sip is hard to swallow, then he downs it.

Marta plates boiled roots and grilled fish and yellow rice for her customers. Everything smells like butter and the sea. Music from the village square fills the air as if battling the smells for attention.

"Hungry?" she asks.

"Not yet," Damien says.

Marta sets the tongs on the table and offers her hand. "Thanks for trying to help last night."

"It was nothing." Damien shakes Marta's fuzzy hand limply. "Is there a place you want me to start?"

Marta points to a pile of rags and an apron on the prep table. She bangs a pot and the lid slides off. She fishes around for something with her tongs. "Stay with me for this rush."

Damien ties the apron around his waist and tucks a towel into it.

"Customers are fussy and lack imagination," Marta says, not acknowledging the customers in front of her. "Our job is to serve what is lacking in their world. Basics: color, balance, salt, and acid. Taste the octopus. Squeeze a bead of salsa verde on your fingertip: see how the herbs match the heat? Don't overcook a thing; in fact, you're not allowed to touch my grill for a while."

Marta repeats the orders called out to her as flames lick her forehead, dance on her skin, mark it with black carbon. Damien narrows in and jumps onto the line by instinct—muscle memory. He garnishes plates the way she shows him, spoons a sauce onto each: the spicy green on the mero, crimson coconut with chillo, bright and macerated shallots and minced tarragon in fish oil for the pulpo.

But Damien's body remembers too much; the shoulder ache, the slippy knees, the shock down his right hip into his femur.

When the rush is over, Damien helps Marta clean and restock. A short, sinewy fisherman with a large cooler balanced on his shoulder walks up from the beach. His skin is leathery and dark, his eyes bloodshot, nearly glowing. The grease or blood or salt in his long hair keeps it from moving easily in the breeze. The drain cap on the cooler is missing. A trail of watery blood leads down the beach and back to his mooring.

"Hola, Marta," the pescador says.

"¿Cómo estás, amor?" Marta says. "Tito, this is Damien. Mamá's new cook."

"Ah, sí." Tito puts the cooler down to shake Damien's hand. Tito's hands are thick and weird.

"Tito is my brother-in-law."

Tito sniffs.

Marta spreads her arms out and embraces the pescador.

Damien suddenly feels uncomfortable watching them hold on to each other so long. He does not like affection, or he does, but he doesn't like other people's performance of it. It seems like Marta is consoling him rather than the other way around. Tito seems like a gentle person, not half as crazy as Damien expects these fish people to be. Damien feels terrible for him, all of them, and about Carla, even if he is still numb and hungover.

"Mira," Tito says. "Look." He opens the cooler. It is full of pale pink fish with flesh-colored eyes bulging from the pressure change. They have webbed dorsals with red needles sticking out of them. Their skin oozes something sick.

"Mero," he says, "trés setenta y cinco por libra."

"Bueno," says Marta. "¿Esto es todo?"

"Sí, I don't know if we'll get more today or not."

The largest grouper is too large for the cooler—its head and tail peek over the cooler walls. The other half dozen are half its size. Their gills smolder red and heave slightly. Damien feels for them, yanked from the depths to suffocate here. Such a painful way to die, to drown above water. He wonders if they feel the pain he feels for them. But of course they don't—they're fucking dead.

Tito turns to him and slaps him on the shoulder. "Super-fresh," he says.

Marta grabs a fish by its tail and starts to scale it. Little glittering flakes flicker onto the dock, the underside of the tarp, attach themselves to Damien's shoulders and neck.

"I don't know what to do during my breaks anymore," Tito says. "The fishing's been slow past few days."

Marta doesn't look up. She stares deep into the dead eyes of her catch.

"How about a drink?" Damien winks. "Mescal?"

"Don't drink Ana María's drink," says Tito.

"He's already had it," says Marta.

"That stuff Ana María gave me last night?" says Damien. "It was good. Fucked me up."

"Mierda," Tito says. "Shit's dangerous."

People are starting to line up again. Marta throws on more coals, stirs a few pots, takes their orders.

"Tito," she calls out, "show him around later, por favor?" She hands Tito cash for the fish. He pockets it and claps his hands.

"Sí, por supuesto," he says, then opens his arms to Damien as if ready for an embrace.

"We'll see you tonight, hermano." Marta washes her hands and throws meat in a grill basket.

The pescador follows the blood trail back to his yola.

Swim Home to the Vanished

As Marta cooks lunch, Damien helps himself to the butcher table, where he starts to clean and scale the grouper. Almost instantly, he feels that shock down his legs; his back overcompensates for his weakened legs, and the muscles start to pull away from themselves in his shoulder blades. He knows the order of his body's break-down, and like his body, his mind is trained to ignore it, to use reverie as a kind of painkiller.

But Damien has had difficulty reassembling memory lately. A spate of images returns now as he cuts and guts the grouper: he and Kai hiking miles into pines, stocked with sandwiches and can-teens, getting deeper into the woods, huffing bark and digging up juicy roots to gnaw on, not turning back for home until the sun pushed long shadows across their path.

They never admitted to it, but when they were out there, they were each other's best friend. They would wander for hours in the wilderness without speaking a word, pick up fallen branches along the way, always considering what might make a good weapon in case they came across a mountain lion or bear, or even a skunk. They would have slingshots ready, too. If it was monsoon season, they rubbed mud on exposed skin to protect themselves from the gnats and mosquitoes. If it was too hot, they dug small holes to lie in midday. Even in winter they were engineers, carved tun-nels through snowdrifts, carved intricate rooms where they could await the spring.

Another fish on the table, and Damien sees a flicker of solace, a past difficult for him to attach any limbs to. "Look at this liver, how it elongates beneath a speckled scale, inflated like a puffer." He rubs his fingers along a grouper's skin, scratches at its iridescent scales, lifts a dorsal fin and fucks with the webbing. "You were built for depth," he says, "a swimmer like me."

Kai and Damien preferred to sleep in the woods near the creek after their parents disappeared. They would get up while it was still dark. The air was cold and smelled of fresh water. Kai was six years old, Damien nine or ten. He held Kai's hand as they hopped along the rocks upstream.

"What do you think Mom is doing?" Kai asked.

"She's writing a story about the fish here," Damien said.

Kai knelt and put his hand in a small pool. "These fish?"

"Yes, not the fish downstream. Those fish are too big."

"Too big for what?"

"Too big to fit on the page," said Damien.

"Yeah, these fish are much smaller," said Kai.

"They should fit on the page just fine."

"What kind of fish are they?"

"Mom will decide that."

"I think she should make the fish talk," Kai said.

"If she could make the fish talk," said Damien, "what do you think the fish would say?"

"They would talk about how they wished they had hair because it's really cold in the creek, and if they had hair they could comb it and they would be more handsome. They would talk about how handsome all the other fish were."

"That's very polite."

"I think so too."

Damien and Kai trekked into the forest every day. Thoughts of home faded the farther they went, and the forest replaced what home meant. Kai still believed their mother was out there some- where, and their father too, in the woods, waiting for them.

Swim Home to the Vanished

They followed the creek all the way to where it bubbled up from the ground, and they whistled and banged sticks and sang in case the bears were around.

"What do you think Dad is doing?" Kai asked.

"I think he's carving us grizzly bears," Damien said.

"Why is he making grizzly bears?"

"Probably because Mom's writing about a place in the forest."

"Are there other animals he's making?"

"Of course. They're in the place we're going to right now."

"Why aren't they with us now?"

"Because they're still discovering it for us."

"Oh. So they'll be there when we get there?"

"Exactly," said Damien.

Damien and his brother dropped black ants into antlion pits, their homes like inverted cones. Kai would hold a leaf while Damien swept the ants into its fold, then Kai would shake them into dozens of tiny craters in sandy areas beneath the pines. The ants struggled to escape, but the sand and angle kept them from climbing too far. The antlions, sensing movement, would climb out and snatch a leg, pull the ant into the trap, and suck it dry. Their jaws were as wide as the length of their prey.

"They're lacewing larvae," said Kai. "Dad taught me. But I wish they weren't larvae and that they stayed like they are now and grow to be giants."

The brothers fed their lions daily. Sometimes it took them hours.

Sometimes, before going out to the forest, they picked grapes from the neighbors' fence line. They were sour and filled with bitter seeds. If the neighbors weren't home, they hopped the veiny fence to climb the apple trees. They liked the sweet ones at the top. Kai would pick them and drop them to Damien. Damien never climbed, because he hated earwigs. He had been told they liked to burrow into ear canals to lay their eggs, and especially in ears as large as his.

Marta throws an empanada crust at Damien to get his attention.

"I've been calling you for like ten minutes," she says.

Damien has absent-mindedly filleted all the mero and has been staring at all the blood and slime on the cutting board.

"How much mescal has Ana María poured into you?" Marta asks.

"Enough to forget," says Damien.

Marta shares agua de coco and sliced mangoes with him. The way her mouth moves when it is full of fruit almost makes him smile.

Paola rolls up with her guagua to restock the line and load up trash and take the empties for cleaning.

"You look pale," Marta says. "Maybe you should take a break while Paola is here."

Damien is exhausted but won't admit to it.

"Thank you for cutting those fillets," says Paola. "You didn't have to work, Ana María should have told you. Why don't you go for another swim?"

Damien nods, surrenders. Where has Ana María gone? Left him here with daughters ready to kill each other so soon after their sister died. One more thing he does not miss about the kitchen: how cooks can feel each other's aggravation, the tension palpable in such small quarters, like bones boiling, even if they have a view of the scintillate ocean. Brujas, he thinks, that's what cooks were.

Damien walks down to the end of the dock and stands at its edge and shades his eyes. Below the water's surface, the pylons are bright green and fuzzy. Twitchy minnows swim as if they have secrets they are desperate to tell, kiss the algae where they keep their whispers hidden. Larger shadows creep below, hunt the littler ones, await the table scraps.

What kind of fish is Damien? The kind barely paddling along, waiting to get gobbled up? He dreamed of those fish in the mountains. Big fish gasping with smaller fish in their mouths. What a way to die: choking on air, in water. He thinks of Kai beneath the surface, one of those big fishes, something between hunter and scavenger, just beyond the reach of light.

Damien drops to his hands and knees and dangles his head over. The old wood splinters into his belly and palms and knees. He adjusts himself, rips a chunk of greasy wood to toss into the water. A big shadow rises to sniff it, scattering the minnows. Is Kai down there somewhere? Damien inhales, holds the stinging air in his lung sacs for as long as he can, counts his heartbeat, the pulse in his cold belly. His mouth is so dry. He feels like he might throw up again. He spits into the water. This time the minnows squirm closer to take a whiff.

Marta turns to check on Damien at the end of the dock as she sloshes a bucket of cold soup into a pot on the stove. "Only a couple hours' work and he loses his appetite," she says. "Did you bring more posole?"

Paola shoves containers of par-cooked octopus legs and fresh anchovies into tubs of ice.

"We're changing it to fish heads again," Paola says. "Mamá's request."

"I hate fish heads," says Marta.

Paola loves her family. Unconditionally. It is her biggest weakness. Paola wonders what the point is, though, when it feels like she is the only one trying to keep the family from falling apart.

"It's symbolic or something," says Paola.

"She thinks people love fish heads as much as she does."

"Let her do her thing for now; we all need to cool down. Let us grieve before we make any rash decisions."

"How do you not want to fucking drown her?" says Marta.

"She would have to be down there a long time," Paola says. "Quiet. Here she comes."

Ana María bursts through the kitchen with a black trash bag slung over one shoulder, a branch of plantains halfway to yellow slung over the other. She breathes heavily, dragging all that weight plus her own around. She heaves the bag onto the prep table, knocking everything else off, and drops the branch beside one of the coolers leaking icy bloodwater.

"Mamá, you can't put those there. Health hazard," says Paola, "and we already have tons of tostones cut and smashed. What are we supposed do with these?"

"Figure it out," Ana María says. "Make a special."

Marta's face goes red; fury makes her mouth twitch weird. Paola squeezes her arm.

"Can I get you something to eat, Mamá?" Paola asks. She offers her mother a ramekin of ceviche she's tasting for salt.

The thought crosses Marta's mind to add crushed shrimp shells and pin bones to the ceviche for her mother to choke on; but of course, Paola would never let her, the little mouse.

"No, mi amor, I will wait until I'm less warm," Ana María says. She thinks it all stinks like slaughter and tastes like metal, that all this life we gut, cut up, and sell by the handful feeds only nausea.

"Where the fuck have you been?" say Marta.

"Out for a hunt," says Ana María. Her flowery muumuu is sweat-soaked around the collar and armpits.

"Thirsty?" Paola asks.

"What is wrong with you? Stop trying to be nice."

"Mamá, we have to talk," says Marta.

"¡Qué calor! Can it wait?" Ana María cries. She slumps into a chair at one of the tables with an umbrella sticking out of it.

"That speckled brown trout you ordered," Marta says,

motioning toward Damien, still prone at the edge of the dock, "do you think it might be going rancid?"

"Some fish do seem happier in the shallows," insists Paola. She wonders if she could preserve Damien in a small aquarium.

"Sometimes they prefer the surface," says Ana María. She spits off to the side, but the heavy phlegm catches on her sleeve.

"Yet he drowns on the surface," says Paola.

"That rain better come on time." Ana María shifts her body to show she's not interested in talking. She points her dumpy snout from under the shade of her straw hat and fans the sweat between her neck bellows.

"Going to be clear this weekend, though," says Marta. *Still unfinished business between us*, she means. A sharp knife is all Marta needs. Belly, back. Back, belly. Guts in the bucket, blood in the water.

Ana María wriggles around in her chair to scratch an unreachable spot on her back, which is most of it.

Marta bags the mero heads, careful to shake off the excess blood. She rubs her bloody hands together, keeps her thousand eyes on Damien from under a shroud of flies.

Ana María looks up. She knows from Marta's twitchy antennae her lies, that she has already listened for Damien's heartbeat, confirmed that his heart pumps braising liquid, now, mescal. His bits are to simmer and tenderize, absorb all the goodness before breaking down into soft, chewable pieces. Except, maybe there is no goodness anymore. Maybe all that has pickled.

"What do you want for him?" asks Marta. "The pickled brown trout?"

"¿Por libra?" Ana María laughs. "There is no meat on those bones!" She waves away a bee.

"True, he seems worthless," says Marta. "Look at him."

"Mamá, you said it yourself," says Paola. "If he has no life left in his bones, then what use is he?"

"It's fine, mijas," says Ana María. She raises a hand, swollen and itchy from a hunting injury. "Mind your business."

"What happened to your arm?" Paola asks.

"There is no saving the trout, okay? The trout is mine. Find yourselves your own."

This is not the way Ana María wanted it; she is not her daughters' enemy, not the bruja they think she is. Let them taste her long tongue. Taste her and tell her that they are not also her.

"Where is Damien now?"

"He was out there screaming a minute ago," says Marta. She points her lips to Damien as he volleys off the edge of the dock, arms flailing. He is underwater for some time, long enough to worry Paola.

Ana María expects him to rise, but if he does not, who would miss him?

Soon, bubbles rise several meters from his wake. Damien pops up, runs his hands through his hair, and spits an arc of water before kicking into a backstroke.

Paola releases her breath.

Ana María snorts.

Marta thinks she sees a smile on Damien's face.

Damien rolls, back to belly, spreads his arms and legs and floats there like a water strider, or a cadaver. Then he skillfully swivels, keeps his feet tight as he dives beneath the splash of his mediocre dolphin kick.

"How many breaks have you given him?" asks Ana María.

"What breaks? This was supposed to be training," says Marta.

"That wasn't training," Paola says, and goes over to Ana María, "because you never told us about what's going on."

"He jumped on the line, started cooking without asking," says Marta. "I thought you wanted us to torture him right away."

"What torture? Go tell him I have something for him," says Ana María.

Swim Home to the Vanished

"Tell him yourself, he's right there," says Marta. She waves her knife, scatters the flies for a better look. Inky lines of fish blood melt into the hot planks of the dock.

Damien swims back to shore and wades into the shallows. He stares at the horizon. He reaches into the water for a rock the size of his fist and throws it as far as he can. He yells at the kerplunk: "Shut up, shut up!" he yells.

He turns and sees Ana María, Paola, and Marta watching him. He waves and starts to laugh.

Paola turns to her mother. "See?"

"See what?" says Ana María.

"He's crazy."

"Mamá," says Marta, "why the fuck weren't you at the service yesterday?" Marta imagines peeling her mother's thick eyelids back and stinging them with a poison sac.

"I told you, I went hunting," says Ana María. Her lips curl.

"Yeah, but you didn't. You were here." Marta wipes her heavy knives dry and slides them into her knife roll in case she needs to make a run for it.

"Marta, please," says Paola.

"Why does it matter?" says Ana María.

"I will never forgive you for killing our father," says Marta. "You weren't there for us then, either."

Ana María snarls, straightens her back, and takes a breath. She makes herself look larger, her sloppy composure suddenly aggressive. Anger exposes her soft underbelly.

"Mamá, take it easy," Paola says. She pushes her guagua between Marta and her mother.

Marta's voice rises. "We live in the same house, Mamá. You can't ignore me."

Ana María lunges and wraps her meaty hands around Marta's greasy elbow. She drags her daughter to the sea-grape bushes, within which is a type of red ant known to devour large bumbling beasts that trip and fall into it.

The ants are now crawling up Marta's unprotected legs. She struggles to escape, but Ana María's strong claws keep her from worming her way free. Marta kicks to rub at the burning stings on her ankles. Her mother shakes her harder. Marta shrinks, and her eyes well up with tears.

"I could not go to the funeral," Ana María says, "I couldn't do it. I had every right not to go. I am as broken as you—*more so*—about Carla . . . more so . . . Try to see it from a mother's perspective, mija? Your own mother?"

"Okay, yes, I'm sorry, Mamá," cries Marta. She sucks a breath and stores the rage in her body with the rest of what she has harbored since her father's death.

Paola has seen enough. She runs over and yanks Marta out of her mother's clutches.

Ana María spits and returns to her napping chair.

Paola walks around with Marta until her sister cools down and catches her breath enough to speak.

"Are you crazy?" Paola says. "Why would you bring up Flaco? Why are you instigating a fight?"

"Testing her defenses," says Marta. She rubs at her bruised elbow and smiles. "I'll have to learn how to hold my breath a little bit longer."

<hr />

Marta watches Damien wade out of the shallows and race across the hot sand like a thin-skinned lizard. He towels off his skinny body. His shoulders are burnt red, nearly purple. He isn't yet a fish. He is still in the process of transmuting, Marta thinks. Here is a man without a family, without a home. Here is a man who thinks he is on his way out like we all know we're on our way out, but his exit is sooner than ours. Here is a man who has given up, and it doesn't help that his new boss encourages this coward to remain cowardly in the shade of her garden, her love, love that raised Marta to hate. Here is a man a woman could love, but he cannot love back. Here is a man who wished he knew what to do, but he is not a whole man, he is an incomplete man who cannot make decisions for himself anymore. Here is a man who is becoming a fish. After all his travels, after all the loss and missing parts, here is a fish who nearly found his last sip of air from the seas, hardly able to breathe above or beneath. Here is a fish Marta wished she could pity, but he is a pawn, a prawn, a fish to be sacrificed on behalf of the queen, and who else should the new queen be but Marta?

Damien throws his shirt and apron on and returns to the grill, where Paola, Marta, and Ana María watch him curiously, annoyed that he is dripping from the waist down onto their work mats, but relieved he did not witness their fight.

"Are you feeling better?" Paola hands him agua de coco.

Damien swallows the coconut water in one gulp.

"See, he's fine, girls," says Ana María. "Damien, I have a special for you." She shoves her way into the prep area. She unties the rope around the trash bag she hauled in earlier and removes a pig carcass the size of a terrier. She rests her fat fists proudly on her wide hips.

"Well, what do you think?" she says.

Paola lays her forearm against the pig to measure its length.

Marta strangles a floor mat to free it of soggy crumbs and debris. "She missed Carla's service to nurse a piglet," she mumbles.

Damien picks out the grains of sand from his fingernails in the pump sink. He dries his hands, and as his fingers plump back up he feels anxious being back on land. He grabs a boning knife and hones it on the bottom of a ceramic bowl.

"Brine the hind legs and cure the belly," he says "Save the shoulder for grinding and head for pâté." Lucky for him the guts are gone, its hair singed and shaved except for a few stragglers on the pink patchy ears. He reaches into the pig body, touches her slippery rib cage before he rinses out her cavity.

"Sí, claro, mi amorcito," says Ana María. She rings out a wet rag and wipes the back of her neck.

Marta thinks the pig's flesh looks human. This is what the dead smell like, too.

"This little piggy has such soft skin, and an even softer layer of fat beneath," Damien says. He leans in, nearly close enough to kiss the carcass. He slips his butcher blade along the fold of her hind legs, the line where leg meets hip. He slices through ligament to release the ball from its socket, then divides her body into quarters.

"And this?" Ana María pulls a liver from the trash bag and hands it to him. It stinks like lead and shines like copper.

"Cut it into cubes and grind it with the shoulder and fat," Damien says. He places the liver on a towel to blot away the blood, then seasons it heavily with salt and pepper.

"Qué rico," says Ana María.

Damien breaks down the rest of the pig, preps it for tomorrow. He helps Marta clean while Ana María micromanages, but once it is clear he knows what he is doing, she turns on the radio, and a song she happens to love is playing. *Luna, luna, luna llena menguante*, a voice wails to a spooky slow strumming and howl. Ana María rocks lightly on her heels at first, then she places a hand on her belly and closes her eyes, and her big hips begin to orbit. Marta holds a few fingers to her mouth, trying not to laugh, and looks to Damien, who is watching her mother. He is placated by her flowery dress, the playful dance. Ana María opens her mouth to the sky like a lizard in a trance, and Marta laughs a rare laugh before taking the chum buckets to the water for one last rinse.

Soufflé of Sea

Sometimes Damien imagines grief like it's stuck in your throat and you can't swallow or cough it up, and you can breathe but only barely. The thing in your throat is not sharp or a loogie. It is not some foreign object or food or a hair or a fly. It is not your tongue or the words you can't say or a tooth. Your neck gets thick, grows out sideways as if around the thing that's stuck in your throat, like how a tree will grow around fencing wire and the wire becomes a part of it. It happens when another tree is in the way; they become entangled before they become one. Tie a bicycle to the trunk and wait twenty years and see what they turn into: each their own but not the same. The thing that is stuck in your throat becomes you, and it takes a long time for you to feel the hurt because it is an incredibly slow process, not unlike the birth of stars.

This is also how memory works. Loss, the ache of the past, drips down your nasal cavities into the back of your throat and gullet, where it lodges, nests, takes a nap as it swells. How else could he explain it? You can't eat a fish whole and expect it to slide on down to where it's supposed to go for proper digestion; you can't wash it down with liquor. No medicinal syrup can loosen the phlegm. No smoke from tobacco or weed will whisk away its bitter sting.

If you try to deceive yourself of its existence, you become a monster, because if you no longer exist you must be a monster. Deny that it has metastasized and it will spread from your tree rings into organs whose purpose you have long questioned. It is not like the pain in your back from kitchen work—it is far worse to have something stuck in your throat. Soon you'll have sappy tumors like the ponderosas. Your neck will grow its own neck, and a new throat will open up.

But that's not how it works, or it is, but growing another throat won't remove the hurt. If you grow around the thing and it grows into you, resisting makes it hurt worse. There is no removing the thing in your throat. You live with it, you die with it. Perhaps you find a new way to breathe, but the thing will still be in your body.

Then grow hard skin, scales. Amputate every piece of you, remove the unnecessary offal, the extra-chambered heart. It doesn't matter. It doesn't matter if he is tree or fish or man or bee. We bleed and cry and die. We lose.

There is relief in water. Damien thinks he can breathe better down there. It will take practice breathing this new way. His sense of smell is more acute in the desert, but in the briny waters smell is taste, taste is smell, skip the middle sense. If he thought he could taste without a nose, this is what it would be like: watery and mystical and heavily salted. Soufflé of sea. He is blind in the water, and when you eat blind, flavors change. He is to trust what falls into his mouth with his life and hope there is no hook.

Part II

THAT WHICH HATH MADE THEM DRUNK HATH MADE ME BOLD.
WHAT HATH QUENCHED THEM HATH GIVEN ME FIRE.

—Lady Macbeth

THAT WAS A LONG TIME AGO, BEFORE I WAS BORN, BEFORE
THERE WAS THE REMOTEST CHANCE OF MY BEING BORN, INDEED
IT WAS ONLY AFTER THAT THAT I COULD BE BORN.

—Javier Marías, *A Heart So White*

The Lure

Over a month has passed since Ana María took in the delicious stranger, though the lazy days slither in and out of summer's serpentine heat at a different pace here. Today, like most days, Tito arrives in the afternoon with the last haul of the day, which has not been as much as he has promised, lately. Damien and Marta start cleaning the fish right away so they can finish before dark.

One of the big dorados has a large lure dangling from its bulbous mouth. Damien twists the barbed hook from its jaw with a crunch, spits on it and wipes away the blood, unwraps its metal clasp. He admires its intricate design, the thin silver wire wrapped snail-like around a glass bulb, a swivel of waxy tails soldered at the end. It almost looks like a pendant his mother would have forged. He misses his mother now, her smell: roux. Flour browning in butter. He remembers his fingers getting caught in the holes of his mother's tattered apron trying to get her attention when she stared off into the distance, stewing over a brooch design, or planning her great escape.

"What did you find there?" Paola asks. Paola has stopped by to get an early start on cleaning the day's dishes. She points to

Damien's found object, his slimy lure. He nearly drops the lure back into the fish's belly.

"Reminded me of my mother's work," says Damien, startled. It hurts his heart, but his heart aches for something other than his mother's return. He does not want her back, not really. He despises her for leaving Kai and their father and him. He wants to blame his mother for their disappearances. Neither an apology nor a ghostly cameo would wipe the slate clean.

Marta takes the lure and laughs at Damien. "If you were really fish, this would be your irresistible ruse?"

She throws it at Paola. The lure's barb punctures Paola's finger, but it doesn't faze her. She knows Marta is trying to start something, but Paola hasn't decided when the right time will be to confront her.

Paola picks up the lure and scrapes away the wax with a fillet knife, then rubs the wax until it softens in her fingertips. She smells it before she touches it with her tongue.

"Cheese," she says. Damien looks confused, disgusted. He must think it a peculiar way to see a thing, not by its smell, but its taste, no matter how deeply ingested by a strange fish. Has he been missing out on life by not touching everything around him with his tongue? Sounds like an easy way to get punched in the face, thinks Paola. But if Damien could ween himself off the mescal, he might realize that his previous life tasted as if preserved in a moldy film, hiding its true flavor—its *essence*, his *aboutness*.

Damien pinches a bit of wax for himself and takes a whiff. "Gouda," he says. His look of disgust becomes one of being intrigued. His memory has become so fragmented he considers this to be his mother's smell, something like smoked cheese, a fish's mouth.

He cleans them daily: atún and dorado, langosta, mero, chillo. He was pretty good at cleaning fish before, but since his arrival, Ana María has shown him how to fillet with efficiency. The catch is so fresh that carcasses sometimes flinch, nerves quake muscle even after the blood has been drained and the intestines ripped out. He breaks them down, one after the other, rinses the meat in salt water, throws the extra bits into the sea. A pot of water stays boiling on the gas burner, for blanching the langosta and washing the cutting boards and worktable. He has lost count of the days and weeks, the weight and measure of bodies slung across his prep table.

"I'm a tasty crustacean," he says to a massive tuna on the prep table. Sometimes an old fish like this shows up with scars across its cheeks, permanent impalements and slashes on its back from a half dozen hooks and missed gaff-shots. Damien likes to check what they have been eating. Smaller fish. Sardines mostly. Hooks can get lodged in the stomach or esophagus. He occasionally finds toys stripped of paint, bouncy balls, candy wrappers, beer tabs, toe rings. Fish aim for most things shiny.

"You're right," he says, "I'm nothing like a crustacean."

Damien spanks the tuna.

Perhaps this is how his brother felt in his last few weeks, hours—that he belonged to the river, because life above was not worth swimming for. As least fish have a path. Water carves them a story from springs rushing into creeks and rivers into bigger rivers before they reach the ocean. Fish only return after they've been out there for years, feeding, fucking, darting in and out of larger mouths. Only a few species return alive.

Damien heaves another tuna onto the table. Blood drips onto the pier, his shoes, his apron. The tuna twitches. He runs a finger under the blackfin's dorsal, rubs in his tears. He stares into its shiny black eye, his reflection in it. It shines black like Marta's.

Sometimes when Damien's eyes droop and he starts talking to

himself or the fish, the women will encourage him to jump into the ocean. He won't refuse a chance to swim. His body moves more naturally in water, though not yet like a fish. Or like a fish, but a fish without its air bladder. He says he becomes his brother in the water. His brother became a fish. Out of water, Damien feels like a stinking body of meat, waterlogged and wrinkled.

One problem is that his body still seems as out of place in water as it does on land, like a thing of the desert pretending to be a thing of the sea, but nobody has shown him how to be either one. It is not the skin-to-scale ratio, that is not what slows him down in water. He does not have webbing between his toes or unreachable fins on his spine or ventral. If he did, there is still no guarantee he would make a decent water creature.

Knife into belly, ass to fin, fin to head. Around the collar, along the back, under the belly, and down the lateral line. Sometimes he chops the heads off first, but if the head is left intact, the bones make for an easier toss into the ocean. Some heads Ana María saves to feed the caimanes; the extras are rinsed, bagged, and placed in ice for the fishermen's families. Ana María says she has to keep them happy. It is how she earns their trust. Share the scraps. Pretend it is a high form of generosity.

Marta asks Damien if he wants to go to the bar when they're done cleaning up.

"Maybe later," Damien says. He does not want to go to Eddie's again, though he craves the mescal. How can he, when he knows it keeps him in this fog? "Isn't there someplace else we can go?"

He washes his gross cutting board and gazes across the rippled colors of the ocean and out to the horizon, where the storm clouds gather and gloss the water gray. It conjures a strange feeling that his brother is near but falling away, like a tannin, vestigial and bittersweet. The same feeling frightened Damien when he jumped in the ocean his first day here. The image of his brother underwater, reaching up not out of need but as an invitation, haunted him. He has not seen any apparitions since then, maybe because Ana María has kept him sedated. She helped him accomplish what she thinks he came here for. To find oblivion and forget what haunts him most.

In spite of Ana María's attempts to frighten him with stories of dangerous creatures who live in the ocean, the water beckons Damien. For him to breathe. To clear his mind. To rinse his mouth and wet his gills and swim as far as he can to find Kai and join him in his weightlessness. Damien thought he didn't want to live like that, but maybe he does, now. Is it possible to want life and death at the same time? Perhaps he is greedy to want both.

Marta, Paola, and Ana María have noticed Damien getting progressively fishier as he cleans the fish. Ana María has tried to convince Damien that she cares for him more than she does for her daughters. He has been lost in the haze of the work and heat and mescal for some time, but somewhere deep between his slimy organs and rusted ribs, he likes it, she is sure of it.

Damien finds some comfort in the transparency of Ana María's manipulations. She has shown a stranger kindness. Making him forget was a kind of sadistic sympathy.

"Sorcerer's solicitude," Damien says to a fish on his cutting board. "Compassionately cruel. Who else would make a fish clean fish?"

It is not entirely her fault he is under her spell; Damien is as much to blame. He is comforted by people who care for him, even if it is performative; it allows him to maintain detachment, like while sitting in a restaurant there's a barrier, an agreement: swap money for kindness and some eggs. Kitchen work offers a similar distancing. He believes getting lost in the monotony of a task, of routine, will keep his heart beating through this hazy cycle of drunk and hungover. The problem is that he has become their proxy—an appendage.

He does not trust any of the brujas. At this point he only trusts that customers return to eat every day. Sometimes it seems as if their purchase is an offering, a tribute, not one of hunger. Perhaps the villagers feel the same way as Damien does about his own existence. Maybe they too do not feel confident about which side of living they are on. He sees fear in their eyes. The tortilla ladies and pharmacist and fishermen used to nod and say buenos días to him, but now they must sense he has become tainted by the brujas.

Paola had gone home and returns now with a pitcher of agua fresca. Damien looks up from the cutting board. His prep station is bloody and flaked with dark guts, his hands are wrinkled and red.

"Thirsty?" Paola offers him a cup. *Trust me*, her gesture begs. Bits of fish meat rub off on her hand as Damien accepts. Paola pours another for Marta and leaves in a way that keeps Damien watching.

"She's never brought *me* cucumber water before," says Marta. She coughs up a mint leaf. "You must be something special."

If Ana María and Marta's feigned interest comforts Damien, he does not quite know how to act when Paola exudes true warmth. He has tried to distance himself from Marta and Ana María by burying himself further in the work, and in what's left of his memories. Smells his mother's lamb stew braising in the oven, deep and steely with a spark of lemon rind. Feels the weight of his father's hunger and heavy wheezing in the evening. But there is ocean, the pressure of ocean, smothering it all like an aspic.

Another fish on the table, and Damien smells the scent of singed fingers holding a line, another finger burn. He imagines himself on the other end fighting against annihilation, until up pops Damien, a fish out of water, look at him gasp, eyes popping, gills heaving, trying to spit Hello!

Damien puts the knife down. He runs his thumb along the tuna's rib cage to rub away an artery. When the grief gets stuck in his throat, his blood pulses fast and he squeezes his eyes shut. His mind leaves his body to cut the fish alone. Anything could happen to his body before he is returned to it. He does not know the extent of the stories he shares while he cleans the fish and chops their bodies into little bits. Only when the feeling passes will he be able to unlock his jaw and release his fists.

With Paola gone and Ana María snoring, Marta feels bold enough to touch Damien's arm. His fin is cold and sticky, with the stench of sweet iron.

"¿Dónde está el dolor?" she says.

He doesn't quite know what she means, but he presses a scaly hand to his chest anyway. That memory is moss now. Stinks of mildew.

Marta reaches for his face. Flies weave around them. He no longer flinches or flips a fin at her touch.

Damien looks down. He shoves the scimitar into the tuna's anus.

"You're a sack of guts and plasma wrapped in shiny flesh," he says to the fish, "made sturdy with sharpened bone. Perfect for carving through ocean."

"Tell me what's wrong," says Marta. Why doesn't he trust her yet? She has been nothing but kind to him, she thinks. Are her attempts to allure Damien as obvious as her mother's? How embarrassing.

What's *wrong*? Maybe what's wrong is Damien is enamored and under the brujas' spell, which is like being underwater, which is like being awake in a dream where you can't stop struggling for breath. He resists, but the strings to his heart have been cut. You want me this way, he thinks, you need me like this, like clay, cold and moldable. A scapegoat. A fish out of water.

"The longer I stay," Damien says, "the more I forget. But the grief is still there."

"Maybe that's not such a bad thing," says Marta. "We can't be deprived of something we no longer have in our possession."

"To grieve by forgetting? What if losing a memory is another little death? If we no longer have the past, if we don't have those stories, we are nothing."

Marta is worried about Damien. She suspects he feels trapped and isolated, which her mother remedies by getting him drunk all the time. Marta was hoping he wouldn't come up for air so quickly. It's time; Marta needs him to trust her.

"Maybe you're right," she says. "Damien, listen to me. Did you ever ask Ana María for help?"

"No," Damien says.

"Did you ask her for anything other than water?"

"No."

"When did you start forgetting?"

"I guess when I got here."

"When she gave you the mescal."

"Yes."

"That's right, she did not want you thinking clearly. She poisoned you."

Damien shoves his hands into his hair and pulls as hard as he can and nearly rips out a handful. Then he slaps himself beneath his ears and gills. How could he have been so blind?

"This is not your fault," says Marta, "this is my mother's hold on you. On all of us. Let me see."

Damien removes his hands from his neck and lets Marta inspect his itchy gills. Marta wishes Damien could see her for the bruja she wants to be, but he has made clear he has no interest in staying here any longer, no interest in brujas, prefers another flavor to the kind of liquor they distill and sling. Too bad; she had hoped his convincing would not require violence.

"I'll protect you," Marta says, petting Damien's salty hair. Her proximity to Damien, her promises, will upset her mother, stir the fire. Marta rests her fuzzy hand on Damien's shoulder. His face goes hot.

"We have another hundred pounds of fish to clean," she says.

⸺

"¡Qué calor!" Ana María croaks herself awake from choking on her saliva or a fly. She smacks her tongue and finishes swallowing whatever swam into her throat.

Marta's voice changes to a bossier tone now that Ana María is awake. "Look what you've done," she scolds Damien. "Mamá's fussy now. Let's finish up so we can get out of here."

Damien sniffles, scrapes silver scales from his arm with the back of his knife.

"It's too fucking hot," cries Ana María. She struggles to sit up from her chair to adjust her sombrillo.

Damien stares at himself in the tuna's eye. How small his reflection has become! Bloody knife, bags under his eyes, scabby apron. He thought he ran away from this kind of life. But he looks like he has all but surrendered.

"Don't let those heads go to waste," says Marta in a deep voice.

"I would never," he says. Wasn't Marta being nice to him just a minute ago? She so easily switches allegiances, Damien thinks.

"They're worth more than you know," says Ana María.

What am I worth to you? he wonders. Marta has successfully gotten to his head. Ana María scares him more in this new light.

Marta leans into Damien and, making sure her mother is watching, whispers into his ear: "Don't drink her drink."

Swim Home to the Vanished

The proximity of Marta's mouth to Damien's ear successfully irritates Ana María.

"Go wash the buckets," Ana María says.

"*You* take the fucking buckets," Marta says.

"When's the last time I did that?"

"Exactly." Marta flinches but doesn't shrink. "No, I'm just tired of your—"

"Tired of me?"

"I'm not your servant." Marta points to Damien. "Ask him to take the goddamn buckets."

Ana María inflates her body. She rises on her haunches and flexes her exposed belly and chubby scutes. Marta turns white and backs down.

The borrachos are right, thinks Damien. Ana María is a god-damn lizard, they say, don't trust her. She's more the caimán, they say; she's nature herself. If we fill her with trash, she poisons our fish. Burn her and the hillsides'll collapse. The villagers dream it all the time.

Marta retreats, knowing now is not the time for a fight. Better to stay on Mamá's good side, like Paola said. What Paola didn't say was how to catch her off guard.

Marta lifts the five-gallon buckets, one in each hand, huffing and puffing.

"That's my baby," says Ana María. "I may be slow, but I have sharp teeth." She decompresses her body and shoves her snout into a bag of fish heads and inhales their sour salt and iron tinge.

Marta carries the heavy buckets of scraps far down the beach to the rocky outcropping where she feeds the eels and crabs. She takes her time throwing guts into the sky. Gulls and frigates hone in, grazing her skull. The birds are masters; they know the smell of meat on the wind. Ana María is an enemy to birds. Sits under a nest, waits for their eggs to drop. The impatient chick's first flight. Ana María slurps them and their shells—she's a sucker for texture. Eggs and feathers and crunchy bone. The birds will laugh at how she is flightless, but they won't laugh long. Crunchy bone and sweet beaks. Even their feet Ana María picks her teeth with.

Marta's rise to the top will be simple—she need only convince the villagers that their destinies are no longer linked to some cold-blooded, tiny-hearted mouth breather like Ana María.

She will inspire gifts instead of fear. If only Damien would cut out her mother's tongue and present it to Marta in a hollow coconut shell—*swoon*!

Perhaps, in lieu of fear, Marta will lead with grace and beauty, qualities her mother lacks. Just look how longingly Damien gapes at her, probably pictures what her body looks like beneath her shiny exoskeleton. How agitated Ana María got when Marta buzzed around too close to Damien. He turned red, attracted to such a young wasp-waisted thing as herself. He won't even make direct eye contact with her he's so enamored.

Marta dumps the remnants of the trimmings. All the blood and bits turn the ocean the color of a bruise.

She looks up at the sky. Dark clouds pucker above her, the gulls and frigates suddenly vanished.

⁂

Ana María waits until Marta and her buckets of chum are out of earshot before she apologizes to Damien for her daughters' behavior.

"It's obvious they make you uncomfortable," she says. "They're upset about something." She blinks strangely, like she has a third eyelid.

Damien found a green coconut down the beach and is looking for something to pry it open with.

"They lost their sister," he says. "Maybe they're in pain."

Ana María stretches her snaggletooth smile. "You've been spending too much time with my daughters, ungrateful fucker. Do I not provide enough for you? Should we have left you in the desert? They don't know real pain." She stares at a small, temperamental cloud about to break open in the distance. "And I hope they never do."

The dullness of the tiny machete Damien found slows his progress on the coconut.

"Family is everything," she says. "I taught my daughters good and fine, but only Paola absorbed more than a thing or two. Which is why I'm glad you're here, Damien. I hope you'll stay."

The rain falls. The heavy tapping on the tarp forces Damien to raise his voice.

"You and your daughters have been generous," he says with difficulty. He has to draw a line somewhere. "Thank you for all you've done, but I can't stay here any longer, I'm sorry. I have to move on."

Ana María inflates herself aggressively. She clicks her reptilian tongue from the back of her throat in disappointment. "Of course, we'll manage without you," she says. "Your existence is not necessary for our survival."

What does she mean by that? Damien panics. Why did he have to say something? He sees his body, like Carla's body, left down by the river, an unsolved crime of passion. Damien puts down the dumb machete.

"We appreciate you," says Ana María, "but I got what I need from you. I have enough to worry about, a business to run, orders and prep and fish and everything . . ."

Damien bites his tongue. Paola and Marta complain about how Ana María doesn't do shit. In fact, it's one of the few things Marta and Paola seem to have in common, the grievances over their mother.

"Wait, I don't understand," Damien says, "am I free to go or what?"

"Sí, claro que eres libre. Did Marta try to convince you to stay, as well? She's a bit of a romantic like me. Don't let Marta scare you. She doesn't have the greatest social skills."

Damien feels relieved, but confused, like everyone's been fucking with him, or maybe it's just because he's paranoid and hungover again. Has he been free to go all along? He doesn't really know what to believe. Everything is still hazy. They have helped him, though. He is grateful to have had these splintery oars to cling to when he was a castaway, but they are a family interested only in preserving themselves. He has grown accustomed to their strangeness, but not to their lies and deceit. Sometimes from beneath the sedation, he realizes he is being used. But I don't have anywhere else to go, he thinks; what choice do I have?

Ana María leans on the counter and holds out her cut-up arms. Maybe he'll stick around longer if he learns the truth of what happened to Carla, she thinks. Perhaps that's what's scaring him—no one seems to have explained anything to him. He no longer wishes to be left in the dark.

Damien backs away. He hopes Marta returns from the jetty soon. Her mother is making him more uncomfortable than usual.

"Look at this," Ana María says. She squeezes her chubby elbow and twists it around for Damien to look at, as if the bruise is still there. "Carla wrenched my arm when I was smoking out on our deck."

Damien inspects the wound closer. It does look like somebody with sharp nails pierced Ana María's thick hide. He thinks back to when she presented Damien the pig as a gift.

"You didn't get hurt hunting that day," he says.

"No," says Ana María. She drops from her heightened state back into her frumpy position. She adjusts herself, feels awkward wearing clothes in this humidity. "Carla was brave, but she never acted out like Marta. She barged right up to me. Her teeth had gotten sharper; I was proud of how gorgeous they'd become. I tapped the ashes of my cigarillo, and I said, 'Mija, what a bold little beast I raised.' But Carla was not her usual self. Someone must have set her off. She said, 'Mamá, why does this world seem built only for its destruction? It feels like in order for us to thrive, everything, or everyone, must die.'"

Damien's arms tremble, suddenly cold. He shoves them under his apron and paces around the grill in order to keep his distance from her. Ana María grabs a chair and brings it under the tarp. She sits down and lights one of her cigarillos. There is no shame in survival, she tells Damien; she built this world for them, her daughters. They have lived through attempted conquest, have so far slipped by unrecognized, saved, from the unwanted courtship of capitalists. It does not mean their land and people won't be raped or enslaved for profit eventually. But Ana María's job—*their* job—is to protect the village from these tragedies for as long as possible.

Ana María smushes a nostril with her thumb and blows a stream of snot out the other. She continues, "Carla wrapped herself tight in her shawl, and she asked me a bunch of questions: 'What happened to Flaco? Was he in your way? Why did you do it? Do you know what you did to Marta by shipping him away?' Carla wanted vengeance based on rumors, lies, one of Marta's fever dreams."

Damien feels sick to his stomach.

"I did not want to hurt Carla," Ana María continues. "I swear it was the smell of fish, like blood in the water. Carla smelled like her husband. Her husband smells like fish. My instinct was to punish her for smelling like our prey. For loving a fisherman more than me. But can you blame me for being protective? I didn't want her marry Tito because I don't like those pescadores. My father was a shallow, violent, worthless drunk of a fisherman, and that's exactly what Flaco became. Turns out I may have been wrong about Tito.

"So, I stabbed out my cigarillo, pressed my forehead against Carla's, pushed my chest to her chest sternum to sternum, matched her heart to heart. Carla's blood was warm, warmer than mine. She attempted to pull me into the house, where her sisters could have helped her, but I am too big, I tore myself away. I slapped her hard. Her eyes were cold. Those were my eyes staring back at me, I wanted them back. I yanked at her hair and pushed her down the porch steps and kicked her in her rib cage. I grabbed her, and . . . I smashed her head against the ground. Thin skin and soft bone. On the road her blood. On her head her blood. Hair. I wanted my eyes back. I remember thinking: I silenced the last man with any power, my daughters are the only threat to me now, don't they know it isn't their time yet? And I threw Carla, unconscious, over my shoulder and carried her to the Red Clay River."

Damien has heard of the Red Clay River, probably from Benny one night at Eddie's. It's where water performs daily, sometimes from the rains, other times from the springs. The water dances, sings around sandstone cliffs. Carves out canyons before it runs down the wash into farms, feeds the maize, drowns the mice burrowed deep, and disappears into a sparkling earth. No water striders, bullfrogs, thirsty birds, not even the sky can escape its blinding shine. It tastes like dirt. Salty, too. Not the same salt as the sea. Ocean is flavored where it touches blue, not from the creatures below, which is how they say the Red Clay River tastes.

Carla, still flopped over Ana María's shoulder, stirred awake. She chomped down on her mother's back hip. Ana María screamed and dropped her. Carla was able to sweep her mother's leg, but Ana María was more powerful on the ground, postured on all fours. She caught and clenched Carla's leg in her mouth and twisted into a spin with the weight of her enormous body.

Carla's flesh was her mother's flesh. Ana María wanted it back.

Swim Home to the Vanished

Blood soaked through Carla's clothes like the belly of a thunderhead. Her breathing slowed, her body became motionless.

Ana María claims that she came back from a darkness. When she realized where she was, she didn't know what had happened, and she left in a panic, leaving Carla bleeding out on the riverbank.

"I did not want Carla to die," she says. "I was triggered by the smell, I swear." Ana María falls to her knees; her entire body arches and shakes as if to discharge a bone or a biscuit, but her stomach has nothing left to chuck.

Damien is nauseous. He drops his head between his knees and breathes—it's too much for him to handle. She isn't so much telling Damien a story as reliving it.

"I am so sorry, Carla, mi amor," she sobs, "I didn't mean to hurt you like that." Ana María starts to dry-heave. She grabs her belly and punches herself in her kidneys and spits, then spits some more.

Damien briefly thinks she is having a seizure, or that she is choking on her saliva or her tongue, and he hides behind his prep table.

She finally falls flat in the rain after several convulsions, but before he can decide if he should get close enough to check, Ana María shoots her neck into the air and kicks herself over the dock belly-first with a colossal splash, and dives deep into the green water until she is shadow.

Damien does not see where she resurfaces, or whether she does at all. He is convinced now that she has a lair beneath the docks, a nest in the reeds someplace near the river's mouth.

⁂

Marta returns from the jetty, running now in the rain with an emptied chum bucket hoisted upside down to keep her hair dry.

She usually rinses the buckets in salt water, but the downpour must have caught her off guard; a pink-hued residue drips a ring around her shoulders. Marta shakes the rain off beneath the tarp like a mudfish, splashing sweat and fishy oils all over Damien and his shining prep table.

Damien is pale, his eyes bulging and wet.

"Hey, sorry for dirtying your station," says Marta, "but you don't have to look at me that way."

"It's not that," Damien stutters, "it's just—" He points in the direction of the river's mouth.

The rains stop, as if by the turn of a spigot, and Paola arrives to help close. The skies have opened; the thunderhead continues on its way. Paola immediately recognizes and misinterprets the tension in the kitchen. She thinks she can lighten the mood by humming a song and swaying her hips.

"Now isn't a good time to dance," Marta says.

"What's up?" says Paola. "Let's do this." Marta may love mornings, but the closing shift is Paola's favorite part of the day. Marta has usually stopped talking by now, and Paola can stalk around her without a fight to restock the line for the morning shift, load the cart with dirties, pour the last contents of each container atop the fresh ones: first in, first out. Some of the fish scraps will go into a stew or get cooked down for empanadas. All that work: fill orders, wash and chop veggies, make all the sides and sauces, plan all the time-sensitive curing and smoking and baking, only to see it shoveled into desperate mouths, many of them toothless, disappeared in a matter of hours. It should be a source of frustration. If Paola focused on futility alone, she'd go mad. But she loves the rotation. Her heart flutters at the sight of the washed and sanitized containers stacked, organized, everything in its spot, mise en place. Paola's management relies on consistency and order, unlike her big sister's. During Carla's tenure, the goal was for their little grill to run itself so Carla could clock out early and go exploring and take naps after long afternoons playing in the ocean. Paola's focus, in the kitchen at least, is on experiment and revision. Rather than risk stagnation, she updates the menu if she feels the slightest bit of boredom. Carla's death inexplicably gifted Paola with a sense of pride in her talents. She accepts her inherited kitchen duties with a whole heart. On behalf of Carla, yes, but Paola finds fulfillment in a precisely executed meal, no matter its simplicity. Rather than being a mere collector, Paola can create something out of nothing, recipes now boundless in her cauldrons.

Paola checks a list, fuming that she can't dance. Marta preens herself in front of customers admiring her from a distance. Damien sinks, still in shock from what Ana María revealed to him about Carla.

Damien wonders what kind of darkness took over Ana María. He feels bad for her, if her story is true. What is the point in telling Marta and Paola that their mother killed their sister if it's only going to stir them up? He is terrified of Marta, and Paola too, just by proxy. If he was unsure about leaving earlier, he is ready to go now.

"Damien, what's wrong?" Paola asks.

The whole conversation with Ana María has made his insides itchy.

"Your mother," Damien says, rubbing the back of his neck. "I don't know if I should tell you this."

"Made up a sin rather than confess to one of her real crimes, I bet," says Marta.

"What did she say to you?" Paola asks.

"She told me that she killed Carla, or *thinks* she did," says Damien. "She said Carla started a fight with her and it got out of hand."

"I knew it," says Marta. "It's written all over her face."

Paola turns to Marta. "Is it guilt you see, or shame?"

"She claimed it was an accident," says Damien.

"Of course she claimed it was an accident," Marta says. "You are so gullible."

"I don't know, I kind of believe her," says Damien.

"Round her up," says Marta.

"Hold on," Paola says. "Don't get ahead of yourself."

"What? She confessed." Marta nods at Damien. "Excuse us, you are a guest here: Ana María manipulates people for a living; it's difficult to know when she's telling the truth." This confession plays right into Marta's hands. The village will agree, Ana María must go. Cinch the ties, light a fire beneath Mamá's feet.

"Why did Mamá tell you what happened in the first place?" Paola asks.

"I don't think her purpose was to incriminate herself, if that's what you mean," says Damien. "Maybe she simply couldn't hold it in any longer."

"Or it is because"—Marta raises a blackened finger—"she knows we would find out eventually. Mamá wants to make sure her version of the story sticks. Paola, what's wrong? Why is your face so purple?"

⁘

Paola restocks and makes tomorrow's order. Marta scrubs the burners, waits for the grill machine to cool safely enough to fold the doors and bellows away into its tortoise-like shell. Damien hoses the mats down for a scrub. Oil strained and fryer cleaned, Damien throws the last box of trash into Paola's guagua and walks away. The sisters have been arguing the whole time.

He does not wait for them like he usually does. He knew he

should have kept his mouth shut. Did Ana María *want* him to share her story with them? Is she trying to inflame their tempers more than they already are?

Damien follows Tito's watery blood trail to the old marina, where along the beach, up high near the ant bushes, old wooden vessels in varying degrees of decomposition lie upside down like exhausted beetles. Most seaworthy boats are down near Tito's yola tied to the dock; his is the best maintained. Tito straddles his yola with short, muscular legs, struggling to untie a line. He is able to slip the knot and push away from the dock, and with a kick of his heel he revs the smoky engine, then motors the yola around in a loop and onto the beach, where the sand hisses at the boat's cool touch.

"Hola, ¿qué tal, Damien?" Tito says, galloping the reins of his yola.

Damien hesitates. He is not quite sure why he wandered out this way other than to get away from his corrosive work environment.

"You don't look so hot," says Tito.

Damien steps up to Tito's yola and touches the scars on its bow. The boards are wide and pockmarked where beetles have attempted to bore their way in. The trees must have been old and resistant to infestation; Damien imagines a species of pine gone extinct. The draft is painted bright white, and several barnacles clasp on for the ride. The hull is sealed with several generations' worth of marine paint, a sloppy patchwork of forest greens. Inside, the railing is canary yellow and the benches are a deep red.

"Those women spook you?" Tito asks. He lifts the heavy motor into its resting position and locks it into place.

"I don't know if 'spooked' is the right word," says Damien.

"If 'spooked' isn't the right word now, it will be," says Tito.

"It's like a bad dream."

"I don't remember my dreams." Tito wraps a bundle of fishing line around his hand until his hand turns purple. "But I'm sure they're all about fishing, staring at my hands all cut up from sharp fins, barbed hooks, fast lines. That's what I think about when I'm not working. I stand around; I stare at my hands. The smell never comes out."

Tito snips the fishing line twice, ties the threads onto coat hangers, which he then folds into little windmills. He attaches one at the stern and another at the bow to keep the gulls from shitting on everything.

"How long did you live with them?" Damien asks.

"Wasn't too long, after we got married. It was one of the reasons we had to get married, so I could move out of my tío's shack. It was temporary, just until we could escape."

Damien pokes his head into the boat. Blood-tinted bilge-water sloshes around with dark flecks of fish organs, scales, large hooks tangled in loose line. Empty beer cans rumble around with swim bladders that float in the red water like atrophied jellyfish. Damien wonders how anyone could live with the smell, but figures Tito probably doesn't notice it anymore.

"My wife was going to take me away," Tito says, "show me things I've never seen. Now I'm back living with my uncle, the Pallbearer, who can be a bit of a sad drunk, always talking about the Criers. Doubt I'll end up going anywhere now."

Tito removes a caneca of rum from under a flotation device and uses the float as a seat cushion. He takes a long pull.

"Where'd you sleep, in the hammock?" Damien says.

Tito laughs. "One of the first things I took was our mattress so I didn't have to sleep on a pallet at my tío's. It still smells like her."

Tito stops. He suddenly realizes he hasn't made sure that Damien had nothing to do with Carla's death. Damien showed up around the same time. Tito remembers seeing him in the church the morning of the funeral. He looked too weak to pick up his own feet. Besides, Tito knows these brujas, he lived with them long enough to know they can be ruthless. They are fully capable of this kind of cruelty, especially Ana María. For reasons beyond Tito's comprehension, she has always despised him.

"Conoces a el Portador del Féretro?" Tito asks Damien. He raises his muscular arms and swings them high and spreads his fingers wide, then he widens his bloodshot eyes as big as he can get them, miming the Pallbearer's monstrosity, perhaps his madness.

Damien laughs. "I don't recognize the words, but your impression is spot-on."

"Have you ever killed anybody?" says Tito.

"No. Have you?" Damien asks, wondering why Tito would ask him such a question.

Tito shakes his head, passes the bottle to Damien. Damien unscrews the cap, takes a whiff. His gills shrivel up. He hands it back.

What happened to Carla? Damien wants answers, since her family can't seem to get their stories straight. But it's clear to him Tito is not thinking about the how because he is still dealing with the grief.

"What was Carla like?" Damien finally says.

Tito hops out of the boat and, barefoot, drags a rope up the beach and anchors it to a palm tree.

"What do you want to know? That she was a saint? Not at all. Like I said earlier, I don't dream. It is possible we inherit the dreams of our ancestors, but Carla willed hers to me like some curse. Fucking brujas."

"What do you mean?"

"I think I dream *her* dreams. If she dreamed of ships that carry disease and green metal horses with stowaway viruses, if she saw the greed and bloodthirst of pale skins floated here from where the sun rose angry, which I'm sure she did, now I have those dreams, some so real Carla must have felt like she was there, which is *here*, hundreds of years ago, before they came, what this land was before, what thriving life! Don't you wish you could return the prospering giant forests here from the beforetime?"

Tito's descriptions of Carla's dreams, their familiarity, trip something inside Damien. His mind floods with an onslaught of images from Dinétah. Magnificent forest fires every year lighting the skies into amazing colors, blazes with so much heat they created their own weather systems. Rivers unclogged by dams, flooding and ebbing. Metals clash; he hears violent screaming after laughable diplomatic gestures. Witness to genocide, the ramifications of the attempt. And what of the ground shaking under the weight of hundreds of thousands of hooves, the dust in their wake?

Civilizations depend on every strand, braid, tributary, from the headwaters in the mountains to the deltas below. Now it's all dried up, siphoned off to slake unquenchable groves of fruit meant to be harvested, dried, and packaged in a petroleum product and sent via petroleum product to someplace far from its birth. Or the water, which is slurped by a particularly thirsty species of grass designed to soften the fall of a little ball you hit with a stick and manically encourage to roll into a little hole. You can't eat the grass, or the stick, or the ball, or the hole. The water is stolen from civilizations who nurtured it for thousands of years, and who now need it the most; then it is delivered to irrigate the fields of ungrateful, unflowering culm.

The memory unlodges a deeper sickness in Damien. "I thought I was trying to remember a place to return to," he says, "but it might not be a place worth remembering."

"That is why I don't really have a permanent home," says Tito. "I live solely on the currents. My skin gets darker every day. Pero Carla, mi amor, Carla, Carla, por favor—I miss her aguacate on my face (she said it heals), jugo de nopales on my skin (she said it replenishes dead cells), and mantequilla on my burns ('Who should need a scar to remember?' she said). Been only how long since she died? And already I'm a burnt sardine." Tito sits in the sand.

Damien hops onto the yola's bow and dangles his legs. He rubs the back of his salty neck, which he tastes now through his gills. Sand exfoliates his thin, damaged lamina, burns his already blistered skin. He checks his elbows and they're just as ch'izhi as Tito's.

"One thing I've learned living with my uncle—he hangs out with Criers all the time—he'll tell you that when we lose someone or suffer somehow, we change. More than anger or sadness. Something happens to us, our bodies. Our bodies change because they can feel before our brains do. Tío sees it all the time. He buries everyone. He knows the Criers more than anyone alive. He knows the dead even better."

Damien wishes he knew how to comfort the pescador. How does one like to be comforted in times of grief? One would think he would know by now.

"At least the fishing is going well, right?" Damien says, trying to lighten things.

"Sure." Tito's voice cracks. "Sort of. But no, not really, it's not."

"No?"

"I've been told to keep it a secret."

"This place and its secrets, man," says Damien.

"Listen, let's just say I'm not the great pescador I appear to be. I mean I'm great, but there aren't any fish in our waters, not since Flaco died ten years ago. Do you know why he and Ana María got married in the first place? For the fish to return, and it worked. But after Ana María had Flaco . . . you know what I mean—it was clear she has something to do with what happened to him. But with Flaco gone, the fish left the water empty."

Tito stands, his salty hair ungiving in the shore breeze. Damien likes Tito. He recognizes the pescador's desperation, but where do the fish Damien's been cleaning come from?

"Mira, I shouldn't be telling you this—but I can't be the only one carrying this burden. Sorry to pull you down with me, but you know when Ana María says she is going hunting? She's actually out haggling for fish in other villages . . . it's all a façade."

"Wait, what? Why?"

Tito looks down the beach and sees Marta approaching, kicking sand, all cleaned up and shoeless. Damien bets she can't scrub the stink of fish from her skin either.

"Brujas, all of them," whispers Tito. "Don't trust those fucking brujas. Quiet around her, cuidado."

"Hola, Marta, mi amor!" he says.

⌐

Marta has watched Damien with some mix of pity and curiosity while they work together, but he rarely looks up from his tasks during the day. Maybe he has been careful *not* to pay attention to her. She is cautious, too, with this game they are playing, or is it all in her head? She wants to convince him they are the same, that maybe they are not as much confused as they are lost. They must have that in common.

When Marta walks up to them on the beach, Damien is leaning into Tito's stories, his crazy hands and wild eyebrows doing all the work. Marta has admired those furry black things since she was a child, wanted to clip some off to add to her own. They carry the weight of his horrid expressions, on a face perfect for the sea. Chiseled and solemn one minute, haggard and clown-like the next. He was a good brother-in-law, Marta thinks, but she always thought Carla could do better than another pescador. What other choice did they have, though? Damien turns and smiles at Marta, and it throws her off. He looks better than when he arrived. It will make her plan easier to execute.

"Tito was just telling me your sister was haunted by the past," Damien says. "Not just hers, but the way-*way* past."

Marta shoots Tito a confused look. "¿Le dijiste eso?"

Tito's eyebrows arch their backs and hiss.

"You drunk already, Tito?" Marta laughs. It is a grittier, higher-pitched laugh than the men expect.

"No siempre, no," Tito whimpers.

Tito offers his caneca and Marta takes a swig. Damien waves it away.

"Do you mind if I borrow him?" Marta asks. She pokes Damien's arm.

"Sure," says Tito. "He just showed up here, take him." His eyebrows fold into a V, his fingers get twitchy. His lies are easy to tell.

"Of course, no problem," says Damien, "I was only taking a walk."

Tito pats Damien's back.

Marta watches them suspiciously.

"Bueno," Tito says. He raises his bottle, swishes the last sips around. "See you at the chinchorros." He starts up the beach and takes a shortcut across the goat meadow.

"Do you want to go with him?" asks Marta. It's hard for her to comprehend why he wouldn't want to go drinking. Maybe he finds her pushy and he'll leave as soon as he finds space to move and breathe on his own. Her mother warned her about scaring him off.

Damien feels pulled to Marta, against his will. "No," he says, "something wrong?"

"Come, let's walk," she says.

Marta takes Damien's arm and leads him farther down the beach where the sand turns to coral and rock. They balance on the backs of slick boulders, toss stones at gulls. They find a place to sit in a gentle alcove just beyond the boulders, where tepid water gets trapped in natural bowls. Waves crash and roll to shore from far out, gently draining and refilling the baths, carved into stone over the course of millions of years.

"I can breathe a little easier here," Damien says. He wipes a bit of the sea-foam off his cheek.

Marta scoots closer to him. Their feet splash in the warm water. She wishes she could talk, to share with him or anybody who'll listen the abject pain she feels, but it's always so mushed up inside and hard to decipher. Maybe her aggression makes him nervous, maybe it's getting in the way of how this is properly done.

Marta reaches for Damien's hand. He rejects it.

Damien turns to Marta, admires her strange face. The sea beads down her strange nose, her sharpened cheekbones. Maybe she is soft-shelled. He is drawn to her segmented neck, all rope and pulley, spiked with thick black hairs. He thinks of the woman in the big-ass hat from the funeral, and Tito, both warning him about the brujas. Damien toils to pull his gaze away.

Marta peeks over her shoulder once more to check if they were followed, then she threads her arm through his and rests her sweaty cheek on his wet arm. They squint at the sun's last-minute dip into the sea. The sky lights up like a strawberry before it fades into blue.

She has claimed his arm. Damien is unsure what to do. Sea spray rolls down his cheek and drops on the furry patches on the backs of Marta's hands. He wonders what they would feel like if she dragged them across his burning skin.

Marta senses Damien's desire and trepidation. She takes his other hand, but she, too, does not know what to do with it, or where it's supposed to go.

Damien succumbs. He slides his fingers into her black hair, squeezes it gently, then pulls it hard. Marta's eyes narrow, her mouth opens, enough for him to see the gloss of her tongue.

"You better hope nobody's looking," she says.

"Don't worry, nobody's around," Damien says, his voice quivering. He imagines slicing his tongue on her sharp cheekbones, an urge he does not believe is reckless or impossible. The desire he yearns for is desire itself, he thinks, and to be desired in return. Marta, on the other hand, seems to know a kiss would annoy her mother. Is that all she cares about? Making Ana María's life more miserable than it already is?

Marta does not think she has ever been in love. Damien is gentle—his heart beats warm blood, if a smidge too fast. Even a crooked soul like Marta's needs a bit of love and rejuvenation; only a loved one can you ask for help pulling a tooth. She wants to pull Damien's teeth, now. How did she become so fond of him? Perhaps it is because of the state he is in now. He is regaining control of his body, peeling himself away from her mother's control. Marta turns her mouth to him.

Damien releases his grip, but his mouth remains partly open, which makes her want to dive into him. She wants to know what it smells like, tastes like, in his cavernous body. Flip her tongue on the tip of his fishing lure (he acted disgusted earlier, but she noticed how fascinated he was). She needs Damien to stay here a while longer, to taste everything as if for the first time.

"You're shaking," she says.

"Sorry, I don't mean to," says Damien. He backs away.

"Don't apologize. I like it." Marta scoots closer. She takes Damien's arm again and pulls him away from himself. She cannot tell what he is thinking. It's too dark to read his face.

She pushes her ear into his shoulder. Her neck pops.

A trio of pelicans glides inches above their own fading reflection in the twilit water.

What is he thinking, letting her lead him on this way? Damien changes the subject. "Do you hear bees?" he asks as he flounders around, exaggerating a search as if a bee crawled down his shirt so Marta doesn't lean on him anymore.

"The bees are our friends," says Marta. She looks for the bees but can see only the earliest stars like holes poked through dark canvas.

"They've been following me since Carla's funeral. Should I be worried? Am I delusional?"

"They are not in your head."

"Do I look like flowers to them? What do they want?" Damien backs away.

"Nothing." Marta laughs. "They want nothing." She listens for his breathing in the dark but hears only his fidgeting. What waves were splashing them before have subsided.

Damien turns to her. "I think several of them have become attached to me," he says.

"Maybe you should ask them if they like you like that," Marta says.

Damien throws his fist to the sky and yells, "What do you want from me?"

Marta laughs again, but the bees say nothing.

"The bees carry our grief," she says. "They are the village. The grief of a grieving place."

Damien feels sweaty again.

"They are fond of you," she insists.

Damien looks up and sees a light bobbing in the distance, some night fishermen searching for bonefish or tarpon. The urge to swim out to them burns in his legs and hips again, but if he did he would be devoured, even in these gentle waves. He doesn't think anybody would swim after him, not even Marta.

"Damien," Marta says, "I want you to trust me."

How? Damien wonders. "Why?" he says.

"I told you before, for your own protection." Marta scratches an itch on her tall forehead.

They stand in silence. Damien looks up at the stars.

"We should get home before your mother suspects something," Damien says.

Swim Home to the Vanished

"I think she already does," says Marta.

"But nothing's happening."

"Best to assume she ignores the truth and proceed with caution," says Marta.

Damien does not quite know where to start, but when he finally feels able to tell Marta about his brother during their walk home, it's because he wants her to trust him. He feels like his life might depend on it. Damien does not tell her everything; not much at all, just the circumstances. He and Kai were close when they were young. They didn't get a chance to say a proper goodbye. He feels guilty, like he could have saved him somehow, but he knows he couldn't have. He just wants answers. About the circumstances surrounding Kai's death. About his family's history, his connection to his grandfather, the whole lot of blood and death of the past and yet somehow he survived. For Damien's mother, for him, for Kai. He feels obligated to return the favor, the gift, of survival.

"I understand," Marta says. "Our people experienced something similar. There used to be an estuary with a mouth many miles wide, a rich source of swimmers and grazers and fliers and grain, enough for several large civilizations to survive on. It is now vanished. We are all stained."

Marta stops along the trail. She tells Damien she has heard some of his stories already, that he speaks to himself when he is mescal-drunk at work. He does not know what he divulges when under the influence of a reptile.

"What do you mean I 'divulge'? Am I sleepwalking?" The thought of there being something else in that mescal makes Damien furious. "Your mother is poisoning me?"

"I am not like my mother," Marta insists.

"That's not what I asked," Damien spits.

He is shaking again. What is it about Marta he can't let go of?

"If you're not like your mother, who are you like?" Damien expects the answer to be one of her sisters.

"My father," she says. "I think you would have liked him."

Are you kidding me? he thinks. Damien seethes at the comparison. He has heard only damning things about Flaco. What would make her think they would get along?

"People say my father was flawed," she says. "I say we all are. They say he was a drunk, but he was never mean to me. My father was the only one who paid attention to me."

Damien starts walking faster.

"*You* pay attention to me," Marta says, following him. She won't let her prey just walk away. "Sometimes, when you're not under her spell, I see you see me, Damien."

"I don't know what you're talking about," Damien lies. Maybe he does watch her, but Marta's got the wrong idea. She doesn't understand how on edge he feels, watching his back all the time.

Marta sees through Damien's lie; he's not very good at it. She takes his hand and slows his quickened pace. Damien flushes red. She leads him home, without pushing him beyond what he is capable of. She thinks she has softened him, if only a little. Enough to ask him to do something she cannot.

⋯

The snores of a sated caimán welcome Damien and Marta home from their beach walk. They tiptoe upstairs and stand in front of her room. She leans back against her door, expecting him to lean in too. She looks up. Damien is sweating profusely. He does not know what she expects of him, and he no longer wants to find out. She terrifies him, which makes her all the more enchanting.

Marta plays coy, kisses Damien's cheek, then retreats into her bedroom with the click of a lock, leaving him alone in the hall. He goes to Carla's room, slips into the hammock, and wraps himself in her old blanket, but the thought of sleeping in her room makes him colder.

He tries to sleep, but when he closes his eyes he sees all the fins he wrestled with today. Their memory swims circles in him. He rolls and twists until the shawl is one thick rope, then he finally gets up to scrub the blood off his hands, attempt to brush the stink from his nostrils with a toothbrush, but none of it will come out.

He hates those goddamn fish. He loves them, too. The beauty of their shine, their luminescent scales, as if a blue flame glows behind each one. He used to like to eat them, but it feels cannibalistic now. They are his brothers and sisters, aunts and uncles. They understand him. They are torpedoes of lustrous muscle; Tito informed him his first week here that they have no purpose on the surface, but in water they are elegant creatures whose silver dorsals flicker when they spin.

Damien returns to Carla's hammock, stares again at the ceiling. He watches spiders in the corner, who seem to be dancing in unison with the crickets cricketing outside. Most of Carla's things had been ransacked by her sisters the day he moved in, but Damien's been careful not to disturb Carla's remaining possessions, or the lurking insects and arachnids, but tonight he snoops through her collections of shells and hoop earrings in a cigar box. Finds a stash of tobacco in a drawer next to postcards of snowy mountains that must be hundreds of miles from here. What looks like Tito's belongings, remains of their life together. Shiny lures dangle like earrings from a small mirror in the corner. A collection of Carla's favorites, maybe. In a beat-up shoebox, old mariachi cassettes are piled with Elvis and Rachmaninoff, but the tape deck looks beyond repair. In another small box, Damien finds pictures of Tito and Carla posing by his yola—him hoisting high a dorado bull nearly as tall as him, blood from the gaff running down his tan arm and splattering his freckled chest.

Damien tiptoes downstairs to the kitchen, reaches for food in the fridge but retches. He pours a drink, but his legs go soft, the whiff of sugars threatens to migraine him. He opens the pantry, but he is scared of the tubers, he burps at the radishes. When he thinks of smoke from the grill he itches from the inside out.

He goes to Marta's bedroom door and listens for movement before he raises a knuckle to knock. Marta cracks the door open enough for him to sidestep in, then she softly clicks it behind her. She stands behind him in her underwear, draped with a shawl inspired by one of her mother's muumuus, no doubt.

Damien peeks and spins away. "Sorry," he says, "I couldn't sleep."

Her room is clean and dimly lit, decorated with tiny shells, a jar filled with dried-up spider bodies, a giant iguana's shed skin staked on the wall.

"It's fine, it's early," says Marta, wrapping herself tighter in the shawl.

Damien marvels at a wall painted entirely glossy green, adorned with desert flora and fauna sketched in ink and crayon, their Latin names scrawled below them in colored pencil. One drawing catches Damien's eye: a contortion of mangled roots snaking their way out of calm water and exploding into a canopy of waxy leaves.

"*Rhizophora*," he reads aloud. "I've never seen those before."

Probably never will, Marta thinks.

Damien fumbles with a photo on Marta's dresser. Paola is in the mountains crunching her way out of a forest with a bundle of firewood and something of a smile. Marta has sleek, sharp features, and Ana María is a frumpy lizard, but Paola has a beauty all her own, even under that pensive, serious face. In the photo, Paola's mouth is contorted like Carla's was in the casket, but Paola's lips curl with joy, and she steps lightly, confidently, like she belongs in the forest. In another photo, Carla is in a one-piece and snorkel gear, a purple speargun raised triumphantly to the sky, Tito next to her grinning ear to ear and holding a towel around his waist, his eyes pinched shut in a laugh.

"They seemed happy," says Damien.

"They weren't," Marta huffs. "He's as suspicious as Mamá, if you ask me."

"Carla is all he talks about."

"Yeah, he's obsessed because he's guilty."

"What if I did it?"

"You, I know for sure did not."

"Why do you say that?"

"You're weak." She points to her skull, taps her temple. "And too stupid to get away with it."

Damien sits and sinks into the corner of Marta's little bed. She is right—he couldn't kill anybody. He gets lost in a small fresco on another wall of a creature getting stabbed through its open, vicious mouth. It has a carapace, a serpent tail, a lionlike face with bear pads and giant talons. It does not look like it belongs on land, nor in the sea.

"And that?"

"I drew it when I was little," says Marta. "My father used to tell me a story about Santa Marta, who supposedly saved a village from a Tarasque—some half-beast, half-fish monster—by parading it around on a leash."

What kind of person would kill a living thing for its strange skin and odd features? Damien considers his own deformities. Doesn't everyone in the village have strange skin and odd features?

"My father said it was unlike other creatures," Marta continues. "The only thing people thought they knew about it was untrue—it did not eat people head-first. And Saint Marta happens to be a sister of Lazarus, the man thought to be asleep who turned out to be dead, then was resurrected, though was most likely asleep the whole time? Now the saint is a crumpled statue in a dry, penniless fountain in the square."

Flaco shared this story with Marta before he died. She sees herself in some distorted version of it. She is as enamored of its spell as she was enchanted by it as a child.

Damien remembers the statue; he ran to it looking for water his first day in town. He can't tell who she identified with more, the savior or the misunderstood monster.

"Let's go," Marta says. She's already dressed and tying her shoes.

"Where to? It's late."

"I want you to meet Carla."

"Okay." Damien smooths out the covers on her bed where he made a dent.

"Perhaps we can ask her what happened ourselves."

Communing with Worms

The night is cool and breezy, the prelude to a storm. Eddie had predicted a big storm several weeks ago. His customers tend to ignore his premonitions despite the accuracy of his whiskers when sensing such things as changes in atmospheric pressure. The problem is that Eddie's calculations of a storm's landfall can be erratic. Catfish are, most likely, not magnificent spatial thinkers.

On their way to the cemetery, Marta says she needs something from Eddie's and runs in. Damien waits outside among the stream of chubnose minnows who are peering through clouds of green smoke like they are hunting, or spawning, in stirred-up shallows. Shoals of borrachos splash in and out of the loud bar with frightening, bloodshot eyes. A confused rooster coughs up a funny noise somewhere in the distance. Patchy-coated dogs roam by with confident tails and giant balls, psyching out rats by bursting briefly into a sprint (all bluster, no bite). Marta returns via the side door, crunches through the alley of broken glass with a caneca of something clear and label-less in her hand. She crosses the street, takes a huge pull, passes it to Damien. He caps the bottle and slips it in his back pocket without taking a sip.

"Not drinking today?" Marta says.

"Not feeling well."

"Go ahead, it'll make you feel better."

Damien takes out the caneca and pretends to swig it in an over-eager motion, then spits it out when she turns around to lead him down another darkened alley. The narrow cobbled road turns toward a hill and becomes a single-lane dirt path. Porous concrete steps, their shapes resembling cactus roots and barbed vines, crumble like broken saltines. The path is lush and tropical, but then it ends at the base of a mesa, where a neighborhood of shack homes pieced together with corrugated tin are weighed down with rotten upside-down yolas. They climb the switchbacks to the top of the mesa, stopping every so often for Damien to catch his breath.

Marta clears vines from a locked gate, but the lock is just for show. The hinges are rusted and overgrown. The priest had insisted the fencing around the cemetery property was to keep the wild-armed cacti from escaping, not for keeping intruders out. Damien swings his legs over the gate, mimicking Marta's motion.

The cemetery is quiet. Its darkness opens up for them. The village below twinkles with lantern light. Lonely lights of fishermen flicker with each bounce on the water, as if mirroring the stars in the sky. But the sky has become overcast. Damien believes Eddie—a storm is definitely coming, but so far doesn't appear to be as destructive as Eddie thought it would be.

Damien stays close to Marta as she navigates the dark shadows and uneven earth. The grounds are wet and squishy in some places, drier in others, so lumpy it looks like prairie dogs oversee the interment of their dead. Most gravestones are either lopsided, sunk in, or uprooted completely. The markers of fishermen, though, are simple crosses hand-tied with fishing line and rope, decorated with a flourish of green grass leaves tied into ribbony bows.

"There are still bones under those weeds and stone," Marta says.

Swim Home to the Vanished

"Pardon me, pardon us," Damien says, dancing over the ruins on his tiptoes in search of a path. Damien is being so cautious that when he looks up, Marta is gone. "Why?" he whispers. He tries not to panic, but his heart is already in his loins. He listens for her feet crunching in dead leaves. He finally calls out for her.

"Shh! I'm right here. Careful not to wake the dead." Marta is only several feet behind him.

Damien, embarrassed, waits for Marta to pass and follows her down another row. He trips on a gravestone, pretends he trotted on purpose even if in the dark there is no one to laugh at him. Marta stops at Carla's grave, which is still covered in flowers, all shriveled and rotten except for the glass vases full of fake plastic daisies. Her marker is a small, unpolished square of concrete, with a texture like bleached coral.

Marta kneels, wipes clean the block and stone. She piles up dried petals from old bouquets, rips the weeds from the edges of the marker. The silhouettes of tombstones gather round. Damien sits across from Marta in the warm grass, Carla in between them. The wind changes direction, steadier now, no longer those impatient jabs. Thicker clouds have rolled in and rubbed out the waning moon. The hesitant leaves of almendro trees and the fronds of royal palms sway anxiously, anticipating a storm's thrashing.

"It's an excellent resting place, but I'd want to be closer to the view," Marta says.

"Did we have to take the stairs?" Damien is still out of breath. "Looks like it's going to pour on us—maybe we should go."

Tiny dried-out bees rest in Carla's engraving. Marta sweeps them away with a clump of crabgrass. She can't shake the image of worms wiggling inches below, the music they sing as they fidget and feed.

"It's a shame," Damien says, half to Carla, half to Marta, "what happened." He pats the ground with his palm, and the soil thumps hollow.

Marta kisses the tips of her fingers, then plunges them into the earth. The mound is still soft, but it has lost its shape, deflated like overproofed dough.

"Your sister here is going to avenge you, isn't that right?" he says.

Marta whips around and stares him down without removing her fingers from the grave.

"Am I wrong?" He feels a few drops of rain land on his face, not enough yet to rinse away the stench of ocean and salt crusted on his skin. Marta shoves her other hand into the softest part of the grave, brow creased, focused.

"What are you doing?" Damien doesn't like that scary face she's making, as if disgusted at what her hands find, though intent on finding what she's searching for.

She says, "I need you to do something for me, for us, the village."

Damien sits up straighter.

"Where are you?" she says. Both her arms are now plunged elbow-deep in the mound. "Ah, finally."

Marta removes from the earth a leather roll the length of her arm, tied with a strap of buoy line. She shakes off the dirt, undoes the straps, and lays out the knife roll in the grass beside Damien. She unsheathes a long fillet knife, the only knife in the bag. It looks tarnished except for its sharpened edge, which has been filed down after years of use.

"This was my father's fishing knife," says Marta. The white handle is bone. Scales permanently coat the hilt, lending it a mother-of-pearl finish. Marta runs her finger along the blade, then flips it and catches the spine between her calloused thumb and forefinger. She presents it to Damien butt-first.

"We have to kill Ana María," she says.

"Are you kidding me?" Damien stands, steps back. The rain trickles harder. All this time tonight he thought she might have had real feelings, swooped him up from Tito's talk as if to apologize. Bringing him here as if on a date. What was he thinking?

"You said so yourself, she confessed to killing my sister. For the sake of our village, for my safety and yours. I will help you with whatever you need, do whatever you want. I'll leave with you." Marta is having a hard time coming up with nice things to do for someone; she's out of practice.

"Have you been planning this all along?" says Damien. "Do you know how crazy this sounds? Why would you think I'd do this for you? Why does it have to be me? Where would we even go?"

"Ana María is going to try to kill you," says Marta. "You're too stupid to notice."

"Ana María has cared for me," Damien says, surprised to be coming to her defense. "Brought me in when I was broken. She may have even saved my life."

Marta laughs that high-pitched snorty one again. "You think Ana María is your friend? Sounds like she's already gotten to you. Her mescal did its trick, don't say I didn't warn you. But she's a fucking liar, Damien, I thought you understood that. I don't know what else to tell you."

Marta creeps up to Damien and reaches for his throat. She is able to squeeze his larynx before he can jump away.

Here he is, scaredy-cat fish-man. Tarasque. Hair full of grease and sea bream.

Damien tries to swallow, but the muscles in his throat catch on her bony fingers.

"You think we're all just fish," she says.

"Yes," says Damien, choking a little.

Marta runs her other cold hand up his jawline and lightly strokes his gills, a few itinerant scales glittery on his chest.

"Fish can't change their fate like we can," Marta says.

"If I could change my fate, I would've been happier a long time ago," he says.

"Fate isn't interested in happiness."

"Whose fate are you hoping to change?"

"The village's," she says. Marta unclamps him. "Mamá is out of control."

Damien falls onto one of Carla's neighbors. Marta has really lost it, he thinks. She is on her hands and knees now, circling Carla's grave. Something about the way she tilts her head, clicks her tongue, reminds him of a cricket or some other hard-shelled insect, chirping away its nerves.

"The fate of the village depends on this," she says. She understood there would be some pushback, not that he might sympathize with her mother.

Damien rubs at his neck and throat. Ana María wouldn't put that kind of pressure on me, he thinks. She tells me I'm expendable—that's much less responsibility. He was, until very recently, unassuming, pretty much worthless, especially in his drunken stupor. Nothing special about him other than that he prepares a good tuna skewer with fried rice. Shows up on time nine times out of ten. Excellent knife skills.

"Imagine," Marta says, "starting a new life here. Destroy the thing that haunts you most." She tries to explain why it has to be him, but stops short. She doesn't need to explain herself anymore.

"And then what would I do," says Damien, "cook? I won't do that anymore. I left that behind."

"I'm sure we can arrange a dishwashing shift," Marta says.

"This is not for me, Marta, you've got me made out all wrong," he says.

Marta thinks his left-turning lazy eye is a tell that he is lying.

Damien wishes it were true, that he was incapable of harming another creature, except as children he and Kai went after the

Swim Home to the Vanished

sparrows (slingshot), blinded a squirrel (pellet gun), broke necks of mice with spring traps (loaded with peanut butter), though none of that was quite the same as stabbing a person. He reconsiders his argument.

"We have suffering in our blood," says Marta. "It's okay to unleash it."

Damien dips his fingers into the mound where Marta made a hole. He scoops a little soil and rolls it between his palms. Now he smells like worms, he thinks, which makes him think of all the bones underground, which reminds him there is violence buried deep and fibrous in the pith of him. He understands only that it is there—he doesn't speak its language yet; doesn't know whether he should unlock it for Marta's use.

Damien gets up from Carla's grave and goes to the edge of the mesa, and he looks out across the water. He wants a beer. No, he craves the stronger stuff, the mescal. It makes his dreams seem true and life less so. Makes him forget a lot faster. Marta's bottle is still in his pocket.

"Mamá clamped her jaws around you too easily," Marta says, her dark figure stalking behind him. "Ana María pulled you under with your eyes still open." Marta can no longer picture Damien as a tongueless man howling into marbled canyons on the other side of the mountains, creeping along cracked highways with his big webbed thumbs. Every town out there might be melted down like the rest of the world, doctored and duct-taped to hold the chimneys up, a hundred coats of paint to hide the grime. Damien has nothing to go back to; she hopes he is beginning to understand that.

A fisherman's light bobs like a firefly in the agitated swell. Damien removes the bottle from his pocket and throws it over the edge of the mesa. There must be a different way. Why does it have to be him, not one of the villagers with their own pent-up anger issues with their matriarch?

"How about Benny? I bet that crazy fucker would do it."

"If she does not die, all of us will. She's going to destroy the village, Damien. It's happening now. You'll be a hero. This is how you find communion with your dead."

Damien turns and reaches for Flaco's blade. Marta hands it to him and he takes it, cautiously. He can't trust any of these brujas. Look at her eyes, how can they be so black and shiny at once? So twitchy, too.

"Imagine all the little fishies it has sliced open," says Marta, "all the bones it has cut through. She'll be its biggest fish yet."

Damien raises the knife to feel its weight and balance. It is no wonder they wish to keep him in a haze. Without it, he no longer sees Marta as *Apis florea*. She is not elegant like a bee, no ravager of nectars. He now sees her as *Ammophila procera*, a wasp who paralyzes her prey with a sting and lays an egg in it, then buries them underground, where the egg grows wormy and eats its way out. Damien learned about this from Paola, who enjoys impressing him during lulls in their shifts with her encyclopedic knowledge of all the local flora and fauna.

"I am after more than vengeance," Marta says. She'll need all the reasoning she can muster if he is to trust her. She has only been nice to Damien, she thinks. Sure, maybe she prefers him drunk, but who doesn't?

Damien is unsure if he should run. He is more frightened of Marta now than when he was too drunk to notice her motives. He feels connected to her, though. Damien and Marta share an obsession with the dead. They cannot forget. They won't let go. They don't know how to let their memories die, allow the bones to take root and the ghosts to do what they need to do.

"You are no different than your mother, it's so obvious now," says Damien. "If I did this I'd become just like you, and you'd welcome me into the family with open arms, wouldn't you." Damien's hands shake. He's not sure standing up to Marta is a good idea.

"Don't fucking compare me to my mother!" Marta shouts. She might be a little drunk.

She says Ana María was born with a soft skull like everyone else. The only thing separating brains from air is thin skin and bone you can poke a finger into. An easy thing to break, crack, bore. Around the temple, the back of the neck, the base of the jaw, sutures on the fontanelle. Ana María feeds them meat. Sea meat. Bird meat. Land meat. Her calloused feet lost the color of skin, her fizzled skin felt like skin once but then were lizard legs. They preferred to climb trees over Mamá's lazy sit-and-wait method. For the nectars, and the eggs. Bird crunch bones.

Naked bumpy chicks. "We stuck our tongues into blossoms," says Marta, quietly now. "Our tongues grew longer every year. I warned Carla about the bees, but she said the bumbles didn't mind. She stuck her face so far into blossoms her cheeks were permanently pollen-stained, like she tried to swallow a constellation but missed her mouth."

Jardín

Whenever anyone drinks Ana María's mescal they have a difficult time remembering, like yesterday could have been Damien's last thirty yesterdays, nothing has changed except the amount of fish he slaughters, the new scabs acquired from the sharp pinwheels of grouper fins. Ana María's liquor worms its way through their blood and bodies, keeps them in a state of inertia, stamps out any semblance of free will. Damien did not drink it last night, though, first time in weeks. The poison nearly made him forget the egg-shaped hole next to his heart where it feels like he is missing another heart. A companion heart, like his heart needed a heart and the hole wanted to keep growing and swallow everything, but the bigger heart will not allow it. Side effects of this battle may cause chest pains, belly cramps, constipation, consume one's entire being if one is careless enough to ignore the cause. Perhaps he still retains a capacity for healing.

Paola had no trouble sleeping last night, in spite of the raucous waves and the strange dreams. In one of them, she and Damien were bees in a nebula, a mess of proboscises and limbs stuck and folded one atop the other. Paola had difficulty breathing through her exoskeleton, no match for bladder sacs or iron lungs or real lungs. All the froth and gleam of lips and fingers in the nebula excited in the swarm a murmur of prayer, and they twirled, stung, buzzed, bit each other with no preconception of what was flower or petal, no notion of entomophilous transfer of pollens or nectars. An invertebrate bundle of nerves, from foot to heart to brain, submerged in a bright light. Instead of attempting to become a singularity, their bodies dispersed into gaseous tentacles of their most basic elements, through which stars will endlessly birth, a tangle of roots and limbs and spit resembling the phlegm of space coughed up from the back of the throat of a black-mandibled monster.

Paola is no soothsayer, but the message is clear when she wakes. A dream less premonitory than about work-life stress. She had already planned to go to Wilmarí's farm today for restaurant supplies, but now she needs to make sure she has enough food to feed the village during the coming storm. Paola is low on honey, too, and her favorite hive resides there.

Paola stomps into Damien's room, knocks after entering. "Hey, you hungover again?" She shakes Damien's snores out of the hammock.

"No, I'm not, leave me alone," he slurs, and rolls over. His eyes are swollen shut; drool has dried white at the corners of his mouth.

"I need your help."

"What's wrong, am I late?" He scrambles. "It's Marta's fault, she kept me up all night."

"Wasn't the waves that kept you up? They were so loud."

"Sure, the waves too," Damien says. "Just couldn't fall asleep. Neither could Marta. She took me to Carla's grave." Damien rubs his eyes, and the crust falls to the tiles below. "Didn't sleep much, but once I was out, I was *out*, best sleep in days."

"It's disgusting," Paola says, "the way Marta drools over you."

"What do you mean?"

"She plays games, but she doesn't really know what to do with you."

"It's not like that, Paola."

"She can be very convincing. Those big buggy eyes."

"Stop. Do you know what Marta asked me to do? Kill your mother. Your *mother*. Can you believe that?"

Paola shakes her head. "I keep sticking up for her, thinking she might change for the better. She hates our mother so much that she has become her."

"I know I should stay out of it, but I feel like I should warn Ana María," says Damien.

"Whose side are you on?"

"Yours, I guess?" Damien scratches his head, and a chunk of hair comes out. "I don't see why I need to choose sides."

Paola kicks Damien a shirt and a pair of scummy pants. "I need you to help me go on a run to Wilmarí's," she says.

"Do I have a choice?"

"If you don't want to help, fine," says Paola. "I think we might find answers out there. The storm made landfall, and it's expected to pick up—we don't have a lot of time."

Paola draws invisible circles with her fingers, sketches how the arms of a storm spin. She squints out the window, pretends she can fly up to the outer bands, see how fat they are with moisture, rotating slowly. The worst of it is still a day away probably, Paola thinks. They have to be prepared even if the eye misses the village.

"Or," Paola says, setting her fist on her hip, "would you let Marta talk you into something you don't want to do? Perhaps you'd like to hang out with Ana María. She's probably in the swamps, waiting for you . . ."

"Okay, point taken," Damien says, and dances into his pant legs. "Who's Wilmarí?"

"A neighbor—you'll like her." Paola tosses Damien's satchel. "I packed breakfast."

Swim Home to the Vanished

The wind is not as strong farther inland as it is on the bay, and the rain has ceased for now. The trek to Wilmarí's takes Damien and Paola over muddy paths, then nonexistent ones, forcing them to hack through wild cornfields and spiny greasewoods. The greasewoods eventually unfold their arms to reveal a meadow of tall sweetgrass and a grove of old fruit trees: apple, apricot, peach, plum, twisted and knobby, healthy but frightening. The orchard's arms and half-eaten leaves stifle the overcast sky. Damien stays close to Paola as she navigates around the piles of rotten fruit, peels open overgrown branches heavy with moss. Beyond the ancient fruit orchard, awkward papayas and gawkish palms loiter around a perimeter of mangoes three times as tall as everything else, their long limbs hoarding biomes of ferns and obnoxious insects, chatty birds and cunning orchids.

Paola explains to Damien that she and her sisters stayed with Wilmarí when they were young, after Flaco died. The villagers believed that Ana María was heartbroken because she disappeared for so long, but she was actually trying to outsource fish from other villages; imagine all the work and lies necessary for her to put such a scheme in place.

Wilmarí helped Ana María only because the waters were overfished, and because it was Flaco's fault. Wilmarí hated that the villagers blamed Ana María for the fish leaving the ocean empty because they thought she broke her vows. The fish weren't coming back, no matter what caimán married whom. Wilmarí kept her secret from the village, thinking the village's ignorance would save them from having to lose respect for their heroic pescador. But somehow the fish scam only made things worse. The vacuum made Ana María more powerful—she had a monopoly on their supply.

"Tito said the fishing has been poor around here lately," says Damien.

"I bet Wilmarí can clear things up for us."

"Who is she?"

"She is my aunt. Ana María's sister."

⁓

Paola and Damien march out of the tropical patch and over a berm, where the land becomes a field of red soil adorned with hunks of a rusted old tractor and giant clay pots lying shattered and overflowing with wildflowers and sage. The sculptures surround an octagonal house, which to Damien resembles a hogan, only adapted to these strange lands. The covered porch is bent up at sharp angles, constructed by someone with little to no geometric knowledge. Pampas grass waves from the roof garden in between the skylights and the maze of snaking pipes that drain into garden beds, inside the house and out. Behind the hogan are a patchwork of gardens in beds and tiny greenhouses sprawling wildly along the grounds, guided by pathways formed by someone's careful step. The farm stretches along the warm base of a mesa. Another cornfield expands down the valley to the edge of a wash. Damien and Paola pause to lend their hands to a few sheepdogs for a sniff.

Wilmarí is on her crooked porch, rocking in her rocking chair. Her mouth and nose are squished into a sour face. Once she spits the seed of a stone fruit artfully over the railing, her wrinkled face finally relaxes.

"Hola, Wilmarí," says Paola. "You look well."

"Not as deft a liar as your mother!" says Wilmarí. "I am old and ugly, but not dumb."

"As hideous as the lizards who sprung you!" Paola's face brightens.

"And I hear we taste like chicken." Wilmarí laughs.

Paola runs to the porch and hops onto her aunt's lap and wraps her arms around her sinuous neck.

Swim Home to the Vanished

"Ah, careful," cries Wilmarí. "You may be light, but my bones are hollow."

"You act like it's been a million years since you've seen me. I was here a couple weeks ago, remember? You losing your memory already?"

Wilmarí points to Damien with puckered lips. "Who's this cabrón?"

Damien introduces himself with a shy flash of his palm. "I like your home," he says.

"We're only here to stock up for the storm," Paola says. She jumps off Wilmarí. "We'll stay out of your hair."

"Nonsense, no. Stay here, eat—I made soup." Wilmarí rocks back and forth, at first with diligence, then with speed, until the rocker launches her to her feet.

A gust of wind carries the stench of bruised fruit from an orchard floor, and sheep bleat to the beat of bells around their necks, but there is not one sheep in sight. Damien kicks at the ground, shakes the foundation beams, leans on the misaligned angles of the porch and pretends to admire its sturdiness.

Wilmarí takes them inside and puts on a kettle and a pot of soup to warm on the woodstove. The spade-shaped door opens and steps down to the open eight-sided room. It is cool belowground, and the air is dry and smells like nixtamalized corn. At the center of the room is a fireplace with a small, patient fire. The stovepipe runs up along a vertical beam and out through the center of the conical ceiling. Skylights warm the room with glassy light. Old pine beams radiate from the middle one, similar in style to the village church's decorative logs, only paler, less glossy.

The entrance faces east, and to the south a glass door leads to a greenhouse full of succulents, ferns, bananas with blossoms dangling low like horse penises. Piles of newspapers and magazines and dusty books partially block its entrance. To the right, a pile of wool blankets rests on a thin mattress, its corners curled like fists on rusty springs. The small kitchen nests on the north side of the house with a wood-fired stove, a card table with wobbly-looking legs, and a long three-sink system that drains to the gardens.

"It's a little messy right now," says Wilmarí. "Only me and the dogs do most of the work now, since the sheep and bees don't know how to earn a living."

The three of them return to the porch. Paola finds her favorite swinging chair. Wilmarí circles the crooked porch and reappears behind Damien with an extra stool, then races to her rocker as if Damien's about to steal it. Wilmarí's hair, thick silver and black, plunges heavily down her back and shimmers as she pushes herself back and forth with her little feet.

"What can I help you with?" she says to Damien. She knocks a tobacco pipe on her crusty heel.

"Not him, Auntie," says Paola. "I need your help. It's about Mamá."

Wilmarí packs her pipe, lights it with a long match, passes it to Damien. A sheepdog sidles up to him and rests her head on his foot.

"Ocean's churning up like before," Paola says. "But I think it's Marta this time."

"Of course it is—she always loved poking the hive," says Wilmarí. She serves them the bubbling stew.

Between noisy slurps, Damien compliments Wilmarí on her soup's balance of acidity and salt. The carrots and potatoes and onions were harvested from the garden, she says, the herbs picked this morning; the sheep she butchered last spring. Damien closes his eyes and deciphers the soup's layers like limestone on a canyon wall, tastes eons in the soil. Tastes the blood, and the stars before.

"I'll take you out there," she says. "Harvest whatever you need." She turns to Paola. "As for your mother and sister, I'm not sure what options we have."

Swim Home to the Vanished

After her guests devour the stew, Wilmarí weaves them into her overgrown gardens. She points out the herbs: sprawling oregano, tenderhearted tarragon, lazy rosemary, flat-leaf parsley, clumped here and there, filling space where the sprawling squash and tomatoes cannot reach. Eggplant and chard and kale are strategically planted between tobacco and calendula and mint to ward off bad insects.

Wilmarí explains how to let it go to seed, it is how she grows—leave it wild and trust that seed in soil with rain and sun to nourish it into some respectable, edible thing. The plants know what to do. Her job is not to control them, only to steer them in the right direction. Some little guys like it better in shady corners, others prefer direct light. The berries she lets take over the irrigation ditch around the perimeter; root veggies are harvested when the weather cools. The sheep tend to keep everything tidy. Peach trees have always struggled, but they enjoy it here too; Wilmarí knows by the notes they leave in the wrinkles of their stone fruit.

She introduces her guests to mysterious plants, congregations of ants, worms warming in cocoons. So many peppers—tiny angry hot ones, giant sweet things, the color of either *eat me* or *I am poison*, each looking crispier and shinier than the next. Paola trails the other two, filling her sack with berenjena and calabaza, herbs and peppers. Damien wipes a bit of drool from his lips with shaky hands.

Paola plucks dandelion heads at the edge of the garden and stores them in a jar in her bag with her other memories. She imagines gluing the seedlings into miniature forest fire dioramas, squeezing the bitter milk from their stems to replicate the poisoned streambeds. She will not know the name of this feeling: the urge, an impulse, to pick dandelions and blow the seeds into Damien's face. She cannot fathom the reason that feeling has been churned up in her, not until she returns home to catalog and examine the contents of her jars. Was that feeling flirtatious or mean or simply childish? What would his response have been? She wants to pester him, flick his earlobes, trip him from behind. She had no such urges in the kitchen, except lately she has been tempted to spill boiling red chilies down Marta's back for acting like an asshole.

The dozen or so pastel beehives sit on chubby logs, alive with hums. As they approach them, Wilmarí places a net stitched onto a loop of willow branch over Damien's head. Paola laughs.

"You look like a homeless bride," she says.

"The veil will protect you from the bees," says Wilmarí.

"Where's hers?" asks Damien.

"I don't get stung," says Paola. "We've always had top bar hives. They've been in our family a long time. The bees adopted us after Flaco died. The girls, too."

Damien spits out the netting caught in his mouth. "Is that why the bees been hovering around me, like I've been adopted?"

"They're more like memories that don't let go," Paola says. "Some people get along better with bees than with people. We are cozy with their grief, or they find consolation in ours. They're our connection to this place."

Damien is reminded of the old man he met in the mountains. He'd said something about this being a land for the grieving, that Damien might feel at home if he's not careful.

"The Goatherd?" says Wilmarí. "My crazy old man. How is he—did he look healthy?"

"Good, really happy, I guess," says Damien. "Tired, too. Ishka the mule appeared only slightly better. She peed blood, I think."

"Ishka the mule! Poor old thing." Wilmarí hocks a loogie over the railing. She packs her pipe and hands it to Damien. He puffs the pipe and attempts to tap the ashes on his heel like he saw Wilmarí do earlier, but the cherry singes his skin.

"Good thing you'll be walking home in the rain—it'll keep those fires out!" Wilmarí cackles and takes a bite of peach.

"Did the Goatherd have anything to say?" Paola asks. She pets the black stripe on the sheepdog's nose and up between her eyes.

"He gave me something." Damien digs through his bag. "I said I'd deliver them, but they aren't here . . ." He spills his bag.

"It's okay, I have them." Paola removes a little glass jar from one of several clinking pockets in her vest. The bees remain lifeless. "You dropped them at our house the night you arrived." She hands the jar to Damien.

Damien's hands tremble, shaking the bees like butterless popcorn. "That man may have saved my life at the very moment I decided my life might be worth living."

Damien passes it on to Wilmarí.

"His idea of a romantic gift." Wilmarí giggles. She raises the jar to the sky. "He is a strange man, the Goatherd. He used to be a priest, did you know? A philosopher-poet clown who rounded up any animal who would follow his crazy ass up into the mountains to become a trafficker of stories and goods and tongues."

"Tongues?" asks Damien.

"Languages."

Wilmarí packs her pipe again and smokes, mentions something about his rambunctious goats and her lazy cats. The wind blows a few strands of hair in her face. She notches them behind her ear.

"Father G ran," she says. "The church was not for him, or he was not meant for it. Excommunicated himself for violating those silly Bible rules. He struggled to subscribe to only one way of thinking. He fell in love, had an affair—with me!—crazy man. He was heartbroken that the church did not listen to him, that they were not interested in seeing the world in new or different ways, so he acquired some goats and moved into the foothills. Worked the old trading routes up and down the coasts and across mountain ranges. Before he left, he relocated the old graveyard because he was scared his belief was false.

"The Goatherd said he had a plan. He said God spoke to him, or if it wasn't God it was something God-like, and he saw in a vision some great hurricane was going to wipe everything out. To keep the dead from bubbling out of their graves, he had to move them to the top of the hill. A relocation. Others say desecration. The religious folks drove Father G out before he could start.

"Some of us try to do good, want to do good, you know? Even brujas. Yes, they are angry with history. They despise the past because it has been so hurtful to them, and now they feel the need to destroy it. They are vengeful—they have every right to be. But it comes at a price. They don't seem to know or care about the consequences and collateral damage. Ana María only had power in the village because they trusted her, but that was a long time ago, when she married Flaco and the fish returned. The village must be turned against her if she's to be dethroned."

"This must be Marta's plan," says Paola. "What better way to persuade the village to hate Mamá than to blame her for Carla's death. They believe it already."

Damien glances at the sky. Rippling clouds push from the southwest. The day is growing dark even though it is still morning. He fears time is running out.

Wilmarí loads the smoker with coconut husks and demonstrates for Damien how to pry the combs and check for brood nests. The smoke sedates the bees. Sheets of honeycomb hang from the closest dividers; some of the cells pulsate with larvae. Paola rips up fistfuls of grass to sweep the bees away from cells capped with honey.

"That one's ripe," says Wilmarí.

Paola brushes the rest of the divider free, and when Damien cuts it free the comb drops into a bucket.

Wilmarí rearranges the combs so the bees have enough room

to build on the empty dividers. "Here, a queen cell is capped," she says.

"You can tell when the bees are inclined to swarm," adds Paola, "when there are larvae in the queen cell cup." She licks a honeyed thumb.

"They are nearly ready to found a new colony," says Wilmarí.

"But we want them to stay," Damien says.

"Aha! You're not dumb after all!" Wilmarí slides the brood nests and the combs capped with honey into a new hive, then she finds the queen, pinches her by the wings, and places her in there too. She brushes in a handful of nurse bees to care for her. The larvae and the queen's capped cell remain in the first hive to build the new colony.

Paola and Wilmarí harvest the best combs. Damien breaks his comb in half and lets it drip into a glass jar. He wipes his hands on his veil. His fingers get stuck. When he tries to shake the veil away, his hands look webbed. He used to be terrified of what his body was turning into, scared of his transmutation, because he had yet to understand its necessity. Now he welcomes it. His brother became fish; Damien will grow into fish, too.

The bees also transform, change. Abejas are brujas, brewing elixirs from regurgitated nectars. They metamorphose into adults; their mutations are encouraged. Their livelihood—their existence—depends on it.

There is something about this garden that lessens Damien's worry, diminishes his terror long enough for him to let his guard down for two seconds, respite from the fatigue of needing to know answers to unanswerable questions.

Seconds later, Paola notices the panic grip Damien's body. She knows his body better than he does simply by working next to him in the prep kitchen, but her guess is as good as his as to what causes his freak-out now. What they don't know is that the smell of the soup is so vibrant it sweeps Damien away, seizing him by the tongue, which is connected to his heart. Damien is convinced he smells charred starch about to burn on the bottom of the pot; the stew is overcooking. He recognizes this anxious feeling from his time in the kitchen. Heat rises in his face; his stomach turns.

Paola snags Damien's arm to keep him from fainting and falling, or fleeing, when all he wants to do is stir Wilmarí's pot of stew and scoot it over to a cooler side of the stove.

"You're away from all that now," Paola says.

"Let go of me," he says.

"There are no burning meats, no sickly employees, no one to yell at. You are safe and sober in this garden."

Damien closes his eyes and tries to imagine living out here as Wilmarí does, perhaps a place to name a home. Chew on this sweetgrass, gather insects as they flutter around the lamplight. Inspect cacti for grubs, dig for roots, just as he did with his brother. When Kai was a teenager, he began writing to Damien about how magical the world was for a child. He wrote that it seemed necessary for the world to become that again, but it was futile. He wished people saw the world like he did, like they did when they were kids, before grief glossed a façade over everything, before adultness dismantled their uninhibited instincts and replaced them with consumer goods and money worries and social functions. For what? Kai wrote. There were no connections in our systems of reality, no existential reason to pursue that kind of made-up life. We must make up our own—you taught me this, Damien. Why can't we be like that forever? How come people are not as curious as they once were, as children?

The letters were written not to reminisce, but as if to say simply, *I am alone. I am not made for this world*.

Damien has been forced into the bay when he gets these attacks at work, usually at Paola's insistence. But, to his surprise, the knot unravels. Damien is able to contain whatever was eating the skin beneath his skin.

Swim Home to the Vanished

It is the garden, he thinks, Wilmarí's home (funny, how fitting, that it resembles a hogan)—this is what he craves. Perhaps it is also what his brother needed. This silent contact. Solitude.

"The Goatherd," says Damien, "he said the bees weren't dead, just resting."

"Paola, why don't you take another look," says Wilmarí. She unscrews the cap and hands the jar to Paola.

Paola smiles and shakes one of the crispy bees onto her palm. She brings it her nose to admire more closely. Damien cringes, anticipating the bee rolling over and stinging her in the nostril. Instead, Paola extends the tip of her tongue and licks the bee's lacy wings, and the bee wakes. It stumbles drunkenly to the edge of Paola's fingers and splays her pinions and shakes off a strange dream. One by one, each woolly leg unfolds and stretches like a yawn before settling on the sticky surface of Paola's pads.

"Holy shit," says Damien.

"Told you," says Wilmarí.

"Do I have to lick all of them now?" Paola asks.

"Maybe," says Wilmarí.

El Dedo Perdido

Nearly two months ago, Paola was at the river's edge, a muddy place, dangerous because the river is known to snag the unsuspecting, but the river leaves her alone because she has been collecting cattails and sweetgrasses and red clay there all her life. She was crouched there when she heard Ana María walking toward the low part of the bank, chatting to herself. Paola hid in the reeds, careful not to rattle them more than the wind.

As her mother approached, Paola realized Ana María was not speaking to herself but to something heavy suspended from her shoulder. Not screaming or wriggly. A body, motionless.

Paola let the sound of the river enter her, calm her. She felt she probably shouldn't confront her mother. Paola held her breath and let herself sink into the red mud.

Ana María dropped the body near the river's edge. Paola could not hear much over the rush of the river, though when she tried to peel away her mud-stuck boots, the slurping sound caused Paola to panic and fall quiet. She did not know how long she waited before Ana María stopped whimpering and limped home. She had never seen her mother look so defeated.

Paola left her boots in the mud in order to slither closer. It was

Carla. Paola gurgled something and nearly stood and ran, but she slipped in the reeds, where, mere inches from her face, a water snake hissed and curled its glistening black back against a nest of eggs. Paola, frozen, was able to peek through the grasses to see Carla's silhouette rise and fall with shallow breaths.

Carla was still alive. Ana María had not finished what she seemed determined to do.

Paola attempted to circumvent the snake, but her warnings, and the river's, were clearer this time, and she listened. She flattened herself, nearly fully submerged in the muck. Seconds later, Marta came down the trail twitching like a wasp. Paola wanted to scream: *Mamá did this! Carla needs our help!* but her voice was stolen by the wind.

Paola writhed enough to see Marta—her black hair shining like a shell, her dark eyes twitching, buzzing—hunch over Carla's broken body. Marta pulled Flaco's fillet knife from under her waistband. Paola recognized the curved blade, the worn bone handle, glittery with scales. Marta stung Carla, plunged the fish knife into her soft body, below her rib cage. Marta twisted the blade like a key. Fate unlocked, Marta buzzed off as quickly as she arrived. *No!* Paola cried, but her throat closed up, as the coiled snake beside her swelled at the scent of her fear.

Paola shook, was shaking, in the reeds. She coughed up fear, dread, mucus. She spit on the snake and the snake spit back, but she had already propped herself up and stomped bootless across the muddy banks. She kneeled and rested her hands over Carla's face and cried.

There can be no remorse, only shame. Swirl, fish, flower. Paola used to think she hated her sisters equally—just let them figure their shit out on their own. Same with her love for them—equal parts pain and sweetness, like her spicy pickles. In fact, Paola loved her sisters so much she keeps parts of them hidden in her room. Perhaps Paola played along at the funeral because it played to her advantage. Is it possible she is no different, no less ambitious or conniving, than Marta or Ana María? Paola believed keeping what she witnessed a secret would save her family from falling apart. Was that not one of Mamá's jilted phrases, that family is not just something, but *everything*? Is Paola as guilty as they are for Carla's death? She could have saved Carla if only she had been able to shimmy herself out of the reeds and mud and the charms of snakes.

Instead, Paola did the only thing she thought she knew how to do: embalm the present tense in little glass jars. She snipped her sister's digits. Swirl fish, swim pinkie, swim toe. She once felt shame for taking without asking, but now she's glad she did.

The Blind Albino Miner

A mining village in the mountains was overrun by malicious deer years ago. These were a people who lived and died in the mines. Burrowed so deep and for so long that their eyes were the color of milk, their skin translucent. They ate only roots boiled to a mush because they liked the taste of dirt. They were born in the dark and mined in the dark and fucked in the dark, scrunching up their whiskered faces.

Wilmarí met a man from this town, a miner, the son of a miner, who had come across the edges of her property, guided only by his bamboo stick. Thicker glasses couldn't help his beady eyes. His ears were tuned underground so he had to wear earmuffs above. Like the sun was mean on his eyes, the birdsong must have been relentless.

A woman came to visit him, the blind albino miner told Wilmarí, and she warned him and his family to leave. He told the miners to stop hurting her body, but what else were they supposed to do? It was all they had ever known. They did not believe she would go so far that she'd turn the earth against its own inhabitants!

His village had miles of tunnels, so many miles they had their own weather down there. Breezes battled, bickered back and forth, in one end and out the other. They ground their yellowed teeth in their sleep. His people grew thick hairs on their arms in order to feel the shivering earth. This man would not let anyone touch him; he said there was a screaming in his ears anytime someone did. Those hairs helped him see in the dark, waving in the air like sensitive suckerfish.

The blind albino miner explained how his town was driven out by the deer that year. Even after what he considered a good rainy season, there wasn't enough to share. The deer remained hungry. They went for the farms and gardens before they attacked the villagers, furious vermin eyes pooled black, their spirits possessed. The deer bit and spit and trampled anyone who tried to intervene.

He showed Wilmarí a soft indentation on the side of his head the size of a hoof. Scalp stomped, he said. Nature took over. Squirrels chirped and jeered from the tops of trees, bombarded them with walnut shells. Mice moved in—fearless, vengeful mice. His people punched and kicked, but they were not prepared, for the herd came for blood.

The miner claimed he didn't know why. It was as if they were under the influence of some other power. What once was a village carved into mountainside was now grown over with bromegrass and aspen saplings. The mines had already weakened the integrity of the town, so when the animals turned on them, so did the earth, and soon the ground opened wide and swallowed everything he had ever known, except for the hungry deer and the sole survivor, the blind albino miner.

Cariña Marta

Dear Marta,

We went to Wilmarí's today. It reminded me of how much you love it here, how you couldn't or wouldn't speak to any of us except for the bees after Flaco's death. The bees have an affinity for people like you, like us. For Damien, too. They help me understand people when I normally can't. They know you saw Mamá ship Papá out to sea. I think I understand the feeling now—a rage festers. The darkness grows, takes over, limits how we see. But I visited our bees today, the offspring of the bees who raised us, all these generations later, and I listened. The bees can guide us, remember? Or have you stopped listening?

Ana María is consumed with hatred for her father, and look at her now, scarred, hard-skinned, reptilian. The Goatherd's torment nearly forced him to unbury the dead, he believed he could have saved them from a future storm, but they were dead already, and the church was explicit about which dreams they get to interpret as true, that they must come from a creature of devotion, which the Goatherd could not profess to be. Take a look at Damien; he's more than a little fishy. But all three of them—Mamá, the Goatherd, Damien—their grief is no different than yours or mine, it only manifests in us differently.

You want to kill our mother to ease your afflictions? Nobody wants to suffer her any longer, you're right. But will it solve our problems? I am not defending Mamá, I only beg you, for the sake of your sisters, and our bees, to reconsider the purpose in retaliating. Be careful of becoming the thing you hate.

We are too young to remember Mamá at her best. You witnessed something horrifying, you have every right to hate her. For that, Carla and I are sorry—we should have protected you, but we were busy struggling to win Mamá's respect, too. Do not let your pain consume you. We didn't know how to tell you the truth about our father's violence. We thought we had more time before you got reeled into his daily beatings, the psychological abuse, the lies, the way he treated our mother. Carla and I were not upset about his death, you may remember that more than everything else. You are lucky not to have been subject to that life, the way Carla and I were raised.

Grandfather Ché was a cabrón, it runs in the blood of men. Women, on our side of the family, we are charming and independent and brilliant, though our power comes at a cost; that is the nature of power. Wilmarí said our grandfather forced Ana María to trim the bougainvillea when they were children. Made Wilmarí watch Ana María's small hands get tangled in a sea of spine and tentacle. He said Ana María needed calluses if she was to be a woman worthy of a man. She bloodied them on the bramble. When Wilmarí offered to wrap her sister's wounded hands in gauze, Ana María insisted she bleed, that she grow calluses—but not for marriage. It was to protect Wilmarí from their father's abuse.

Perhaps you recognize some of the scars on Mamá's arms, the ones you thought were from a vicious monster. She ran away as a teenager to the mangroves and grew a protective skin; that's where they say she transformed into a caimán. She became of the land, adopted by it, nurtured. She could control the vines, command birds to chew the crud off her back, order fish to swim right into her mouth. Grandfather Ché once went looking for Ana María in the swamps, perhaps feeling guilty one sober afternoon. He never returned. The village says he was her first victim, and they agreed he deserved punishment for his crimes. They felt

Ana María had prevented something far worse from happening in the community.

The pescadores by then did not yet realize the waters had become overfished. If they knew, they continued fishing anyway. Pescadores like our father and grandfather, they were disrespectful of the ocean. Fishermen who stole from her belly without asking. Some people do not change their ways, simply because they are used to doing things the one way they have always done it, rather than adopt radical solutions to try to preserve their way of living. Like the miners searching for colorful stones and bright metals who poison our rivers and eat our mountains. Oilmen who siphon black carbon from earth's body, causing excruciating shocks of pain from her liver down the side of her leg.

Humans over the years have lost their ability to commune with the ocean and desert and mountains, everything below and beneath, all the sacred directions. From the overfished waters to the now-empty mines, the polluted rivers now conduits for oil, the slashed and burned forests choking out what lungs we have left. It is only a matter of time before we are all evicted. Might be too late to stop the storm, but not too late to hide.

Nature suffers daily trauma, Marta. She has a way of fighting back. Disasters are retaliatory. Mamá once believed there must be balance, like the ocean has: for every mouth she feeds, she takes one back. When Mamá grew angry, the ocean swelled. Villagers, spurred by a fatuous church, believed prayer offered answers; soon they believed those answers came in the form of dreams, and in one of those dreams they were told their only redemption was to marry their best fisherman, Flaco, to a caimán. The ocean will return life to their reef, they said, the storms will settle down.

When Flaco died, and we moved in with Wilmarí, you were forced to fend for yourself. I am realizing too late that you assume Carla and I had each other, but Ana María didn't know how to raise us, either. We grew so fast, forced into responsibility, into survival mode, before you were even born. If you ever felt like your big sisters abandoned you, that was not our intention. I am sorry. But then, did you try to be our friend? Too bad, we're your goddamn sisters. Sisters aren't supposed to be friends.

It is time to let go of your violent intentions and find another way, Marta. While I wish to hurt you, I do not; see how easy that is? Damien does not belong here—remove him from your list of inessentials. He is not interested in what you are selling. He should be seasoning shanks, boiling bones, picking parsley. He finally seems to be realizing where he is, that he has a choice about who to become next. Have you ever thought that his arrival was meant to teach us something? To show us something we haven't previously experienced? I thought he was incapacitated, that he needed something from us, desperate, but he learned we are as miserable as he is, and that has been enough for him to feel less alone. We might take that shred of light. You are not alone, Marta.

We are leaving Tía's soon. I've asked her to deliver this letter should we get separated by the storm if it's going to be as bad as you need it to be to exact your revenge. In any case, if this gets to you before then, let me warn you one more time: you've picked a battle with nature you have no chance of winning.

I saw you kill Carla. I watched you plunge a knife into her heart. I am going to show Mamá something I've kept a secret from you all. I need to tell her the truth about you, about what I saw. I need to keep things from going from bad to worse; I am trying to keep our family from falling apart. I hope you understand, and that Mamá's reaction will not be as violent or drastic as yours. Or is it your plan to keep her agitated? That's a terrible idea, bent on destroying us all. We love you, Marta. Carla and I both. Mamá, too, though she is no good at letting us know.

Wilmarí told me and Damien some stories, Marta, ones we haven't heard before. Mamá destroyed a village for a lot less than you blackmailing her. Our mother survived near extinction, keeping you and me *alive this long. She has a rage, yes, we know, and look how difficult it is to control.*

We have it in our bones, Marta. I forgive Mamá. She has suffered enough.

You, I wish I could forgive, but don't know yet if I can.

Besos,
Paola

Subaqueous Foragers

Paola had nearly forgotten about the jar of dandelion heads she imagined blowing into Damien's face. The rain picked up on their way home from Wilmarí's, they heard the ocean from miles away as it breached the seawalls. Once home, Damien continues walking, citing a need to witness the storm, while Paola goes inside to unload her finds of the day. In her room, she places her findings on secret shelves next to neighbors floating in cloudy liquids, and below the bees and wasps pinned to corkboard, the moths twinkling from strands of fishing line.

A door slams downstairs. Someone battling the wind and rain. Paola recognizes the drag of her mother's tail in the kitchen. Paola runs to the stairs, watches her soaked and snarling mother. Winds rock the shutters. The rain sounds as if it is being tossed at the house one barrel at a time.

"Mamá," Paola says, "I have to something to show you."

It takes some convincing (and a shot of pitorro) to coax Ana María upstairs. Paola escorts her mother to her bedroom closet, undoes little locks and chains behind the false wall. First, she presents a drawer of lures lined according to size and color like exotic candies (marlin have a sweet tooth). Another drawer: paws, appendages, mostly limbs of small animals. Larger items float in gallons on the floor; the smallest containers are up top. Grass-hoppers, a tick, a praying mantis, and several kinds of wasps and bees dangle from the ceiling on fishing line like beaded curtains. Hanging from boat line are two panes of glass clamped together with clothespins, between which several dozen mosquitoes are smashed into hilarious positions.

Ana María sighs, nods, runs her hands over the shelving, touches the labels Paola created by pasting ginkgo leaves onto toothpicks.

"The felt lining is a nice touch," she says.

Paola folds her hands behind her back and fixes her gaze to the floor, holding back a smile.

"Why would you hide this? Do the others know?"

"No, we are scared of you, Mamá," Paola says. "I didn't know what you'd do if you discovered this."

Ana María bobs her large head and scratches her bumpy chin. There might even be some moisture in her dry, slitted eyes. "It's beautiful," she says.

Paola reaches for Carla's phalanges on a shelf of jars organized by date rather than by taxonomic classification. She swishes them around in front of her mother. "I saw you with Carla," she says, "so I hid in the reeds. I saw what you left behind."

Ana María attempts to take the jar. Her hands tremble. She can't seem to get a good grip. Her tremors form bubbles in the embalming fluid.

Paola touches her mother's hands, holds them as if to cup water, and in this way they caress Carla's toe together.

Ana María cries. Her hands are cold. "I am so sorry, mi amor," she weeps. "I don't know what happened. It was her smell, I swear. The smell of fish on her like my father, and Flaco! You must despise me!"

Paola holds her mother's hands tighter to keep from dropping

Carla's toe. "Mamá, I do hate you, but not because of this. This is not your fault."

"It is, it's all my fault," Ana María sobs.

"You shouldn't have left her behind, you shouldn't have hurt her at all! But she did not die because of you, Mamá. It was Marta. I saw Marta sting Carla in the heart. She swept in right after you fled."

Ana María's hands harden in Paola's clutch. Paola does not let go, even as her mother's skin begins to slip out of her fingers. She looks into Ana María's eyes but can no longer see a reflection. A white film has closed beneath her eyelids.

Ana María drops to the floor of her daughter's room. The skin of her arms dangles from Paola's fingertips. She dry-heaves, then bawls, and contorts her body in a strange way, like she has been falling for some time and the landing has knocked the air out of her. Her eyes bulge from her skull. Her arms are now fat and short and thick, and her claws attempt to grip something in the air and she holds them clenched there until she starts breathing again. Ana María rolls her hefty body like an agile corkscrew, the momentum driven by her meaty tail. She crawls down the stairs, coughing or gagging or both, and when she reaches the door it does not budge, it is too busy protecting the old house from moisture, a broken screen door, a hurricane. Ana María drags herself out a back window and slithers into the night, into the flooded street.

Part III

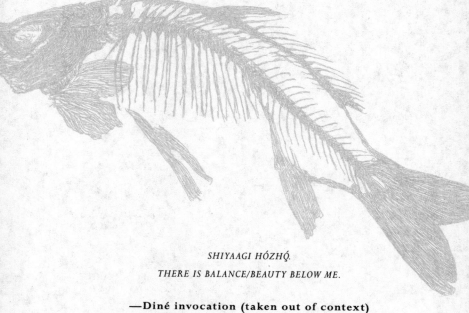

SHIYAAGI HÓZHǪ.
THERE IS BALANCE/BEAUTY BELOW ME.

—Diné invocation (taken out of context)

DO YOU EVER SUDDENLY FIND IT STRANGE TO BE YOURSELF?

—Clarice Lispector, *The Hour of the Star*

The Storm

The unceasing wind has picked up, the ocean now more vicious than the rain. It has become a plastic sea, rough and grumbling shit tossed from the world. Cans and clothes, bottles and buoys, doors and masts. There will only be more debris. No Kai, though, no fish of any kind.

Damien left Paola, deciding to see for himself the wild ocean. The wind threatens to peel his face off before he reaches the docks. The surge has breached the seawalls. Everything smells like a dirty body of water, a cocktail of shellfish and chocolate. Corrugated metals buckle and wheeze in the heavy wind, windows threaten to pop from the pressure change. Trees bend horizontal to the earth. Palm fronds grate concrete and squeak on tin, raising the hair on Damien's neck. He dodges palm fronds and branches that slice the heavy air and he leans against the wind with all his weight into the square.

Damien squats behind the statue in the plaza, temporary relief from the airborne detritus. He looks up at the saint. She once held something magnificent, but her broken fists now form a hollow grip on the sky, a boxing stance. Fisticuffs. Damien tries to remember the story Marta told him, that this saint was some kind of savior for her own people far away from here, whoever they were. Marta thought their destinies were bound because they had the same name. Marta's version of the story made the saint out to be a hero. Marta's version of the story is a lie.

A corroded brass serpent is coiled at the statue's feet, looking poised as if to strike the woman, except Damien notices that the serpent is actually the woman's tail. He examines the markings on the statue's ankles in the dim lamplight of the plaza, eroded by cacti invading her well. Damien brushes away the crumbling plaster and mud and salt to find a creature that is something half-beast, half-fish, like a salmon with a cat face. The creature is coiled at her feet. If it had been pinned down, the weapon she once wielded must have been a spear or a trident, something long to quell the creature below.

The Tarasque, though, pants dopily. It isn't growling or biting. It isn't attacking Santa Marta at all.

Damien wipes away at something shiny in the wet dust. A plaque that broke off the base of plaster reads: *Santa Marta*. Beneath the inscription, somebody scribbled in cursive with a thin blade: *Destroyer of Serpents*. How long ago did Marta vandalize this? Damien wonders. How long has she been planning to trigger this storm?

The rain is piercing his skin, now, but he is scared to go back to the house; it's about to get swept away, too. He doesn't know if he will be able to find his way back, but there is no point in waiting, either. Damien folds his fins against the warm breath of the hurricane and smells his way home, hoping something doesn't stir up and decapitate him in the dark.

The village suddenly goes dark, as if it has lost consciousness. Within minutes, the valley hums and stinks of petrol from the gurgling croon of generators lifting the village from darkness. Damien can see better now: the roads rivered and within them wooden toys, empty beer cans, broken-winged umbrellas flashing down the hills, piling up and creating dams. Trees are naked, leafless twigs. Dogs chained to rooftops bark at villagers blaring music. The storm forces everyone to gather and drink around their wind-up radios, because if they are to wash away, if their town lifts up and sets sail, they might as well sing.

The stormwaters from the hills meet with the tides of the ocean, a confluence at Ana María's door. Is she in the house? Damien wonders. Candles near their demise flicker dangerously low on the stair banister and around the kitchen. A bright gas lantern shines on the dining table. Damien pummels and kicks the back door, but the humidity has swelled it permanently shut. Damien finally is able to climb in through the back window.

Paola is in her prep chair, shucking corn. She tries to blow her bangs with a puff of her lips. A bag of peeled onions fumes in the corner. Shelled runner beans sit piled beside their own skins on the table as if they have undressed for supper. A box of fingerling potatoes await their turn. Paola sweeps the hair from her eyes. Her hands drip with corn milk.

"This is what you do to prepare for a hurricane?" Damien says.

"Nervous habit," Paola says.

Damien sits with her and takes an ear of corn and peels a layer of skin with a loud and satisfying rip. Its kernels are jagged purple teeth.

"We need to hide," Paola says. "We're going to get washed away. Whole village is."

"You don't look surprised."

"My father washed out in a storm like this."

So did my brother, Damien thinks.

"Marta wants you to do something she can't do herself," says Paola. "You don't have to do anything. Nothing *to* do except wait out this storm."

Damien rips open another layer of husk and finds a worm curled into an inverted S. The house vibrates as if it is being dragged over a washboard. Water seeps under the door and

Swim Home to the Vanished

through cracks in the windowpanes. The pressure has changed. Their ears pop.

"I know, but—" Damien notices a burlap sack sitting behind her. It is not filled with corn or beans or squash. "Paola, are you taking all this food?"

"I am only taking what I can carry," she says.

Damien looks in the bags and does not see corn or dried beans. He reaches in and takes out a bundle of corn husk, unwraps it.

"What is this?" Damien asks. He digs around the sack, which is padded with freshly husked peas, and finds glass jars filled with weird liquids and arachnids.

"Someone needs to remember us, our past," Paola says. "We must preserve our memories. If we have an opportunity to try again, perhaps we can start over the right way."

"Where are you taking them?"

Paola hands Damien a lantern.

"We should leave now," she says. She hugs him.

Damien holds on to her. She smells like corn silk, like a place his ancestors are from.

⤚

Damien, wading through knee-deep floodwater, turns against the wind and, holding up the swinging lantern, finds Paola is gone. He carries on. Many houses have already been swallowed up in the brown water, the ones made from pallets and siding and twine. He hears a two-stroke motor retreating inland. He crosses the rivered street, dodging pharmaceuticals and a screaming calf, heads for higher ground, for shallower water, where he finds that his huaraches have gone missing. He would have noticed earlier but his feet are bleeding, and numb from the salty water. The waters continue to rise; the safest place in the village might be the church.

He hikes up, sees a candle burning sweetly in the stained-blue window of the church steeple. The church walls are stained dark from rain, like sweaty pits. Damien enters through the heavy wooden doors. The building feels solid against the incessant winds, and it is dark and silent, not unlike the inside of a mountain. The room smells like burning pitch, the flammable sap released from bones of pine.

"Hello, Father?" Damien's voice echoes in the nave. A few remaining candles dance self-consciously in a corner. A bench creaks in the front row. Someone grunts, then slams a book to the floor. Damien calls out, but he does not wait for an answer. He rushes down the aisle, bare feet slapping the tile floor.

Tito, last of the great pescadores, is sprawled and bleeding on a front pew. A puddle of dark water shimmers beneath him. He is shoeless and masked with blood, his chest scraped pink. Damien takes a candle and lights several others to better examine Tito's swollen face.

"Ana María," says Tito. He flinches as Damien dabs at a gash on his forehead. His pants shredded where he was dragged across the coral.

Damien hoists Tito upright. Tito coughs up water, continues coughing. Blood trickles from his mouth.

"I think you've ruptured something," Damien says.

"We hurt her," Tito gurgles. He whimpers forward. Snot and spit burst from his purple face. "We hurt her. She's nursing her wounds. But she took my crew, she took all of them." He tries to catch his breath, flinching again at a pain in his side.

"Didn't feel like a storm yet when it hit, but the water was so clear, 'mano," he says. "I didn't think Ana María could build a storm that fast."

He coughs. Each breath he catches seems to flutter away.

"We motored out and stayed close to shore," Tito continues, "because the barracudas were swarming and we couldn't tell if they were running toward or away from something. The next set was less green, more blue, and the silver head turned amber. Flying fish started to flicker and hiss and spit all around, you gotta duck or those fuckers will cut you, cabrón. I've seen guys with lines cut across their cheeks and slices of ear peeled clean off their heads. Their beady eyes said they were frightened by something in the water, or maybe just by the water itself. I didn't see no sharks, and the 'cudas went ahead, as if the predator got preyed. Never seen that before."

Tito could talk an ear off in spite of his injuries. The pescador tells Damien between coughing fits that when another set came, red light shined through the wave and the sky went dark and the spray was warm. It lifted them way up before they felt its crash. They lost their cast lines, so Tito screamed, "Haul in or cut the ropes, it's time to roll home!" but it was too late. He pushed the motor and tiller starboard so fast they nearly capsized and the guys had to run portside to weigh against the turn. The waves were humongous, at least double overhead. If they had turned the yola earlier they might have ridden the backs of the flying fish and 'cudas. Instead, they made a diagonal cut across the head of a wave but teetered on her crest and fell twenty feet into glass, swallowed whole by the ocean. The sound was of your ear popping, that hiss before a high-pitched silence. Some of his crew bubbled up in the calm between sets, yola still intact, but their poles broken. The boys started bailing water and the engine was stalled, but Tito got it going again in one, two, three pulls. He glanced behind them and there it was. The last wave was no longer green or blue or amber. It was a deep red streaked with foam and bubble, a sea that couldn't rise any more since there was no sky left to hold it. Tito revved the engine.

"We were fucking done, coño," Tito says. "I screamed 'Hold fast!' and peeled off my boots because when you fall in you don't wanna sink, you wanna float."

He turned the tiller and pointed the stern right into the center of her belly—*Hold your gaff high, hermanos!* If his crew was gonna die, best they try and take her out with them—*La bruja, puñeta! Brace yourselves!* he screamed. The crew wrapped buoy lines around their ankles and armed themselves with gaff and spear. With one hand Tito steadied the tiller, in the other he gripped his old machete. They understood this was the end. They smiled to their gums and howled over the wind to make sure La Fucking Bruja could hear them coming, and drove their stern and steel right through her fucking estómago. Their bodies cracked in half like the yola, splintered into a million sticks. Their liquids became hers, sucked clean off the bone. "But we hurt her. We felt it when we hit."

Damien removes Tito's blood-soaked shirt, wrings it out, rips it into sheets to tie around his rib cage. Tito cringes as he crosses himself. He lies down on the pew, rests his good hand across his forehead. He was the only one to surface. He does not remember paddling in. He could not see the shore because it was all underwater, but he swam till his feet touched something, kept pushing through the muck until he found the church.

"We need to save Carla," Tito says.

"No, you need to rest here," says Damien. "The dead aren't going anywhere."

The church rumbles, heeling in these winds.

"We have to get her before the graves slide down and take us all." Tito sits up, cradles his face in his bloody hands.

"Carla is fine," says Damien. He reaches for Tito's shoulder, but Tito bats him away.

"They're coming crumbling out of that mountain soon."

"Who is?"

"They're coming for all of us." Tito closes a nostril with a finger and one by one blows snot and ocean out his nose, then he cries some more.

"Where is your uncle?" Damien asks.

Swim Home to the Vanished

"He better not be digging up my father in this huracán. He'll catch his death."

Damien kneels at the altar. He closes his eyes, submerges himself into something resembling weightlessness. He has not slept much these last few days. He folds his hands and smells the backs of his thumbs and thinks, I don't pray, but I can understand why people do. On the dark side of his eyelid, he watches his deceased dishwasher dancing in kitchen smoke, his cook Johnny peeling shallots, wiping tears. He sees his own hands slice carrots into obliques, and they hurt, so he rubs the meat between his thumb and forefinger now.

Maybe he did pray, if praying is ripping chard leaves from their stems, bathing them in garlic and hot oil. The smell of the butter browning with vanilla bean, the consideration of the viscosity of blood from a young sheep, how similar it is to fish blood. Sounds of shucking corn. The stink of Ishka the mule. The pop of bees in your mouth, the grit left in your teeth, bitter on the back of your tongue.

Tito trips over a broken tile, dropping a pilfered sleeve of Eucharist crackers and one of several bottles of wine.

"I am going to find my uncle," Tito mumbles, his mouth full of crackers. "He is all I have left." He washes down the Eucharist with an obscene amount of wine.

Tito passes the wine to Damien, who is listening to the storm spin like a top above the church, rising in waves. Damien hands the bottle back.

"Carla, too," says Tito. "We have to save her."

Damien shakes his head. "Your wife is gone, remember? We have to leave the dead behind."

"The dead are more than just memories to be washed away!" Tito cries.

"You hit your head pretty hard," says Damien. "You shouldn't go back out there."

214

"The storm will soak the graves, the graves will sink and collapse the mountain and wash the village into the rusty sea and cause a tide to rise."

The heart of this fisherman had been crushed like his boat at the bottom of the sea.

Tito tries to limp away, but Damien snags his arm. "It's too late," Damien says. "What do you think you're gonna find? You're gonna die out there."

"Do not tell me how I am going to die. I will decide that." Tito stops sniffling. "I lost everything; let me save her, and my uncle."

Tito stares at his bloody and muddy and broken hands, no longer capable of hauling in a net of baitfish. He does not see how crumpled they look to Damien because Tito can only imagine them wrapped around a bruja's throat.

How many lives have Tito's hands snuffed out? Damien wonders. Perhaps they have taken enough.

"It doesn't matter whose fault this is. My uncle will die out there. Let me go."

Tito uses Damien as a crutch down the aisle. They lift a bolt and the heavy doors swing open. In one breath the storm blows out all the candles in the church. They stand in darkness. They can no longer see their hands in front of them, only swirls of blood in their eyes like sparklers. Water creeps in; they feel it on their toes. The cactus garden failed to escape the flood, held back by the priest's cruel fence. The roar is deafening. The church's core shakes and may set sail soon enough. Tito lets go of Damien and extends his arms, seeking someone, or something, to lead him to Carla's grave.

Damien slams the doors closed to hold off the invading waters a moment longer.

Gravedigger

The Pallbearer drains his hat into his mouth every time the brim fills, a splash of hope tinny on his tongue. One shovelful at a time, he braces against the wind in the cemetery. His brother Javí is down there; the Pallbearer knows because he put him in this hole and he is gonna pull him out and bury him farther inland with better soil like Father Gáagi should have done with the bodies in the first place.

The rain has muddied up the dirt. The heft of it burns deep in the Pallbearer's back. "I have come to gather your bones, have patience, Javí!" One hand over the other, he digs. Jams the spade, scoops a slurp of mud, turns the suction over. The dead belong to us! Even if Javí is all bone now, the Pallbearer won't let the storm take him. Even if Javí is no bone at all, just soft and wormy, his brother will save him from dying once more in a bruja's storm.

Tito, limping, soaked with red, screams for his uncle among the shivering graves. Damien's tourniquet has at least slowed the bleeding. Tito grimaces into the wind, the shards of plant matter, he digs into the wet earth, with legs made for balancing the great seas, to find his uncle, the Pallbearer, who is grinning gummy against the wind and digging frantically, a lantern beside him hissing in the rain. Tito runs to him and relieves him of the shovel and starts scooping faster than it takes the hole to refill with water and mud. He hits his father's box. The Pallbearer and Tito fasten straps around Javí's coffin, and together they fight the mud to lift it out of the sinkhole. The rotted box bobs up, then down, as if over a cresting wave, before crashing on impact. The Pallbearer removes a couple of cracked boards, and there he is, his brother: meatless, wrapped in a sheet.

"Now Carla," Tito says.

They push against the storm to Carla's soft spot. Tito cries as he digs, then he laughs. It hurts to laugh. In between shovelfuls, he grabs his rib cage and coughs and cries, then laugh-cries, spitting blood.

The Pallbearer's large hat hides his bloodshot eyes, but he is grinning gummy again. He clasps his nephew's arm. He has never seen a master pescador try to turn the earth; he doesn't know how to use any tool that ain't a rod.

They take turns digging until they hit casket. Then they weave the straps around Carla's casket, and this time Tito holds on to his uncle's waist as they pull Carla out. She is much heavier than his father was. She is fresh, still. For every other pull they lose one, and the box descends into the hole. When the Pallbearer finds the strength to yank the line, they both fall backward into a pile of mud, and Carla's coffin lands in the soggy grass.

Tito does not open the casket. Instead, he wraps the straps crisscrossed around his shoulders and belly. He drags the casket east to higher ground; the wet earth and the wind at their backs reduce her drag.

The Pallbearer follows, carrying what is left of his brother in a sheet in his arms like a brained tarpon. "I'll keep you warm, hermano," he whispers. "I miss you. I've missed you so much."

Wasp

Damien listens to the bees bump around in the eaves of the dark church. He feels his way to the front row to look for his blown-out lantern. He kicks it, nearly trips. Damien picks it up and flicks the flint, adjusts the filament's brightness.

An arm juts out from the shadows, and cold, hard fingers hook onto Damien's wrist and pull him to the ground. He slips easily on the wet tile. There is a sharp pop in his tailbone when it hits the floor. He maintains his grip on the lantern to see the dark figure beside him, Marta, with hardened dark skin, a gleaming shell.

She is sitting in Tito's leftover bloody puddle. She looks at Damien, and for a moment does not seem to recognize him, the sleek fish he has become.

"Didn't think you were religious," Marta says. Her voice sounds a bit crackled, as if caught between wavelengths.

"What have you done?" says Damien.

"Where is Tito?" she asks.

"What do you care?" Damien scoots away.

Marta fiddles with the box of stale wafers Tito left behind, takes one out and licks it for salt, but it has none. Her eyes, blacker than normal, bounce around the room as if searching for an enemy, or a snack, or a place to lay an egg. Her hair looks singed.

"No more lies—it's over, Marta."

Marta crawls over and reaches for him; she touches Damien's neck and ears and gills, the scales now permanent on his neck. He is too scared to move, shivers at her cold touch. His body seizes.

He tries to invoke that pain in his marrow, the violence carried in his blood now in his fists. Damien allows the burning inside, the fire in his body. He claims the pain of his dead.

Damien cinches Marta's wrist and twists her arm, but her arm seems to have extra joints. The maneuver does not faze her.

She lifts herself off the floor, but she struggles. She winces, holding her abdomen.

"In the long scheme of things," she says, "we are but temporary inhabitants of this world, dirt and ash, recycled stardust."

"But in death, we become memory," Damien says. "In grief, we're made permanent."

"As long as there's someone left to mourn us." Marta chokes on something in her chest and throat. She buries her face in her palms and gurgles blood and weeps.

"It is far worse to feel nothing at all than to grieve forever," says Damien. "It is too easy to drink away the affliction; to work until your muscles distract you from grief; to forget."

When Marta stands, Damien is shocked by the severity of her wound. Tito pierced the belly of a wave. When he thought he punctured Ana María's estómago, it was Marta's.

She presses her abdomen now; blood flows through her fingers. She tries to leap toward Damien, but he is already back on his feet. She raises her hand: *stop*, it says, or *help*, or *get into striking distance*, but she drops to her knees. She lifts her other hand. Her guts cascade to the floor.

Damien takes the lantern and leaves Marta in the darkness. He hears her fall into the puddle of her and Tito's fluids, sobbing, gurgling for forgiveness.

—

Damien leaves the heavy doors open, wades back out into the night, allowing the stormwaters to come rushing in. As he turns toward higher ground, Damien imagines the corrupted water genuflecting with its own holy self as it floods the church.

Marta, on the floor, cups at the dingy stormwaters with her segmented legs, sips on them, gags, swallows some more, as if to sip away the surge entirely. To drink herself full on her own guilt and sorrow so that when she finally gets washed away she will sink and settle dark-eyed on the sandy ocean floor, begging from her sisters their absolution, and company, in her depths.

Stealthy shadows beneath the toxic surface. Not the company she preferred. Ten, twenty, more form a V; their bulbous backs arch in ripples. Deadened eyes under white protective lids. Tails paddle, hardened hides unfeeling to flotsam and chemical. The caimanes follow a leader with bougainvillea scratches across her back. They swim into the church as if they have been waiting for this day, the waters deep enough to pray.

Hashtł'ish

The earth shakes, crumbles beneath the irrecoverable inhabitants of the cemetery at the top of the mesa. A vengeful mouth threatens to open its gullet and swallow what was once hers, a village of loyalists. Damien recalls Wilmarí's story. What happened to the mining village is about to happen to them now.

Damien moves as quickly as the high waters will let him. Legs weak and out of breath, he lets his body fall as soon as it becomes deep enough to swim. Most of village has fled for higher ground, but many are still wading through the thick waters. Bodies are piled high, damming up downed trees and mules and beds and more bodies, their screams indistinguishable from the crushing noise shaking the village. The earth sounds like it is being turned inside out; it is not the wind or trees or rain, but behind him, and under him, with him, in the water. The sound wraps him like a song.

The rain soaks through the earth into the bones of the dead and loosens them. There is a release, a grumble. The skyline lights up orange. The shock wave sucks the breath out of anyone in its path, and the cemetery hill collapses, a mudslide of the dead aiming for the bay. Caskets ride into the square. Mouths fill with mud and metallic clay and crunchy bits of sand. There is mud in Damien's eyes; he feels bodies clamor under him. He pulls and yanks at whatever body he can, living or dead, to stay above the earth. Some bodies are shoved into ocean, others buried in clay. Some caskets tumble, and out come dancing the shriveled bodies of the past. Like they've decided to come alive just as they've finished dying.

He can't see clearly with all the mud in his eyes, but Damien thinks he sees the silhouette of Benny (everyone knows his shape). The hollow bones of elders float up to the surface—poor Eddie, and El Mariachi, the Hunchback and Lorena hand in hand. He thinks he sees Marta's feet, but they are someone else's long toes, an arch like hers. He can hardly differentiate the dull cries of villagers from their desperate slurps for air, their twisted little hands and tangled feet grasping for something breathable beneath them.

The tortilla ladies float atop the mud, their mouths open in a soundless chorus. The pharmacist is splayed like a water strider on the surface; if she moves she will sink.

"Throw me a line, I'm sinking fast!" someone yells, but it may be Damien's own asphyxiated voice.

More faces rise, too stunned to cry; earless, voiceless. Damien is able to unlock his arms and pushes himself up, but his arms sink on whatever it was he was using to lift himself. He searches for an arm or a leg from the gaspers around him, screams of dead bodies muffled with dried flowers. He howls the names of everyone he has ever known, his mouth full of clay. But he can't help them, either. He tries to dig, but his hands and arms are as useless as fins.

A finless fish wallows first in mud.

Damien tries to scream again, but everyone's ears are filled with mountain. He uses the last of his strength to stretch his limbs, and feels his hands and feet bloom. He swims around with power now. Finds a leg, from a horse. Warm mud. Cold bodies. A hint of sulfur in the air. A soupçon of hair. This hand alive and twitchy. This limb loose and broken.

He finds a whole mess of bottles clinking in the mudflow. A jar of feathers. A jar with a toe. This one filled with cloudy eyes. Another leaks its beans.

⚊

This is an inside-out earth. Listen to mice paddling as if in pudding. Keep moving. Hear ocean. Listen for its lung expansion, its gills to billow. Hear a heart pump one last time, your own heart deepen. Opposite of wither. *Hath burst asunder!*

Lured into darkness, their light a fire smothered under all this grave. But the sky has opened—a dim blue light clings to the low-cut horizon. A ridge has been carved out of the east. Without the cemetery hill, the sun will rise a few minutes earlier. When the water recedes, the shore will be twice as wide. All the boats have been masticated, toppled, or buried. Pescadores flounder in the thickened water, gasping, suffocating at the water's edge, as if their mouths are filled with fish. And there, where the mud thins and slips into ocean, Ana María slithers from the belly of them, blood on her crooked smile.

Damien wants to call out to her. She might be the closest thing to family he has anymore.

He is distracted by a star on the mountain, a lantern light swinging off the edge of a cliff like an anglerfish lure. Is it Tito and the Pallbearer, Damien wonders, cuddling the bones of their dead? He hopes they were able to unbury their grief so they might suffer the delight of carrying it with them forever.

Sand is pushed by big water into bigger water; Damien crawls, belly down. He tumbles under the angry waves. To swim and cool his seared scales.

To be with his brother.

He finally knows what he would say in the eulogy:

Let the current run him off the map and breathe into him new life. From shallows he'll drift to kelp. To find the dead. The lost. Let him breathe again fins ablaze, weightless and quick. Let him fin-slice into ocean, let him swim home to the vanished.

What Fish Remain

As he was swept out to sea, Damien thought he might see his mother's worn-thin dresses and contagious pies one last time or hear the barbarous laugh of his overworked father. But they were gone. He accepted that.

Damien watched as the town was engulfed. He imagined being buried alive, thought there was no worse way to go, that he would rather be buried at sea.

What he did not know about his parents, his obituary might say, is that they were from a place like this. Builders from the bush. Dried-up sea-people. It is possible Damien inherited from his mother the wobbly way she huddled over her obsessions, the temperament of silver, the secretions of copper, the kiss of lead on a soldering iron. From his father, perhaps he acquired vision, mapping space before a home exists—bones to frame up walls, windows, doors. Wiring like dried-up veins. A plumbing system so lovely he wished it did not hide beneath the floors and drywall.

When Damien stood over those fish carcasses and opened up those fish, he studied their framework of thin white bone and crunchy cartilage and bubbly anatomy like they were maps. Gills flared for oxygen, ruby red, etched like a pendant. A maze of kidney, stomach, intestine, polished for his delight. He threw away their heads and innards, while other creatures waited near the rocky shore to annihilate the leftovers. All that time he was gutting them, he was gutting himself.

Now, he has come to join them down below, among the living and the dead. Forced into the sea by a deflated hilltop. The blue chromis and cardinalfish might go for his eyes first. Grunts and angelfish peck at fingers, eels will wrap themselves around his ankles. But the trumpet fish are picky; they would rather suck the scum off a chub.

If a loved one dies and in your grief you become a fish, of course you will be drawn to water. You must learn to breathe differently. You swim through rooms full of everyone you have ever met. Taste things you have never eaten before. Learn to look both ways in order to see right in front of you. Your sense of smell will not be as acute as it used to be, in fact your nose will not be attached to taste. Everything will taste metallic anyway. You'll get used to the salt in no time.

One thing separating the living from the dead is that the dead have no senses.

Now Damien is truly a fish, maybe always has been. He remembers his father's eyes being fishlike, the color of Concord grape. And his mother had a limp, as if uncomfortable with gravity's burden, preferring movement in big water, expansive water: *Tó Ts'ohnii.*

Damien's body is more graceful in water, too, even if he is still growing accustomed to his fins. It does not take much to flip upside down; there is a learning curve to air bladder swimming. What a shiny body he has. New and glittery. Within each scale is blue smoke, iridescent like oil in water.

Circling the seaweed, he searches for Kai. Scratches his scales along the coral. Nibbles at the flotsam. Soon he is digging at the sandy bottom, shoveling with his speckled snout huge plumes of silt, billowing until he is invisible.

Time ebbs, flows. He tries to re-member before he can't any-more. In order for the past to endure, he must sew the body back together, even the parts he wished he could leave out. What are we if all of our stories are erased, even the ugly histories we don't wish to pass on?

He is unfocused, still, but Damien thinks he sees Kai, gangly muscle and sinew, stronger than Damien (he always had been), exploring endless kelp forests, teasing the makos.

The night before he disappeared, Kai had gone into the forest, where he dreamed of becoming a fish. The crunch of leaves under his boots made his mouth water. The sweetness of the decom-posed, the spores from a puffball, wet bark and moss. He heard a familiar sound. His mother's voice. His father's. Snaking in the ivy, tangled in thorny raspberries, blooming on the morning glory, cold and damp with dew.

The earth cackled. A hiss in the leaves whispered him forward. Not to death, but to share with him how it felt, that there was nothing to fear.

Kai stood over the swollen river waiting for it to rise, take him, bathe him, turn him into the fish he wanted to be, had always been. He spoke to the river. "Do shí tá hó t'sii da"—he knew the phrase. A life out of balance.

Damien told himself a million times he should have tried harder to bring Kai home. Tried harder to let him know he was not alone because they were alone together. Like they were sup-posed to be.

But Kai beat him to it, and they made a pact. And Damien grew into fish-shaped grief.

Swim Home to the Vanished

Now I am fish like you. And a fish can drown on land like a man drowns in sea.

He wished Kai had come to him before the river did. It was not anyone's fault, but Damien wanted something to blame other than himself. He wished he had told him: I am with you, we are limbs from the same body.

Watch as Damien grows fat and playful not too far from the shallows. There is a cliff, a drop of forty feet, where the only obstacle to fear is a heavy test line, fluorescent lures, and shiny hooks. Perhaps he will nibble at a few, and when the metal in his lip reminds him briefly of his mother, or the stink of a motor conjures his father, Damien will remember he is only hungry for crustacean, and he will yank himself away, snapping the line, and dive for deeper water.

Acknowledgments

I am grateful for everyone's support over the years, and miles. A solitary task can't be done alone. Thank you to my loving parents, Judy and David, for everything. To my weirdo brothers Keith Basham and Reymont Cantil—I wouldn't be who I am without your music and bullying and art-making. Everything every day to my little brother, Tristan: not a day goes by I don't feel you peeking over my shoulder looking for typos or a decent place to insert a pirate or rhino. Ahéhe' to all my Diné family, Tó Ts'onii, Bit'ah'nii, ancients and elders, grandmas and grandpas, aunties and uncles and cousins, for your generosity and laughter, even in dark times. Same goes to the Bashams, especially Uncle Lynn and Aunt Charlie, whose contagious obsessions with language infected me as an infant. To the DiMartino and Vella clans, a family gracious enough to take me in as their own, and who keep feeding me (and feeding me). To all my friends too many to mention here, but especially Cee Gustke and Gregor Murrell, Bojan Louis, Sara Sams, Billie Dólii, Sarah Flett Prior, Adam Coble, Erin Hiser, Mark Graves, Wes Atkinson, Sherwin Bitsui, Jon Davis, Sam Goldsmith, Liz Velez, and the Baltimore café crew.

Big Fish Heart thank-yous to the Institute of American Indian

Arts faculty, staff, colleagues, guests, and alumni, including Ramona Ausubel, Andre Dubus III, Pam Houston, Toni Jenson, Joan Naviyuk Kane, Tommy Orange, Derek Palacio, Izzy Prcic, Claire Vaye Watkins, Lydia Yuknavitch. Huge hugs to Aimee Bender and Garth Greenwell, amazing minds and workshop leaders, thank you for being such kind and thoughtful readers. Brian Turner, June Saraceno, and faculty at UNR–Lake Tahoe's MFA program; Meg Kearney and crew at the Solstice MFA program. To my students: thank you for sharing your words, wisdom, and patience. Your stories will keep the world treading.

Thank you to the Book Mobile in Flagstaff, and to public libraries and all librarians everywhere. To English teachers who let me hide during lunch to write; people like Cindy Hardy and the Summer Fine Arts Camp at UAF, for encouraging young people to partake in such incendiary acts as writing stories and poetry.

To Puerto Rico, Mexico, Colombia, Ireland, the Pacific Northwest, Dinétah—all the nourishing places and people who helped me along, not to mention the real-life Paola, Goatherd, and Ishka the street dog, whom I met in real life in a jungle somewhere between the mountains and the sea.

To my fine restaurant families: countless cooks, chefs, servers, dishslayers, bakers, owners, and assholes I've worked with along the way, from Flagstaff to Portland, Rincón and New York, Chicago, Olympia; for those of us battling with mental illness; and Ritchie and Sean, two crazy big-hearted crew lost too soon. So much love for Lauren Cravey and the Cravey clan, and everyone at La Copa Llena: thank you for accepting me in my multiple states of mind, for allowing me to be wild and free in the kitchen.

To Erin Wicks, and to Millicent Bennett and everyone at Harper, who acquired and helped shape into something what others believed unwieldy.

Thank you with a million splashes to PJ Mark and Ian Bonaparte, who see something in us fish out of water, in our work, before we see it in ourselves, then urge us on and fight to bring to life a dream. A world without art is a world not worth saving.

And finally, thank you, Lauren DiMartino, and our Little Dog. I am so grateful to be able to call you Home. I love you more than oceans within oceans.

About the Author

BRENDAN SHAY BASHAM (DINÉ) is Tó Ts'ohnii and Bit'ahnii, born for bilagáana (Scottish, Irish, English, German). A fiction writer, poet, educator, and former chef, Brendan was born in Alaska and raised in northern Arizona. He received his MFA from the Institute of American Indian Arts and his BA from the Evergreen State College. His work has appeared in *Puerto del Sol*, *Santa Fe Literary Review*, *Yellow Medicine Review*, and *Juked*, among other publications. He is a recipient of Poetry Northwest's inaugural James Welch Prize for Indigenous Writers, fellowships from the Truman Capote Literary Trust and Writing By Writers, and the Ucross Foundation's first Native American Literary Award. He lives in Baltimore, where he runs a make-believe café with his wife and dog.